When 3.0 0 0 4 0 0 4 8 0 0 8 6 4 **th her.**

She turned to face him, and his pulse sped up.
Moonlight hugged her, showing little of the
details he had beeath.

She had high che_____gh
she was lean, her_____was
lacking in her attit_____ceful,
her skin a smooth,_____eyes,
framed by dark lashes, dominated her other features.
They were a bright Lycan green.

She took a step, bringing her close enough for Rafe
to feel her breath on his face. She said suddenly, in a
hoarse, velvety whisper, "It's you, isn't it?"

Then she waited in silence as if daring Rafe to find
meaning in those words.

Linda Thomas-Sundstrom writes contemporary and paranormal romance novels for Harlequin. A teacher by day and a writer by night, Linda lives in the West, juggling teaching, writing, family and caring for a big stretch of land. She swears she has a resident muse who sings so loudly, she often wears earplugs in order to get anything else done. But she has big plans to eventually get to all those ideas. Visit Linda at lindathomas-sundstrom.com or on Facebook.

Books by Linda Thomas-Sundstrom

Harlequin Nocturne

Red Wolf
Wolf Trap
Golden Vampire
Guardian of the Night
Immortal Obsession
Wolf Born
Wolf Hunter
Seduced by the Moon
Immortal Redeemed
Half Wolf
Angel Unleashed
Desert Wolf
Wolf Slayer
The Black Wolf

Harlequin Desire

The Boss's Mistletoe Maneuvers

Visit the Author Profile page
at Harlequin.com for more titles.

THE BLACK WOLF

LINDA THOMAS-SUNDSTROM

Recycling programs
for this product may
not exist in your area.

ISBN-13: 978-1-335-62958-6

The Black Wolf

Printed in U.S.A.

Dear Reader,

There are wolves in Miami, Los Angeles, Colorado, South Dakota, France and London...in my Harlequin Nocturne series of stand-alone books about werewolves. I love to tell their stories, because who doesn't love those hot, sexy beasts when they are all really good guys beneath all that heat?

My first Wolf Moons book for Nocturne, *Red Wolf*, (and the *Blackout* bonus novella) was released way back in 2010 and first introduced a Miami wolf pack that keeps on ticking with characters that have cameos in most of my books since then. I have received quite a few requests for more of these Miami Weres, and love that readers have responded to the characters so openly and let me know it. That kind of feedback is sheer author bliss.

So here comes my latest wolfish story, *The Black Wolf*, dedicated to lovers of the supernatural for whom werewolves hold special meaning and who believe the terms *hot* and *sexy*, when added to things like suspense and adventure, make for some good full-moon howling. Here, we catch up with the Miami pack and some of the original characters from the first wolf books.

Thank you for suggesting this.

I hope you'll love *The Black Wolf* as much as I loved writing it. And I hope you will look forward to my next wolfish Nocturne, *Code Wolf*, coming November 2018.

Please do check out my website to find all of the books, like *Red Wolf*, *Wolf Trap*, *Wolf Born*, *Wolf Hunter*, *Seduced by the Moon*, *Half Wolf* and *Wolf Slayer*...and to keep track of what's coming up next. Connect with me on my Facebook author page. Join my reader team. Or just stop by and say hello. I'd love to hear from you.

Cheers and happy reading!

Linda

To my family, those here and those gone, who always believed I had a story to tell.

Chapter 1

Hot Miami nights in September were the bane of tourists and locals alike…but they suited Rafe Landau just fine.

Werewolves seldom reacted to heat the same way humans did. With body temperatures so elevated most of the time, a few degrees one way or the other didn't matter. And humidity was Rafe's friend. Sultry nights like this one were perfect for keeping criminals inside in front of their air conditioners. Or so he hoped. A detective's job didn't involve much downtime in a city this big. Having a night off from the usual chaos was a blessing.

Rafe sipped his soft drink on the narrow balcony of his semi-affordable oceanfront apartment, where the crash of waves almost completely masked the more invasive city sounds. Behind him, the blonde he planned to share a couple of hours on a mattress with shuffled toward him on bare feet.

"Got anything to drink in your bachelor pad besides sodas?"

Her voice was grittier than her looks. Rafe liked his temporary bed partners natural, without medically enhanced curves, dyed hair or overdone makeup. His preferences could have been a throwback to the times when wolves ran naked in the wild and nature ruled, but the fact was that he liked to see, taste and feel the women he dated with nothing artificial in his way.

Tonight's date had already discarded most of her clothes; she was down to flimsy green lingerie that looked good on her. Her shoulder-length hair was tousled, her lips pouty. And her current state of undress made her invitation perfectly clear.

"Cupboard by the sink," Rafe said, directing her to the stash of wine people had given him on various occasions, which he never drank. Other than a few swigs of beer on social occasions, the acuteness of his Were sense of taste and smell made alcohol off-limits.

"Wine?" she called out from the small kitchen, and followed that up with, "Warm wine?"

"I wasn't expecting company" was Rafe's standard reply in situations like this. He liked his women to feel special. This one was extraordinarily beautiful and probably damn good in bed, but she wasn't the first he had invited home this month.

He supposed that he had been compensating for the painful memories, finding comfort in random companionship.

He had started feeling sorry for every woman who had caught his eye lately, believing him to be trustworthy because of his detective status and hoping that he might be available. The main thing he needed from a human female partner, however, was something none of them had been able to provide. Not that any of them could help being human. Although he could pass among them most of the time, he wasn't really like them, and he had a secret to guard.

The fact that he was one of more than two dozen werewolves in a tightly knit Miami pack wasn't exactly something he could be open about, and it kept him from any real connection.

He glanced over his shoulder. Hell, he was fairly sure he remembered this woman's name. Brenda? Brandi? Something starting with a B.

Maybe he was wrong about the B. *Randi? Candy?*

He might call her again sometime when he was lonely, even though they had nothing in common, really. It was dangerous for Weres to fraternize for too long or become regularly intimate with a species outside their own.

But available she-wolves were a rarity in Miami and tricky to be around due to that little phenomenon known as imprinting. A lingering meeting of the eyes, Were-to-Were, or one outstanding sexual climax between them, and a werewolf was as good as engaged.

"Do you want some?" his date asked, clinking glasses on the counter.

"No," Rafe said. "You go ahead."

A breeze had come off the ocean to ruffle his hair—hair that was too long for a cop and too short for Rafe's taste. It was a good wind. Felt nice.

He closed his eyes.

The scent of lilac perfume preceded his date onto the balcony. "Nice view," she observed.

"Yes," he agreed. "I'm damn lucky to have it."

He took in the long lines of towering hotels perched along the beach. Lights glistened on the water. Colorful umbrellas dotted the scene during the day. His place was the only remaining small, privately owned building among those multistoried stucco behemoths. A holdout. His refuge. The manager liked having a cop around.

"How much is the rent?" his companion asked, making conversation, interrupting Rafe's communion with the darkness and the breeze. At this point in the evening he should have been paying more attention to the green lingerie, but he frowned.

Some little thing nagged at his consciousness, served to him on that wind. A new scent arrived that was hard to define with Brandi so close. It wasn't salty ocean waves or the usual array of smells wafting in from the restaurants down the street. This was something else.

What?

Rafe's pulse accelerated slightly as he caught and held a breath, searching for a way to reconcile the new scent with the sudden burning sensation at the back of his throat. He set down his drink and peered at the ocean, hoping to attach a name to what he couldn't quite capture, though his unusual talent for identifying and categorizing problems was what had made him the youngest decorated detective in the Miami PD.

Not perfume, he decided. The incoming scent wasn't floral. It couldn't be the warning signal of a wolfed-up Were, since the moon wasn't full tonight, and anyway, he was intimately familiar with the scents of his kind.

The way his body had automatically tensed suggested he would have to find a polite way to send the woman beside him on her way and find the source of the mysterious smell that had taken precedence over her lilac perfume. There was the slightest suggestion of danger in the other scent, and his innate sense of justice demanded he focus on tracking it down.

Mysterious scents were almost never good. More often

than not, they were attached to trouble. Still, he actually would be sorry to see Brandi go when the night had been so promising. What male, human or Were, wanted to pass up such an opportunity?

He just had a bad feeling about what might be out there…and he couldn't let it go.

Cara Kirk-Killion stared out the window of the black SUV, feeling anxious and trapped. She didn't often leave her family's secluded estate. She liked the freedom of open spaces, wind, trees and being alone to commune with those things…and all of that was about to end for a while. The SUV had already entered the city, which meant that she had less than ten minutes of freedom left.

She hated the promise she had made to her father to behave. It was time, he had said, for her to see more of the world…in moderation, and in carefully controlled circumstances. It wouldn't do to turn her loose in Miami without strict supervision, she had heard the Elders say, and she understood the need for such precautions. So she was to see more of the world under the protection of one of the largest and strongest werewolf packs in Miami. Her father's people…though they weren't really people. They howled each time a full moon came around.

Every instinct at the moment, however, told Cara to run in the opposite direction. Seeing more of the world wasn't necessary when deep down inside her so many worlds already existed. She hadn't actually begun to believe she might be a freak until a week ago, when some Were Elders showed up and the plan to take her away became a reality.

That's when the dreams began. And the lectures.

Cities were dangerous places, her father had warned, which was likely the reason her parents had hidden her and themselves in the country. Cara also got the impression that the Kirk-Killions wouldn't have fit in anywhere else. Her family was different, and Cara hadn't needed anyone to point that out.

Colton Killion's body was covered with scars that no one ever spoke about, probably because his Were blood should have healed them. Her father's hair was as white as his skin. He liked to roam in his wolfed-up shape and seldom came into the house. A pure white wolf. Lean. Strong. Fierce. Ghostly.

Her mother was neither human nor entirely wolf. Though she had been born a pure-blooded Lycan, it turned out that Rosalind Kirk also shared her blood and DNA with other types of beings. Her mother's hair was sometimes as black as the night and at other times white. Her features had a tendency to rearrange on occasion, and her deceptively delicate body reeked of old power.

Her mother liked to disappear for hours and shape-shift when the moon was full so that she could run with the white wolf she had lived with for years. The eerie sounds Cara's mother often made—not howls or growls, but something much more powerful—had echoed through Cara's mind from the time she was born.

It hadn't taken Cara long to realize that she also possessed some of her mother's special traits, and that the Kirk-Killions might seem scary to the humans beyond their gates. Because of all that, her parents weren't accompanying her to Miami. There were two strangers in the front seat of the SUV, and they refused to meet her inquisitive gaze.

Werewolves. Both of them. Half-breeds, in that unlike her, they had been human once. Cara smelled the old bites that had sealed their fates and inducted them into the moon's cult a long time ago. They'd probably been warned about her being a freak of nature, and it crossed her mind that maybe she should give them a demonstration. Show her fangs. Bring out her wolf. Give them a thrill and make them turn back so that she could again plead her case for staying home.

She wasn't actually going to do any of that. At eighteen years old, she was no longer a child. She could remain calm and follow the plan that had been made for her. She would try to behave, if only because her dreams had also pointed her this way...to Miami and what she might find there. *Whom* she might find there. The male who had been haunting her dreams lately and had contributed to her current state of restlessness. The guy who had destroyed whatever kind of peace she had been able to find with her unusual little family for the past few weeks.

If she happened to find the guy, she would make him pay for bothering her and piquing her interest. Then she'd go home dream-free.

The city's glittering lights surrounded the car, but Cara stared at the back of the seat in front of her. Through the open window she caught a whiff of a salty scent that could only have been the ocean she had heard so much about. It was a lovely scent, unique, and served to scramble her sense of duty.

Suddenly, behaving herself and allowing these guards to take her someplace she didn't really want to go just didn't suit her at all.

So when the car slowed for the next red traffic light, Cara opened the door.

Chapter 2

Standing on the sidewalk, Rafe stared at the darkest stretch of beach with his senses wide-open. The wind had changed, taking the mysterious scent with it. He listened to the waves and muted music from one of the hotels. There were no police sirens tonight, and for the moment, no noisy tourists. It was just him and the beach.

Nevertheless, his pulse continued to race as if he was about to discover something. He hoped whatever that was justified his reluctantly giving Brandi the heave-ho. She hadn't gone without a pouty fuss.

Rafe buttoned his shirt and tucked it into his jeans. He scanned the beach, looking pretty much like anyone else who might be out for a nighttime stroll, except for the badge pinned to his belt. He hadn't taken the time to put on his shoes.

A half-moon overhead made the wave foam look silver and the sand appear as soft as velvet. Yet all was not so calm beneath the surface. The farther he had walked from those glittering hotel lights, the more his senses nagged about something being different tonight, something he had to pay attention to. If the strange scent had reached him on his balcony, its source couldn't be far off.

When his cell phone buzzed with a text message, Rafe cursed the interruption. Still, the number that came up on his screen was an important one. This would have taken precedence over a call from his department anytime. It was his father asking him to come home. Judge Landau seldom made such a request.

"Okay," Rafe muttered without immediately texting back. His attention was fixed on the water, where a solitary figure had emerged from the waves.

A woman.

She stood near the sand with the water swirling at her feet. He was pretty sure she was naked. Although the idea that occurred to him was insane, Rafe ran a hand over his eyes, imagining that he could be looking at a mermaid.

Of course, there was nothing strange about someone taking a nighttime swim, so he should just turn around and head home. But the feeling of stumbling onto the mystery that had called him here had gotten stronger, along with that unidentified scent.

Using the special abilities that allowed all Weres to see in the dark with more precision than their human counterparts, Rafe stared hard at the woman near the shore, even though his mind issued a warning about infringing upon her privacy.

The moonlight shone on the water behind her, presenting him with her slim silhouette. Her legs were slender. Long wet hair cascaded over bare shoulders.

Though Rafe couldn't see the woman's face in the dark, even with his considerable Were talents, he knew she was looking straight at him with the same kind of scrutiny. The intensity of her attention was electric.

"You all right?" he called out. "Are you alone? The tides can be quite treacherous for anyone swimming solo."

The mermaid offered no response.

"Well, I'll leave you to it, then," Rafe said. "Sorry if I interrupted whatever you were doing."

Maybe she thought he was some kind of pervert for staring at her. Could he blame her? On the other hand, if she did turn out to be a mermaid…

He shook his head sharply, clearing away that ridiculous notion. Again, though, he got the funny feeling this woman was connected to what brought him out here tonight in the first place. Since there was no one else around, he had to consider that she could very well be ground zero for the sensations running through him.

He didn't see a towel or a pile of clothes that might belong to her on the sand. She made no move to turn away or cover her bareness with her arms. Being naked all alone was one thing. Being naked on a public beach was another.

"Do you need something to wear? Maybe someone took your clothes while you enjoyed your swim?" he asked.

The woman didn't speak. Her earthy, not quite identifiable exotic scent floated around her like a cloud.

"You can have this." Rafe removed his shirt and held it out to her, then shook it as an enticement for her to take his offering.

"Fine." He lowered his arm when she made no move toward him. "But you really can't walk around like that. Not here."

"Why?"

Her question rendered him speechless for a few beats. She had a deep, throaty voice unlike any he had heard lately. Sort of a whisper. Almost a purr. It moved the wolf buried deep inside him with the kind of physical response usually reserved for a full moon.

Rafe shook that off, too. "You might scare the tourists," he managed to say. "Or receive a proposition or two that you find offensive."

When the woman shook her head, her waist-length wet hair swirled. Though he wanted to see more of her, Rafe figured she already thought he was a perv.

"There are no strings attached. The shirt is a gift."

"I don't know you," she said.

The sexiness of her tone produced a strange fluttering sensation in his chest, which Rafe also found absurd given the circumstances. Hell, he wasn't going to arrest her for indecent exposure, because he was the only one out here at the moment, and honestly, what he could see of her was quite decent. What he had to do was to go away and leave her alone.

And yet her rapt attention kicked his pulse upward another notch, and the air between them seemed to be charged with ions like those preceding an oncoming storm system.

There was danger here, his instincts warned. He had to tread lightly if he hoped to understand what that danger was.

"I'm with the police," he said to explain his continued presence.

"And you're a werewolf," she returned with way too much insight and confidence.

Rafe was stunned. "Werewolf, is it?"

She spoke again. "I've heard that Weres around here have to try to fit in. You look human."

"Why would you think I'm anything other than human?" he asked.

"Practice."

After waiting a few more heartbeats, Rafe said warily, "If I'm a werewolf, what does that make you for recognizing me as such?"

"I guess I'm harder to define."

"Maybe you can try."

"I've been cautioned not to do that," she said.

"Who cautioned you?"

"One of you."

"A werewolf, you mean, or a cop?" Rafe pressed.

Although a cloud passed over the moon, bringing a brief, temporary dullness to the night, Rafe saw her nod her head.

She said, "The ghost warned me."

Another spike of surprise struck Rafe. Though he didn't have the specific details about this woman, her reply made who this had to be extremely clear to him. The scent that had drawn him here and the prickly premonitions about the possibility of danger finally came to a head. Mystery solved. One part of it, anyway.

"You are Killion's daughter," he said.

This was the female his pack was expecting. She was supposed to be an extremely rare kind of shape-shifter hybrid. Hell, maybe she *could* have been a mermaid.

"Yes," she said.

"What are you doing here, and without your companions?"

Rafe connected this shapely vision in front of him with the text message he'd received from his father moments before. Cara Kirk-Killion must have escaped from her transport and her guards. His pack would be looking for her.

"Those guys were responsible for your safe passage to the estate," he continued.

"I don't need guards. Maybe you've heard why?"

She didn't give him time to reply. With a quick turn

on her long legs, the female that everyone in their pack had been warned to avoid at all costs until proper introductions had been made…just walked back into the sea.

Leaving Rafe to stare after her.

Cara didn't stop to consider the possibility that the Were on the beach would follow her until she felt the pressure of a hand on her arm.

The touch came as a shock. No one had dared to touch her in the past for fear of what kind of shape she would end up in and how far into their souls she could see. One touch was all it took for her to adapt her form to the shape of whatever kind of being had reached out. Sometimes all it took for her to shift her shape was closeness, eye contact or a connecting thought.

Once she had melded to their shape, she could read them easily and see into their souls. She could at times predict their futures and understand their needs.

This Were had broken with tradition. Possibly he didn't know better than to get too close to a member of the Kirk-Killion clan. Yet if he knew about her guards and the estate, he had to belong to the Landau pack and be privy to their secrets.

"It isn't safe out here," he warned, letting his hand drop.

"It's never safe," Cara replied, longing to get back to the silence and buoyancy of deep water, dreading having to go to the Landau place, where more Weres like this one awaited her arrival and she would be fenced in.

"I mean that if you're as special as everyone seems to believe you are, you'd be a hot commodity around here and possibly hunted for your many talents," the Were said. "It's not safe to be on your own in a strange city."

Cara still felt the burning sensation of his hand as if his fingerprints had been stamped on her skin. Did he also feel the heat? Had the call already gone out about the necessity of finding her?

More time was what she needed. Time to herself. Time with the water, which had been lacking at her family's inland estate. Time to experience a few more precious moments without the shackles of Were society.

"I'll take you there," the Were beside her said, skipping over all of the things they hadn't yet mentioned about why she was in Miami and how she had gotten away from the guards. "To the house," he added.

She had escaped one net only to be ensnared by another. The big Were next to her, with his moon-streaked brown hair, lean, muscular build, chiseled features and light eyes, looked capable enough of handling any surprises that were in store.

Because he was in human shape tonight, Cara maintained her human countenance. She also kept her voice. However, she sensed the wolf curled up inside this guy as if it were her own and knew that it was strong, like hers. Being near him messed with her delicate equilibrium. She was drawn to him without knowing why.

He looked at his hand suddenly, as if he also felt the burn caused by one brief, simple touch. Then he glanced back up at her.

"I don't like being caged," Cara said, watching him closely, observing how he fisted his hand and the way the wind played with strands of his hair. He was as good-looking as her father, with prominent cheekbones and wide-set eyes. He was tall, with broad shoulders and moonlight-dappled golden skin. All of those things reinforced the Were's wolfish nature, and yet he wasn't a full-blooded member of the species. Human blood also ran in his veins; she perceived the slightest hint of an altered fragrance. One of his parents had, at one time or another, been human.

"That's what you believe will happen when you accept our hospitality?" he asked. "You'd be caged?"

His voice disturbed her with its low, cautious, controlled quality. The Were's earthy, masculine vibe caused another new ruffle in her widening awareness of the world outside her family's gates. This was her first time meeting a male Were who looked as if he might not be too much older than herself.

"Why else would my parents shun this place and everyone in it, if not that for the fact that they no longer fit in?" Cara replied.

"From the stories I've heard, your parents withdrew from the rest of the pack because it was in their own best interest."

Yes. She knew that. But it was only a small part of why the Kirk-Killions had withdrawn. And she didn't owe this Were any explanations.

"I need time to get myself together," she said. "It's not easy for me to come out of the seclusion I'm used to."

To her surprise, her companion seemed to get that. After a brief silence, he nodded and said, "I'll wait for you on the beach."

Cara didn't know what to make of that. He was going to leave her alone for a while?

"What if I swim away?" she asked.

"Then you will be someone else's problem."

He didn't mean that the way it sounded. Cara heard how his pulse pounded with the effort it took for him to let her have her way. She had no doubt that he would come after her if she tried to leave the area, and that shaking off this guy might be a difficult task. The strength of his inner wolf and all those rippling muscles made him a worthy opponent.

"Who are you?" she asked, more intrigued about him than she wanted to be.

"Name's Landau. Rafe Landau. And I can assure you that though my family's estate has walls, those walls are there only to keep trespassers out."

Landau...

The Miami pack was both run and protected by his family.

She didn't really believe in coincidences, and yet what were the odds she would run into a Were of this caliber so soon after ditching the guards his family had sent to bring her there?

"Can you promise me that's the truth? I won't be a prisoner behind those walls?" she asked.

"I can."

The handsome Were allowed one little thought to slip past his mental defenses, and Cara caught hold of it easily. Neither fear nor anger ruled Rafe Landau's thoughts. He wasn't afraid of her at all. When she saw the image he held in his mind, she smiled.

"I could be one, you know," she said. "If there were such creatures."

He was staring at her openly. His heart continued to pound.

"Who knows?" she added. "Since you're granting my wish by letting me explore the sea, maybe your wish will come true."

"What wish?" he asked, frowning.

Cara's answer was meant as a subtle warning of her power. This Were might be strong, but he wasn't truly in control now that a werewolf-vampire-banshee hybrid like Cara Kirk-Killion was in Miami.

"About mermaids," she said as she dived beneath the next incoming wave.

Chapter 3

"Well, this is going to be a challenge," Rafe muttered as Cara Kirk-Killion disappeared from sight. He feared that the word *challenge* didn't begin to cover things.

She was swimming away, and he wanted to go after her. What if she decided not to return? Would he let her go? Let her become somebody else's business, as he'd said?

Not likely.

He found himself much too interested and curious about her. And besides, his family was responsible for her safety.

Rafe ignored the tug of the outgoing tide on his legs. He needed more time to think. If Cara was anything like her parents, he could sympathize with her reluctance to meet the pack that had helped her family out of a jam so long ago.

Rosalind and Colton had departed from Miami soon after a battle with a particularly nasty nest of vampires that had almost killed Cara's father. Colton Killion had been so severely injured that he had ended up a rare ghost wolf—the name Weres had for survivors of such heinous, life-threatening attacks.

Given Colton Killion's state of health and his appearance after the attack, the wolf's desire to go into seclusion was understandable. But in addition, from the stories Rafe had heard, Colton's mate had turned out to be something even rarer than he was, making it even more necessary to retreat from the city. Now, Killion's sole offspring was here, and heaven only knew what traits she possessed.

Rafe walked farther up the beach and turned without taking his eyes off the ocean. Cara hadn't seemed dangerous, but what did he know? Wasn't it a fact that looks could be deceiving?

He clutched his phone. The next step was to call and check in with his father, who would probably send a car to fetch her. But he didn't do so. Not yet. Rafe empathized with her plight. Cara had to know how different she was and that his pack would be wary.

Still, whatever other forms she could take, Cara was a wolf. Both of her parents had been full-blooded Lycans before the events that had changed them, and Lycans carried the purest blood in the Were world. His hand felt hot. His insides were feverish. It was likely that his wolf was reacting to that part of Cara. Was his desire to see her again due to obligation and the threat of danger in his own backyard, or did it have to do with meeting a new kind of being that he wanted to understand?

Maybe she'd ditch him and appear somewhere else. If she did, where would she go?

"I won't call them," he said as if she still stood beside him. Then he sent that same message silently through the telepathic channels all Weres used to communicate.

"But I won't go away," he warned out loud.

The return of the fluttery sensation in his chest made Rafe stand up straighter. It was as though Cara Kirk-Killion had heard his little speech and had placed her own silent comment inside his chest instead of his mind. She knew he was there, all right, and that he would be here when she decided to be reasonable. She was also letting him in on some of the special things she could do.

The only question now was how long she might make him wait for another chance to see her, and if she already knew that was what he wanted most.

The Were wasn't going away. Cara sensed his determination to corral the guest who was MIA and fulfill his obligation to the pack. She also sensed that he was genuinely interested in her for reasons of his own. This Were male had a different agenda. He seemed to be as curious about her as she was about him.

She rode the crest of another wave, feeling extraordinarily light, but guilt over the promise to behave that she'd made to her father left her nauseous. Her family never broke their promises. Would she be the first to do so? If the Landaus' walls didn't keep her in line, her family's reputation for integrity would.

As the wave that brought her back to shore receded, Cara stood up. Taking a few steps forward to avoid the drag of the tide, she said to the Were on the beach, "You are persistent."

"Persistence is my middle name," he returned. "I've been told it's a virtue."

Cara didn't wipe the water from her face, liking the coolness it provided. "You'll take me to your pack yourself? You aren't afraid of being alone with a member of my clan?"

"Should I be afraid?"

"Not tonight."

"Then yes, I'll drive you to the compound, if that's all right with you," he said.

"Do I have a choice in the matter?"

"I suppose you can do whatever the hell you want, though the invitation to be our guest stands," he replied.

She watched the tall Were brush sand from the hem of his jeans. In the moonlight, his bare shoulders appeared to be perfectly sculpted. She allowed her gaze to linger there.

"One thing, though," he said, glancing up. He held out his hand, offering her the damp shirt he had removed before wading into the water after her. "Nakedness won't do if we meet anyone else on the way to the car. This is the best I can come up with unless you remember where you left your own clothes."

Cara glanced up the beach. "I came from that way."

He nodded. "Maybe you can wear the shirt until we find your stuff."

If she followed his suggestion, she would have to take the shirt from his hand…the same hand that had touched her and given her the first real thrill she could remember. She wasn't sure she wanted another one. She was fiercely aware of his body, and the fire in his eyes held her strangely captive.

She took another step, then paused. The Were's scent saturated the shirt he held out to her, overwhelming her senses.

Seeming to understand her reticence, he closed the distance and stopped an arm's length away from her with the shirt dangling from his fingers. It was a dare. A challenge. She took the shirt and held her breath as she slipped it on. The musky fragrance embedded in the fabric surrounded her body like a cloud until she could barely smell anything else.

"Better," the Were said. "Now let's get the rest of you covered up, shall we?"

Cara only then dared to take a deep breath.

"You have to understand that my family is personally responsible for your safety while you're in Miami," he said. "That was the pact we made, and pacts must be honored. I'm guessing there would be hell to pay if we don't keep you in our sights."

The shirt was soft, well-worn, and the same color blue as Rafe Landau's eyes. Cara liked those details, and she liked looking at Rafe. He was a fine male of the Were species, she supposed. But the way she felt around him was disturbing.

"What if I asked you to postpone the inevitable for a while longer?" she asked.

He said, "I thought you already did."

"Your pack thinks I'm a freak."

"Then you can prove them wrong."

"How do you know I'd be able to do that?"

"Call it a hunch," he replied.

Cara blinked slowly. Like her, Rafe was quick to make judgments. But that didn't mean he was right.

"It's just a feeling I have," he explained.

"You don't know me."

He shrugged those fascinating bare shoulders. "We can walk along the shore to get your clothes. I like the sand. Moonlight makes it sparkle."

Cara expected him to say more. He had to have questions.

"Maybe we can come back here sometime after you settle in," he said. "Would you like that, Cara?"

Hearing a stranger say her name gave her a jolt of pleasure that she tried to ignore. She wasn't experienced in the nuances of male-female relationships, though she wanted to learn. And she could do worse than having this handsome, understanding Were as a teacher.

Rafe Landau didn't know her, though. Not really. Not at all.

So what would he think when he found out her secrets?

The time it took for them to reach the spot where Cara had left her clothes was too short for Rafe's liking.

With Cara dressed only in his shirt, which hung a little below her hips, the whole situation felt too intimate. They weren't lovers out here to enjoy the moonlight. He had become her guard—and her jailer, to hear her tell it. Still, having this rare and beautiful creature beside him made Rafe feel oddly content.

He had to wonder about the hidden dangers Cara represented. Her father had achieved legendary status among those of Rafe's pack. Her mother was only mentioned now and then in whispers. What kind of life could Cara possibly have had with a family like that?

"Are you much like your mother?" he asked, undeterred by the probable insensitivity of the question.

"Yes," she replied.

"Are you afraid of being like her?"

She glanced at him as they walked. "Sometimes."

"Would your family have sent you here if they had suspected trouble for you among us?"

She shook her head. "Only at home can I truly be free."

Rafe said, "I believe… I hope…you'll find that doesn't have to be the case, and that you'll make friends here."

The desire to see her face up close and in better light had become an urgent necessity. Rafe wanted to get to know every line and curve of her body. Cara might be dangerous, but she looked so fragile and delicious in his shirt.

Maybe *fragile* wasn't the right word.

If Cara was anything like her mother, formidable was more like it. Rumor had it that Rosalind Kirk could shape-shift into many different forms any time she wanted to and that few enemies could stand against her. Neverthe-less, if Cara was like her mother, and not entirely wolf, why did his wolf recognize hers? And why didn't he sense any animosity in her?

"I won't be here long. Surely you know that I can't live among you," she said, acknowledging his thoughts as if he had shared them with her.

"How do you know you can't be happy here?" he asked. "At least you can give us a try."

She gave the ocean a long look and said, "I have prom-ised to try."

Cara's feet seemed to skim the sand. She was incred-ibly beautiful. Stunningly so. Yet there was no mistak-ing the powerful aura that surrounded Cara like her own personal fog. Rafe could only imagine how she might use that power if she wanted to.

Despite that, it took all of his willpower to keep his hands to himself. He wanted badly to console Cara, to reassure her that her visit would go well. He knew he was lying to himself about the possibility that she wouldn't want to leave when the time came. For the moment, he tried to stick to the story that they could be friends, though that too was revealed as a falsehood each time Cara leaned into the wind and his shirt clung to the outlines of her sleek, wet body.

When she stopped, he stopped with her. She turned to face him, and his pulse sped up. Moonlight hugged her face, showing Rafe all the details he had been hoping to see. He held his breath.

She had high cheekbones and a wide brow. Though she was lean, her full lips lent her a softness that was lacking in her attitude. Her neck was long and graceful, her skin a smooth, unblemished ivory. Large eyes, framed by dark lashes, dominated her other features. Those eyes were a bright Lycan green.

She took a step, bringing her close enough for Rafe to feel her breath on his face. She said suddenly, in a hoarse, velvety whisper, "It's you, isn't it?"

Then she waited in silence as if daring Rafe to find meaning in those words.

Chapter 4

She knew she had surprised Rafe. There was no way he could even begin to comprehend her remark. But this had to be the Were who had haunted her dreams. Why else had they met like this—him, out of all of the other wolves the Landaus could have sent to find her?

Was there such a thing as coincidence, after all, or had there been some other hand at work here?

Cara had anticipated this meeting with her dream man and had vowed to pay him back for the sleepless nights. Now she wanted this moment to go on, and for time to stop with the two of them right here, near the water.

Eventually, she broke the silence. "Six days. I'll stay here for six days and then I'll go home."

He said, "Are you worried about the moon being full right after that?"

Cara didn't have to look up at the sky to know the exact position of the moon, and that it was half-full tonight. The pull of the moon on her system was a constant reminder of what it could do, and what she could become. She also felt the movement of the tides and the rhythm of the blood in her arteries.

She felt Rafe's attention on her as if it was another touch.

"It wouldn't be wise to stay any longer," she said.

"What would happen if you did?"

He wore a serious expression that made his eyes gleam as he waited for her to explain herself.

"Unwanted guests might arrive," she replied.

"We've had quite a few unwelcome visitors in the past and know what to do with them," he told her. "Have no doubts about that."

"These uninvited guests wouldn't be any of your concern and are merely another part of my existence."

"Are you talking about vampires and what happened to your parents here?"

"Among other things."

He leaned toward her. "What would other creatures want if they did come?"

"The same thing you want," she replied soberly.

"And that is?"

"Me."

Her answer didn't seem to surprise him. He didn't feign ignorance or pretend to misunderstand her meaning. But he took in a breath and held it before speaking again.

"It's natural, I suppose, that I'm interested in you. Wolf-to-wolf attraction has a heady allure, and being at the beach doesn't help any, because moonlight on the water is romantic. Then there's the fact that you're exceptionally beautiful and half-naked. All of that can mess with a guy's head. I'll admit that it's messing with mine."

Ribbons of pleasure wound through Cara with an exotic

flutter. No one had ever told her she was beautiful. She hadn't really been sure how others perceived her looks. She'd never understood why other creatures wanted a piece of her, except for the vampires. Her mother had warned her about that. Having a Banshee's spirit nestled inside her would allow her to lead bloodsuckers to their next meal by pointing out human weaknesses. If caught by them, she'd become a vampire's dinner bell.

The heat caused by Rafe's remarks left Cara uncertain about what might happen next, and what she should do. Her legs felt weak, and that was a first. Her stomach twisted as if the thing she housed had come alive. Rafe had an almost mystical allure for someone who had gone without companionship for most of her life.

They had reached the place where she had discarded her clothes, but he hadn't noticed. Hadn't he said he liked her half-naked?

"You haven't seen a naked woman before?" she asked, noting how he stared at her as she started to take off his shirt.

"I've seen a few," he replied. "But none quite like you."

A shiver moved through her as she brought her head up and whirled around. A new feeling had invaded her senses, and it didn't register as anything remotely like pleasure. It was an announcement that they had company. The kind she had warned Rafe about. Trouble was coming, and the wolf beside her was about to find out what her world could be like.

Rafe spun around, his senses on high alert. Cara was already on the move.

He caught up with her in four long strides as his cop reflexes kicked in and he stepped in front of Cara to block her way while he searched the beach and the sidewalk. She placed both of her hands on the center of his back and applied pressure to move him out of the way.

"Wait," he said to her. "Just wait."

He didn't have his gun. Hell, he wasn't wearing shoes. The shove Cara gave him sent him forward a few inches, but he rallied. Determined to do his job and protect her, Rafe hit a number on his cell phone to call his father and said to Cara, "What's out here that I can't see?"

"Fangs," she replied.

"Fangs, as in vampires?" Could that be right? Had vampires found Cara already? How was that possible?

"One of them," she said.

"Close by?"

"Very close."

"How can I find it?" Rafe asked.

"Smell."

He was supposed to smell a damn vampire when his lungs were filled with Cara's rich scent?

"Describe the smell, Cara."

"Dark earth, dirt and other things more difficult to define unless you've met with vampires before. They're masters at masking those smells, which makes them hard to find if you were to go looking."

"Can we get to the street, or another block down the beach?" Rafe asked.

When she didn't answer him, he took her silence for a bad sign. Keeping his eyes trained for any movement in the distance, Rafe automatically reached for Cara's hand. The surge of electricity that hit him when their skin met was a shock. But he couldn't let it distract him from getting Cara out of there. Even if she had faced these creatures before, he had to guard her with his life. Or try to.

"Follow me," he instructed, lacing her fingers with his

and absorbing charge after charge of electricity that felt like nothing he had ever experienced.

Adrenaline took over. Cara didn't protest when he pulled her forward. "Warn me if I'm heading for trouble," he said.

She tugged at him hard enough to stop him after a few steps. Frustrated by this, Rafe turned to face her.

"It's you," she repeated, but with a different emphasis this time.

Her face came close to his. As she met his eyes, her wet hair brushed against his bare arms, causing alternating heat and chills. Cara, the hybrid shifter he was trying to protect, could adopt a vampire's form if one were to appear on the beach, but the need to get her to safety was strong enough for him to override his fear of that happening.

"What is it, Cara?" he asked.

Her next words shook him up more than touching her had.

"You smell like them," she said.

"What are you talking about?"

Cara didn't honor him with a reply. She turned toward the dark remains of a hotel under renovation, taking him with her. That's when Rafe saw what had attracted her attention. Someone was standing on the sidewalk in front of the hotel. Someone Rafe thought he knew.

"No way," he muttered in surprise. But in the time between that remark and his next breath, the figure materialized beside them…and Rafe hadn't seen anyone move.

Perfume. He smelled perfume, and it was familiar. Also familiar was the tangle of blond hair and the green shirt that did little to hide an exquisite body.

Holy hell…it was Brandi. She was a goddamn vampire?

Shock kept him from moving as fast as he should have. His date from earlier that night was there beside him, hiss-

ing through a pair of lethal-looking fangs as she went for
his throat.

In a flash of speed that rivaled the creature in front of
him, Cara had Brandi's hair in her fists. God, it really was
Brandi…or whatever the hell Brandi really was.

"My problem. Not yours," Cara said to him over her
shoulder.

"The hell you say," Rafe snapped.

Cara was already liquefying. That was the only way
to describe what happened. Her body just seemed to melt
into a kind of being that was Cara, and yet different, as
the fight began in earnest without him.

Cara snapped at the vampire with a fresh set of fangs
that made the creature in her grip hesitate for a few seconds too long. Uncertainty flashed in its red-rimmed eyes
as Cara's hold on its hair tightened.

She felt the vampire's hunger and the incessant throb of
its need to feed. Hunger was everything. Starvation meant
oblivion. Vampires killed in order to feel alive—otherwise
they were merely animated corpses without any real direction. This one was old, and masterful in its ability to disguise itself, at least on the surface. Once the fangs came
out, its human semblance began to decay.

Cara's fangs, on the other hand, brought on a hunger of
another kind—a defensive desire to rid the world of the
monsters she was cursed to emulate.

The Landau wolf joined in the fight. Using his weight
to press Cara aside, he struggled to get one of the vampire's arms behind its back. The harsh sound of a bone
breaking was alarmingly loud as the vampire's arm shattered near the shoulder. Louder still was Rafe Landau's
startled intake of breath.

Fangs brushed her arm, ripping her sleeve, leaving a

long trail of flapping fabric. Cara maneuvered her way between Rafe and the snarling bloodsucker with her own fangs exposed and her hands moving almost subliminally fast.

Rafe, who was incredibly strong and used to fighting, by the looks of things, wasn't to be left out of this fray. He also wasn't going to allow a female to help him do his job, no matter who or what that female was. With great force, he leaned his shoulder into the vampire, and it teetered. The bloodsucker hissed again through its treacherous fangs and spit out his name.

Hearing that made Rafe Landau hesitate. Cara pushed past him. Even a few seconds of hesitation when facing the walking undead meant certain death, and this abomination whose distant relatives had helped to make Cara like them in so many ways wasn't going to win tonight. She hated vampires. She hated when they came to find her, sensing kinship. She hated every time her fangs dropped and she became like them.

Foul black blood spurted from the vampire's shoulder when Cara's fangs found purchase. The blood was evidence of the creature's recent meal. There would have been none otherwise, only a spill of dark gray ash, the same ash vampires dissolved into after being dealt a death blow by a worthy opponent.

"Let me have her…have *it*," Rafe directed. But this was Cara's own personal war.

Cara dug into the bloodsucker's flesh with her fangs. At the same time, Rafe landed a right-handed punch to the vamp's shoulder, and the fanged parasite shrieked, probably not from pain, but from anger. It lost hold of its feminine disguise as it rallied, and the undead creature whose looks previously could have fooled most humans became the bony, skeletal, red-eyed abomination it really was.

Cara felt no kinship with this vampire and refused to acknowledge being like it. This was one of the many monsters that ruled her nightmares. Vampires were the enemy, though this one had likely believed at first that Cara Kirk-Killion, with her pale skin and fangs, might help take Rafe down. But vampires like this one had nearly killed her father. To most of the world, her father had died.

Colton Killion's DNA had been compromised by too much vampire saliva and too damn many bites, and he'd become a legendary white ghost wolf one fateful night here in this city, an albino whose skin and hair would have stood out anywhere as being freakish.

The same thing was not going to happen to Rafe. *Not tonight.*

Though this bloodsucker was fast, Cara moved faster. She possessed a secret weapon that hadn't yet been revealed. Her heritage. All of it.

She snapped her fangs in the creature's face and made it look at her…made it look into her eyes. A far older spirit than this vampire was beginning to show itself. This was death calling. True and final death. The Banshee inside her had awakened.

The shriek that came from the vampire's open mouth when it realized its fate dictated what would happen. One second passed, then two more, and Cara, with her dark spirit's extra push of power, punched through the vampire's bony concave chest with both hands. Gripping hard, she squeezed the blackened heart that had not beat in centuries until the useless thing crumbled.

"Don't breathe," Cara shouted to Rafe, who was beside her and struggling to get his hands on the foul creature. Seconds later, the bloodsucker exploded like a bomb had gone off, and its lifeless body disintegrated into a flurry of foul-smelling ash.

Chapter 5

A dark, sticky rain was falling. But it wasn't rain, really, and nothing that resembled water.

Rafe let out the breath he had been holding and stared at the spot where the vampire had been standing. He was afraid to look at Cara in vampire mode. Shock over witnessing what had happened here made his stomach turn. This was something he would never forget, though the whole event had happened so fast, he hardly believed it had happened at all.

Finally, he did look at Cara. He had to see her to try to make sense of it all. She hadn't just exposed a gleaming set of fangs—she'd exposed one of her secrets. And even with her fangs, pale skin and flat black gaze, she had the ability to mesmerize.

Many features remained of the Cara he had met earlier tonight, only slightly rearranged. She had sharper cheekbones with gaunt hollows beneath. Dark crescents underscored her eyes, contrasting with the whiteness of her skin. The only color she possessed was in the tiny drops of blood speckling her lips, which were half-closed over a daunting pair of unnatural teeth.

The rumors were true. Cara had transformed into this new version in less time than it had taken for him to catch his breath. Rafe found himself equally fascinated and repelled by her new look and by what he had seen Cara do to the vampire. No stranger to violence himself, he sympathized with Cara, and how her life probably consisted of one fight after another. He wondered if she would ever be able to find the kind of peace she might crave.

Hell, he was speechless, and therefore couldn't ask her how a shape-shift like hers was possible, or what it felt like. Plus, it wasn't his place to ask her tough questions or make her feel any more ill at ease than she already did.

Cara Kirk-Killion, in whatever incarnation, had just possibly saved his sorry ass from a date with a vampire. He couldn't believe it Using fangs had likely been Brandi's intention all along. The skimpy lingerie had been camouflage. Lilac perfume had masked the unfamiliar scent. They probably never would have made it as far as the bed.

Cara had freed him from having to deal with his first vampire—a bloodsucking parasite so like a human, he had fallen for its charade. What about the curvaceous body Brandi had sported, and the silky tousled hair? Would he have discovered the truth if he'd gotten close enough to the creature to discover that her chest contained no heartbeat?

And what about Cara? Did her vampire form come with a vampire's thirst? If she had those kinds of urges, she was controlling them well. She stood three feet from him with her hands at her sides, radiating no perceptible aura of danger, though for a few seconds back there, he'd had doubts. His ears still rang with the sound of her fangs gnashing.

"Can you change back?" he asked, slightly out of breath from the recent adrenaline surge. "Will the vamp characteristics fade away on their own?"

Maybe those weren't the questions Cara had been anticipating, but they were the only ones she was going to get from him at the moment. Her eyes were trained on him. She said nothing in reply as he led her down the sidewalk.

In the glare of his building's exterior security lights, Rafe glanced away from her lingering gaze long enough to note the rips in the shirt he had loaned her and the blood soaking it in several spots. She didn't seem to notice any of that.

"We'll need to see to those scratches," he continued, stepping aside so that Cara could precede him to his apartment. "We can make a quick stop at my place if you're up for that," he added. "I have a first-aid kit."

When she shook her head, Rafe paused, then rallied enough of his wits to say, "Thank you, Cara."

Her red-rimmed eyes, still dilated by an interior darkness, met his. The tips of her extremely white fangs seem to glow against the color of her blood-flecked lips.

"That's what you meant when you said 'it's you,' right? You smelled that vampire on me?" With the adrenaline still flowing, he kept up the nervous chatter. "Now that I think about it, I invited that thing inside. What kind of a fool does that make me?"

Cara finally spoke. "I told you they are deceptive in their disguises. Like we are."

Like we are...

She meant werewolves masquerading as humans.

As Rafe watched, Cara's face began to shift back, resuming the beautiful human features Rafe had first seen on the beach. The hollows in her cheeks disappeared, and some color returned.

He couldn't have explained what the process actually was or how it worked. When the redness around her eyes faded, Rafe wondered whether the face she now showed him was what Cara actually looked like, or if its beauty was another kind of stunt for suckers like him to fall for.

In the light from the building, Cara was even more beautiful than she had been in the moonlight. Could he trust his eyes?

Werewolves didn't shape-shift easily. Transformations were always painful. Some Weres shifted faster than others, with full-blooded Lycans being masters of the pain game. Cara's switch to vampire mode and back had been different. It was silent, fluid, as if she had merely coaxed another shape into existence.

She continued to observe him with a keenness that made his inner wolf anxious. *Just another shape-shift in my repertoire of them*, her expression suggested. *Nothing special.*

Hell, did she even know what special was?

"Can you control when you become like them?" he asked, unabashedly curious. "Do you make it happen?"

"It just is," she replied.

Though the fangs were gone, flecks of blood still dappled her mouth. Rafe tried not to look.

"There's no control button or on-off switch?" he pressed.

She shook her head.

"Can you do that with any supernatural creature, Cara? Look like anything that comes your way?"

"For the most part."

"Christ," Rafe muttered. "I see why you'd rather not be in an unfamiliar place when the moon is full. What could your werewolf side possibly be like when coupled with so many other talents?"

"My wolf side isn't much like yours," she said and left it at that.

The weird thing was how much Rafe desired to get closer to Cara in spite of the warning flags his mind was waving. He should have felt sorry for her and her burden, yet she seemed to be up to the task handed to her, if tonight was any indication. Though her family and background were intimidating, part of him needed to see past all that and find the real Cara. He tried to guess whether anyone had ever seen the real thing.

Telling her he'd like to help in any way he could seemed ludicrous, given the fact that she had just killed a vampire with relative ease. Still, when he gestured again for Cara to precede him to the stairs, she obliged docilely, as if she trusted him and they were fast friends.

As they began to move, the soft growl of a well-tuned engine broke the silence. Rafe had almost forgotten about the emergency call he'd made to his father before the vampire attack and had mixed feelings now about how quickly the call had been answered. He would lose one-on-one face time with Cara. There would be less of a chance to get to understand her.

Cara was listening to the same sound. When she turned to him, her eyes were again the color of polished emeralds, flashing with curiosity as she wiped the flecks of blood from her lips with the back of one hand.

"I'm sorry," Rafe said as the musky scent of approaching Weres became more pronounced. "We've got company, but it's all right this time."

Almost immediately, he caught sight of his silver-haired father and Cameron Mitchell, another large Were Rafe knew very well, who was a senior detective on the Miami force. They were heading their way.

"I'll go up and get more clothes for you," Rafe said to

Cara. "We never found yours, and the picture you present in my shirt is…"

Cara tilted her head to one side, waiting for him to finish. He didn't. Couldn't. This hybrid Were was sexy, lithe, strong and more than a little bit scary.

Yep, he was a fool, all right, for sliding into sympathy with her so effortlessly. Telling Cara he was attracted to her, scary bits and all, wasn't going to help their situation and would confuse them both. But that was exactly what Rafe was thinking when he'd only known her for, what? About an hour? As she had said, he didn't really know her at all.

"Rafe?"

His father's deep voice was only a sampling of the kind of power Dylan Landau possessed. Cara looked at the alpha coming their way with a flicker of interest. Before stopping to think, Rafe reached out to offer her his support with a light touch on her arm.

Fire erupted inside him as her eyes met his. More flames licked at his throat, bringing on a whole new level of heat. There was no way to acknowledge the suddenness of these feelings, their origin and what they might mean.

"Cara. Are you all right?" his father asked, slowing as he reached them.

When she remained silent, Rafe didn't answer for her. He was struggling to control his own feelings. Cara had told him she needed time to adapt and get her bearings, and time was exactly what he needed, too, because his heart seemed to stop each time their eyes met. The reaction was not only absurd, it was irresponsible.

"Come with us," his father said, gesturing with a wave of his hand toward the car parked a short distance away. "And welcome to Miami."

Rafe's father hadn't gotten to be a respected judge without having serious social skills. The alpha's tone was calm and free of any hint of chastisement over her earlier escape. There was no anxiousness in his bearing. There usually wasn't.

Between his father and Cameron Mitchell, Cara was in good hands. Rafe should have been relieved to let her go.

Yet he didn't feel relieved. Far from it. He felt as if he wasn't going to allow them to take her.

Cara slowly turned toward the two men without visibly revealing the concern Rafe knew she felt. On the inside, Cara was on fire, just like he was. They shared the flames that had been kindled between them tonight. He should have feared that, or at least been wary of the speed with which this had happened.

Ignoring the others, Cara said to him, "That vampire wasn't after me. It wasn't waiting for me out here tonight."

Rafe gave her a questioning glance.

"It was here for you," she said.

Cara was probably right, Rafe realized. Having missed her earlier opportunity, Brandi had been waiting for another shot at draining him dry, whether or not he had company.

But there was a slight problem with that, if the stories were true about werewolf blood being a turn-off to vampires. He chose not to point that out for the time being. Brandi had been trying hard to seduce him. If it wasn't dinner that wily creature had wanted, what had she been after in her attempt to take him down?

Cara wasn't in a position to protest the presence of the two new Weres, so she tucked those arguments away. She didn't like this interruption of her time alone with Rafe Landau. In less than an hour, she had become comfortable with him. Now, with the other Weres present, she again felt tense.

The stab of regret she felt when Rafe dropped his hand and spoke to the others was a new kind of pain. She didn't like pain. A fresh round of defiance rose inside her over the idea of being separated from him.

"What vampire are we talking about?" the silver-haired Were asked nonchalantly.

His scent was similar to Rafe's. The older wolf was notably alpha, and had to be Rafe's relative. Father? He was tall and handsome. His long hair was tied behind his neck, and he had a younger Were's build that made him appear half the age he'd have to be if Rafe was his son.

Rafe answered the Elder Were's question. "We had an argument with a vampire a few minutes ago."

Cara observed how the alpha moved with the same kind of grace Rafe possessed. However, she could tell the older Were was a pure-blooded Lycan and wore his power like an emblem of high birth and rank.

"Cara, this is my father, Dylan Landau, host for the duration of your stay," Rafe said, interrupting his father's line of questioning. "And this is Cameron Mitchell, a good friend of ours."

"Please forgive the lack of introductions," the alpha said with a polite dip of his head. "We were very worried, and happy to find you in good hands."

The alpha took in the scene through pale eyes, missing nothing, assessing the situation without comment. When his gaze landed on the tears in her sleeve, Dylan Landau said, "Not a heated argument, I hope, with that vampire?"

"Nothing too bad," Rafe lied.

The alpha nodded. "I knew your father and your mother, and I'm glad they agreed to let you visit. I'm sorry you didn't have such a warm welcome, Cara, and would like to make that up to you. Would you come with us to see where you'll be staying?"

Cara didn't look at Rafe. She could have been wrong about the tension that seemed to be building up in him. She knew he wanted her to comply, to reach a safer place than this one. He had worried about her from the start.

Even more interesting was the fact that Rafe's father didn't appear to be too concerned about their encounter with a bloodsucker. Every Were here should have known this was worthy of further investigation.

Unfamiliar sensations continued to flood Cara's system when she stole a closer look at Rafe. The flares of heat were new and something she didn't fully understand.

As if he had the ability to read minds, Dylan Landau addressed her last thought. "Rafe, why don't you ride along with us? Maybe you can loan our guest some clothes until we get her home."

Rafe's father didn't ask how she had lost her clothes in the first place, and Cara felt herself warming to his social skills.

It looked like there was going to be a benign ending to this eventful evening, although she'd now witnessed for herself the vampire presence in Miami and how far this city's bloodsuckers had evolved. The appearance of the one she'd met tonight, along with the fact that it had purposefully lain in wait for Rafe, was highly unusual. Vampires tended to act on instinct when finding their next meal, and didn't usually set traps to ensnare their victims. Yet it seemed to her that this one had.

"Male or female vamp?" Rafe's father casually asked.

"Female," Rafe said.

The alpha asked Cara the question directly. "New or old?"

"Not too ancient," Cara replied. "But talented."

Dylan Landau nodded. "Well, it will be a relatively short ride to our home. It won't take long. We aren't going far."

Unlike with his father, Cara could read Rafe's emotions as easily as she had read the tides. Rafe wanted her to go along with the plan his father had laid out, and at the same time, he was sorry she had to.

Cameron waved a hand toward what Cara supposed had to be the waiting car. She looked to Rafe, whose nod indicated it was all right for her to follow.

She was trapped. There was nowhere for her to run, and she couldn't rely on the ocean to take her away.

"I'll be right behind you," Rafe said. "I'll just get those pants. I hope you like jeans."

Cara followed the two Weres from the beach without argument, already counting the minutes until Rafe would again be at her side. She continued to watch Dylan Landau closely, gauging his strengths, needing to ask the alpha what he knew about her parents, while knowing she'd have to behave and honor his wishes if she were to piece together the puzzle of what had happened to them here nineteen years ago.

Had her mother and father been cast out of this pack for being different, or for being dangerous? What had made them outcasts? Who had been alpha of the Landau pack back then?

Her parents had never spoken to her about these things. Questions about the past were taboo. Getting answers was part of the reason she had gone along with the plan for her to visit Miami. It was the reason she was going with these Weres to the car. Still, there was another path to explore here in Miami as well. The path revealed by her dreams… and the wolf that had haunted them.

Right here, tonight, whether it had been coincidence

or the fates had played a hand, that wolf dream was no longer just in her imagination. The wolf had come to life, and his name was Rafe Landau.

They were in some way connected. Even in the reality of the moment, Rafe Landau was haunting her. His looks, his presence and strength, all pointed to something she had yet to grasp. If events were lining up and falling into place, did that mean she was on the path to get everything she wanted?

The questions she needed to have answered were the reason she had helped Rafe fight off the undead attacker, and was wearing his clothes. Her curiosity had prevented her from making Rafe pay for appearing in her dreams and disturbing her sleep. It suddenly seemed to Cara that Rafe, for good or ill, was going to be the key to what lay ahead. He was the central clue in the mystery of her existence that she had to unravel.

Do you know this, Rafe?

She didn't send that question to him over Were channels because the answer would have been about what lay ahead. If she stayed.

Chapter 6

The Mercedes sedan seemed crowded to Rafe as Cameron pulled away from the apartment building. Cara didn't look at him from her side of the back seat. She had withdrawn. He couldn't read her.

They traveled in silence. The car's interior temperature felt cool, and the leather seat was luxuriously soft. For once, Rafe was relieved to leave the beach. Thoughts of his close call with the vampire nagged at him. He hoped this wasn't a prediction of what the future might bring.

Several things continued to bother him, but the image of Cara with fangs was foremost in his mind. He would have preferred that others in his pack not be exposed to the kinds of things Cara could do. *Freak* was the word she had used to describe herself, and actually, was that so far off?

Then there was the attack itself. Why had the vampire gone after a werewolf when a human tourist would have been much tastier fare?

Rafe kept those thoughts locked away as buildings and lights shot past the window. At this hour, people crowded the streets in search of food and entertainment. Six police cruisers crept by, keeping up a show of law-enforcement presence.

By comparison, the estates on the far side of the city were quiet, secluded and seemingly a world away from the neon and the noise. His family's property was one of the largest in the area. Its three landscaped acres were entirely surrounded by an eight-foot stone wall that was monitored by the pack, and there was a small manned guardhouse at the front gate. A well-respected federal judge lived there. Wolves lived there. The Landau house was a place of secrets.

Rafe stole a glance at Cara as they neared the front gate, thinking she had to feel the heat of his attention even though she didn't turn her head. Or was he just making that up?

He sighed and rubbed his temples, not sure what to expect when they arrived. Who would be among the welcoming committee? He assumed that most of the pack would have been kept from meeting Cara, at least for tonight.

"Here we are," his father announced as the surroundings grew darker and the long stretch of gray stone came into view. Cara had told Rafe she feared being trapped behind those walls. He'd have given a lot to know what she was thinking now.

The car stopped in front of the ornate iron gate and was quickly waved through by a familiar guard when it opened. As the Mercedes cruised down the driveway, his father turned in his seat.

"It's past dinnertime, but you can have whatever you like as soon as you're settled in. You must be famished," he said.

Rafe could almost hear Cara silently say, *What I'd like is to go home.* To her credit, she didn't voice that response.

"Not many of us will be here tonight," Rafe's father continued. "We thought you might prefer some time to get to know the place before we introduce you. Is that all right with you, Cara?"

Cara was looking at his father. She barely nodded her head. He knew this was the moment she had been dreading, probably since the plan for her to come to Miami had first been hatched. On the surface she looked calm enough, but small quakes rocked the seat he shared with her, and every one of them was like a stab to his heart.

"Cara," he said, needing to speak, hoping to ease her trepidation. "Look. See up there?" He pointed at the brick house that rose two and a half stories above a meandering lawn. "Top floor? Can you see it?"

Her eyes glided that way.

"Your mother stayed in a room there. Your father, too. Maybe you'd like to have that same room while you're here?"

He had snagged her interest. The air in the car became charged.

"I'm sure that can be arranged," he said.

"It can," his father agreed.

She was tuning in now and sending Rafe messages over silent Were channels. *"Will I be a prisoner?"* And *"Will you be here?"*

"No. Not a prisoner. I've told you that. And yes, I'll stay if that's what you want," he messaged back over airwaves his father would also be privy to, as well as every other Were within a short distance if they weren't careful with their transmissions. He'd have to warn Cara to erect her own inner walls.

Here, in this pack, where so many secrets had to be

kept, unspoken messages were the normal mode of communication. That didn't necessarily ensure privacy but there were ways to get around being overheard at times.

"After what happened tonight with that vampire, it might be best if you stayed away from the walls for a day or two, Cara. Just to be safe," his father suggested.

The next shudder that rolled through Cara felt to Rafe as if it had been his own. The word *trapped* echoed in his mind like a shout. When the car stopped in front of the columned southern portico and Cameron opened the door for her, Cara got out. As Rafe's mother emerged from the house, Cara paused. But she didn't have to be worried.

Dana Delmonico Landau had turned *casual* into an art form. That showed now in her outfit, a faded pair of jeans and white T-shirt. His mother had never been a fan of anything fancy. She had been a good detective for years and had risen through the ranks to become a captain in the Miami PD. She had only recently retired and therefore had too much energy in need of release.

His mother had been born human. She had also been here when Rosalind Kirk and Colton Killion had briefly been in residence. From the stories of that time, he knew his mother, along with his father, had helped Cara's parents in the final showdown with the vampires, after which both of Cara's parents had disappeared.

Did Cara know anything about that, or about the part his pack had played in those last days? If she housed spirits similar to her mother's, would being in this house seem like déjà vu?

"Cara." His mother had stopped on the bottom porch step. "I'm Dana, and I'm glad you made it here. Would you like to come in, or would you prefer to take a look at the grounds first? Please understand that we're not as grand as this place would make us seem, and we're happy to have you join us here."

Cara didn't speak, but Rafe noticed that her eyes gravitated toward his mother's.

"Rafe," his mother said, turning to him, "why don't you show Cara around while we find her something to eat? Let her catch her breath before joining us inside."

Rafe looked to his father, who nodded in spite of his earlier warning to remain clear of the walls for the time being. Both of them knew the importance of that warning, and also that Rafe would take it seriously.

"Cara, what do you say to a little more fresh air?" Rafe asked. "Just to get the feel of the place."

She nodded. And as though she was merely any invited guest instead of the daughter of two Were legends and potentially as dangerous as both of them, everyone else went into the house, leaving Cara and him in the driveway, alone.

She had never seen a house as large as the one in front of her. Actually, Cara had never seen any house besides the small one she had grown up in. Nevertheless, she sensed a certain familiarity with the Landau mansion that didn't make it seem as foreign as she had expected. There were plenty of ghosts here, something she was intimately familiar with.

"How long?" she finally said to Rafe, looking up at the house. "How long were they here?"

The fact that he was keeping up fairly well with her line of thinking was reflected in his reply. "Your father was treated here after being gravely injured. My grandmother took care of him and helped him to heal. Your mother was also a guest at the time and helped keep watch over him. This was before your parents had bonded."

"My mother was a guest?"

"She was here with her father. Your grandfather. It was also Rosalind's first time away from her home, and she skipped the warnings about remaining inside, and breached the wall. She must have found your father in the park, in a fight with the fanged hordes. It was her call that brought other Weres to your father's aid before it was too late."

Cara eyed the wall in the distance and the trees topping it. "That park?"

"The same one," Rafe said.

"So close?"

"The vampires had infiltrated a section of the park that's still some distance away." Rafe was eyeing her intently. "Does being near to it disturb you?"

Cara shook her head.

"No one mentioned those things to you?" he asked.

"My parents don't speak about the past," she replied.

"Not even to explain why things are the way they are?"

She turned to look at Rafe. Getting to the heart of her parents' past had been a burning desire for as long as she could remember, and Rafe was telling her things she had long waited to hear, but how much of what he knew was the truth, and how much of it was either hearsay or exaggeration?

Rafe probably hadn't been born when her father and mother had been here, and neither had she. To Rafe, the past was just tales. To her, the real story of what had happened and who she was had become the main puzzle of her life.

"Vampires," she said. "Vampires made my father a ghost."

"It took a hell of a lot of them to do so, I've heard," Rafe agreed. "Colton was one of the strongest Lycans around in those days, and also a damn good cop."

"Cop?" Cara echoed.

He nodded. "Your father was a cop, like my mother. They protected Miami's population from bad things that dwelled both in and out of the shadows."

"Until those shadows gained strength," Cara noted.

When Rafe smiled, she was taken aback. There was no humor in anything that had been said, yet his smile was spontaneous and sat as easily with Rafe as his wolfishness.

He said, "We've both sprung from some pretty good genes. My mother was a badass, too, I hear. She's actually pretty formidable even now."

His smile dissolved into a more serious expression. "How did you know that vampire would be after me? I'm asking you because I'm wondering if maybe you purposefully gave me a trail to follow that took me away from her tonight. Could that be right, Cara? You lured me out of my apartment in time to prevent those fangs from reaching my neck?"

When she broke eye contact, Rafe seemed to read into it. "Well, then I doubly owe you, don't I." he said. "And I'm not going to ask how you managed it, because whatever you did worked."

She let that go. Had to. Rafe was looking at her differently now—more warily. Her earlier show of tricks might have scared him. Either that, or he was perplexed by what seemed to be an overly complex plan.

She could read in his expression that he had more to say on the subject. Instead, he changed tack. "We can walk in the grass. In the evening, and this far inland, it's the coolest place around."

"Where are the others? Your packmates?" she asked, wanting more of her parents' story but not ready to ask.

What Rafe had already told her was food for thought, and better than any dinner the Landaus could have served up. Her parents had both stayed here, in this house, and some of these Weres had fought beside them.

"The others will be waiting to be called," he said.

"Will they come tonight?"

"A few of them, especially because of the vamp sighting. They'll keep a close watch on the park. You won't have to meet more of them until tomorrow."

So, she had been wrong about being a freak show for this pack. There was no crowd. She wasn't going to be the main event for tonight. Rafe's immediate family members and the Were who had accompanied the alpha were the only wolves present at the moment. She could breathe easier, and almost relax.

Maybe not too much relaxation, though. Because there was a new scent in the air, and a sense that someone on the other side of the wall was silently calling her name.

Chapter 7

A chill reached Rafe as he watched Cara turn toward the section of stone wall not far from where they stood in a way that made it obvious she sensed something he didn't.

After years of having to protect herself, Cara was probably a master of the art of self-preservation. He'd hate for it to be another bloodsucker out there, though. His grandfather's pack had culled vampire-nest numbers years ago. As far as he knew, there hadn't been a vamp sighting near here since he was a kid.

Rafe maintained his neutral expression while keeping a cautious eye on Cara. The electrical current she radiated eased after he took a few deep breaths, testing the air the way most Weres did when their inner fur was ruffled by a disturbance. Her frozen stance had produced waves of anxiety in Rafe that made his muscles twitch.

Reluctantly, he tore his focus from her to check out the wall. Cara took a step toward it. Though it was only one small step, Rafe sensed that she wasn't going to be chained by any rules governing her confinement, even if they were for her protection. Actually, he couldn't imagine who might stop her. The memory of Cara Kirk-Killion in action tonight wasn't going to fade any time soon.

Ebony lashes fluttered over her eyes. Strands of midnight-hued hair, still damp from her swim, looked like streaks of ink against her ivory neck and the shoulders of the borrowed shirt, which was too large and made her look waifish. In his jeans, Cara seemed even more like a kid playing dress-up.

"What is it?" His voice was low and steady.

"No one is watching us now?" she asked, her gaze intent on the wall.

"I wouldn't say that—" He didn't get to finish. Cara was already heading for the barrier at a sprint. She was more like a streak of lightning than anyone moving on two legs.

Rafe swore out loud. Then he gave chase, hoping to God that he could catch up with Cara before anything else did.

He didn't see her top the wall and didn't stop to analyze his actions in following her. There were eyes on them from the windows in the house and also from somewhere else nearby. He and Cara hadn't truly been on their own, and she must have known this.

He breathed a sigh of relief with the knowledge that backup would be right behind him if it was needed. Uttering oaths beneath his breath and pushing the limits his patience, he followed her into the park.

She was fast. Cara ran like she was on all fours, much like their ancient wolf ancestors. He had never seen anyone go from zero to thirty in just a few seconds on foot. But he was also no slouch when it came to running. Pack training readied all Weres for speed a few nights each month after the sun went down. Plus, he spent a lot of time sprinting after bad guys in the day job.

In his favor there was the fact that he knew every corner of the park that lay beyond his family's property. Most of the officers in law enforcement did, because the western section had a notorious reputation as a gathering place for gangs and criminals. There would be a cop or two on duty out here tonight, keeping watch for illegal activity. There would also be a party of Weres scouting around. It was unfortunate that a place so haunted by an unsavory past was connected to the estates beyond its borders, but that was part of city life.

He ran without breathing hard or breaking a sweat. Cara, just ahead of him, had slowed to a jog. She darted from tree to tree like a bloodhound on the scent, and he still had no idea what she was after.

Damn it…why didn't he know what she was doing? He was supposed to be a good detective.

After nearly tripping over something on the ground, Rafe slowed. Cara had removed the jeans, possibly in order to get around more freely…which meant that she was again half-naked. He was an idiot for allowing her the freedom to get away like this.

He was also an idiot for harboring thoughts of what he'd like to do with all that ivory bareness of hers if the situation were different. And, well…even if it wasn't.

The disturbing scent Cara had noticed was strongest near the trees. The humid air had filled with whispers.

Night had a strange feel to it here, too. The darkness was thicker, denser, as if unseen things took up space in the shadows. The pressure in her ears was a warning. Strange odors left a tang on her tongue. Her pulse thundered, though she saw nothing.

She slammed to a stop beneath an old tree, where her search turned up no one. Ready to shout a warning to some unseen foe, Cara waited a few more seconds to gather what information she could find.

The bark of the tree she stood beside shimmered like gold in the moonlight. Leaves shuddered and fell at her feet, as if the season were changing. There was movement. Rustling.

Cara glanced up.

Her equilibrium wavered. She gave a soft roar of protest. Clinging to the tree's branches was a kind of darkness she hadn't seen before. The treetop had become like a black hole in the atmosphere that was filled with chatter.

She swayed, unsteady on her feet, finally realizing what this was. What it had to be. Vampires were here. Lots of them. The damn bloodsuckers had called to her in a way only they could.

That realization caused the night to blur. Bloodsuckers unlike any she had seen before began to drop to the ground, one after the other. Five. Ten. More kept coming. Too many to count. The sheer number of them took the air from Cara's lungs. For the first time in her life, she felt afraid.

They moved like a monstrous incoming tide of malevolence—a wave of dark disjointed bodies with shockingly gaunt white features and skeletal frames. Things out of nightmares. Throwbacks to ancient times when vampires were nothing more than the walking dead. Their black eyes sank into dark sockets. Mouths were open and hissing, exposing lethally sharp yellow fangs.

An odd sensation of déjà vu hit Cara and rooted her to the spot. Sickness roiled in her stomach as nasty odors churned up unpleasant things inside her. She was going to be surrounded and vastly outnumbered. She'd be dead if she didn't act fast.

Fear of what she was seeing caused her wolf's energy to blaze. She didn't want to become like these monsters and had to do something to stave off a transformation she refused to accept. But could she manage to trick the traits built into her system by avoiding the rules?

Yes...

Like a caged animal finally freed, Cara let a rush of energy take her over. That energy flowed through her like a river of fire, burning everything in its wake. A new, crazed kind of power fueled her fury. Fangs filled her mouth before disappearing again.

"Not like you..." she whispered.

As she raised her hands to fight, Cara felt the sharp pop of claws springing through her fingertips. She called her wolf to the surface and made it obey. The wolf barreled upward and through her with the force of a runaway train.

Her spine cracked. Muscles seized and began to lengthen as she took her first swipe at the darkness gathered around her with preternaturally curved claws that would be a match for any oncoming pair of fangs. The shift was painful because it went against her nature—she had chosen her wolf, instead of becoming like the fanged parasites breathing down her neck. Cara had never attempted this before, and she had to bravely hold on.

Breathing became difficult. Her discomfort turned white-hot. Cara rode out the pain until her body finally accepted the shape that ruled most of her genetics. Werewolf. She-wolf. Not just any Were, either, but one with the ancient European designation of *wulf* that denoted the early masters of the breed who were powerful shamans.

This is who I am. What I am.

The urge to fight roared through her. The need to kill

the creatures that had nearly killed her father here a long time ago became too difficult to ignore. She was strong, fast and fierce. Her wolf shared its soul with the spirit of a Banshee, just like her mother, and that spirit told her she was not going to die tonight.

All she had to do was kill every last bloodsucking fiend surrounding her.

Her blood sang with that goal until her head felt light. But her plan encountered a hitch. The vampires dropping from the trees didn't come after her. Every one of them suddenly moved en masse in the opposite direction, as though they had been drawn elsewhere by something more appetizing. As though they hadn't seen her at all.

There was someone in the distance. Cara turned her head, and the sickness inside her tripled. *Rafe?*

A ripple of horror accompanied the idea that Rafe had followed her, though she should have known he would. Rafe was a protector. He watched over her. As strong as he was, however, Rafe would be vulnerable without a full moon overhead to shift him. Against so many abominations, he'd have little chance of surviving an attack.

She ran, plowing through the haze of vamps, wielding her claws like the weapons they were originally intended to be, slashing at everything in her way and swallowing growls of anger and the sudden fear of losing what she had only recently found. Rafe Landau.

Her claws went through vamp bodies as if they were composed of air instead of strings of decaying flesh and bone. Although the vampires shrieked with terrible, unnatural voices, none of them noticed her. Not one of them fell.

The shock of her inability to stop them tripped her up. Cara stared at the dark moving tide with wide wolfish eyes, seeing clearly, shocked by the sight in front of her and how she wasn't able to do anything about it.

Then her system was jolted with a new awareness. The gaunt creatures were attacking a fully wolfed-up werewolf, brown-furred and massive in size. *Not Rafe. Someone else.*

The werewolf fought the oncoming horde like a pro, swinging his arms, using his legs, snapping his jaws. He fought hard, though he had to realize all that energy was useless against so many sharp teeth.

Cara couldn't stand to watch. She started again toward the rapidly tiring werewolf in the center of the fray and heard a voice in the distance say, "I'm here."

Or...had she uttered those words?

She flew to the middle of the fight, whirled, lashed out and made no headway. The big brown Were, now tiring, didn't once look her way. He looked past her at something she would have had to turn around to see.

Another sound broke through the grunts and growls she and the brown werewolf were making. At first, Cara thought it was a howl of distress or a warning call going up about the fight taking place. But that wasn't it. She recognized what it was. She had heard this sound before.

The shrieking noise seemed to split the darkness into multiple shadows. The power in it sucked the fight out of Cara. She stilled, frozen in place as the scene continued to unfold in front of her.

Helpless to do anything but observe, Cara witnessed the downfall of the beautiful brown wolf as it forfeited its life. Fighting on wouldn't have helped the Were, she realized, because this scene wasn't actually taking place in her current reality.

The brown wolf wasn't here. There were no vampires. What she was seeing was an image projected on the spot where this battle had happened in the past.

Cold gripped her. Energy that had been white-hot now turned icy. She panted with the effort to understand what was being shown to her as her limbs trembled and spasms threatened to drive her to her knees.

The Banshee spirit inside her hadn't predicted death here. The shriek had been a Banshee's cry, yes, but her Banshee hadn't made that sound. Someone else had used the Banshee's voice, but in a different way—maybe not to predict this brown werewolf's death, but to save his life.

And that just wasn't the way things worked.

Banshee spirits predicted death, and this one hadn't. There were no other dark, death-bringing spirits in the area, except the one sharing space in Cara's soul. And yet she had heard that wail.

She stared hard at the scene that she now knew to be unfolding in a different time. Her claws had been useless against the monsters because they were ghosts, like the rest of the images she had been shown. She was experiencing a memory, a projection, an imprint of what had happened in the past, in this spot. And that meant the sound she had heard had to have been made by her mother...long ago.

Others were coming, rushing toward the fight in this alternate reality. She watched with fascination as several Weres flooded the area. They had come to the brown wolf's rescue nearly too late, drawn by the Banshee's wail.

Once the Were pack took up the fight, it became even more fierce and bloody. But Cara couldn't be a participant, since this was a dream. She had seen this battle, had lived it, had experienced the horror of an event that took place long ago...all through her mother's eyes. Rosalind Kirk had been here then and had made the call that had ultimately saved Colton Killion from death.

The park had shown her another piece of the puzzle. What had happened here all those years ago had been so awful that it still resonated in this space.

Witnessing the attack that had made her father what

he was today made Cara's knees buckle. Colton Killion. Ghost wolf. Outcast. Survivor.

But how could he possibly have survived this?

She closed her eyes to shut out the rest of the fight her parents had endured. It was a gruesome thing that made that sickness inside her grow.

Releasing the breath she had been holding, unable to fight the wobble in her limbs, Cara slipped toward the ground without hitting the grass…saved from falling by the strong grip of two powerful hands that had come out of nowhere.

Chapter 8

What the hell just happened?

The question echoed inside Rafe's head as he reached Cara in time to catch her. She was breathless and wolfed up. He had no idea why her heart was racing so fast. There was nothing out here to see. He and Cara were the only two Weres in the area. And yet she, who was supposedly the strongest of them all, had folded up as if life had suddenly become too much for her to bear.

He held a werewolf in his arms. Cara had shifted without the moon to guide her, and without other external stimulus. There were no furred-up werewolves present to initiate such a change. She had taken werewolf form as quickly as she had adopted the vamp semblance earlier. He'd have believed this was also impossible if he hadn't seen it with his own eyes.

She was also incredibly beautiful, and he shouldn't have noticed. In a shape that was more familiar to him than that of a vampire, Cara looked both feminine and feral. Yet she didn't exactly look like any werewolf he had known. She retained more of her human features than was normal for Weres. Same light eyes. Same dark, silky hair. There was no hugely elongated face or altered body shape. Upon closer inspection, it was easy for him to see the female he had met on the beach.

She was taller, thinner, stringier. She had more angles. Sharp bones jutted under her skin, and there were shadows beneath her eyes. Ten curved claws edged her fingertips. Her spine, through the shirt she still wore, felt to him like a string of pearls.

Maybe she had gotten stuck in a partial shape-shift. It was possible her shift hadn't been completed before he'd found her, and because he looked human, her changes had hit a pause button. Whatever the cause of the way she looked at the moment, Cara's uniqueness fell way beyond the scope of his experience.

Rafe sank to his knees, holding her. Cara's eyes were closed. Her face was chalky and pale. He wiped away the tears that glistened on her cheeks and listened to the growls rumbling in her throat. She'd had a shock of some kind that he hadn't been able to share. His eyes had been on her and not their surroundings. Whatever had shocked Cara into her current behavior had been the impetus for this latest version of herself. So, what the hell was it?

"What did this to you, Cara?"

His only concern now was to make sure she was all right. While he wanted to point out the consequences of breaking rules put in place to prevent incidents like this, Rafe didn't speak of those things. He didn't take the time to search the area again in case he had missed something. All he could do was comfort Cara and encourage her to shift back to the shape that best resembled his in case anyone from the pack came looking for them—which would be any minute now.

"Change back," he whispered, his face close to hers as he pressed dark, silky tresses away from her cheeks. "Do it now, Cara. Do it for me."

She shuddered once before he heard the soft sucking sounds of her body realigning that meant her wolf was in retreat. Jutting angles melted back into curves as her tautness eased. Her face blurred back into full human mode, though it remained as white as a sheet. The last to go were her claws.

With them together like this, the moment felt exotic. He was holding a she-wolf in his arms, one he was attracted to in spite of all the warnings and inexplicable phenomena he'd witnessed tonight.

His inner wolf gave a roar that shook Rafe up. He swallowed back an inappropriate human-voiced growl. Were to Were, wolf to wolf was how attraction among his kind worked.

Cara was again only half-dressed in the torn shirt he had loaned her. Her lean legs were bare. Broken buttons on the shirt exposed far too much neck and the graceful sweep of her collarbone for him not to notice.

The scene was as rich as it was surreal. His wolf, tucked deep inside him where it belonged, continued to respond. Pressure built up in his chest, and these feelings weren't supposed to happen. Shouldn't happen. He and Cara were sampling a forbidden closeness that would get them into trouble with their respective families if they found out. Killion's daughter was off-limits. Her presence in Miami was merely temporary.

So why was it happening?

Why was Cara here, uncomfortably out of her element?

Who in their right mind had forced Cara to visit a world she knew so little of?

When her eyes fluttered open, Rafe felt immense relief. "You're okay, I think," he said. "Am I right?"

Chances were that she couldn't talk yet. Maybe she didn't want to. The air around them vibrated with questions he needed to ask her.

"We have to get back to the house, Cara. This is far too dangerous. I'm not sure what just happened, but I'm guessing it wasn't normal, even for you. There are tears in your eyes. You're shaking. Please tell me you're all right."

She reached up to encircle his shoulders with her arms, in what amounted to the first show of vulnerability he had seen in the short time he'd known her. The slide of her palms across the back of his T-shirt felt extremely sensual and gratifying, though he knew better than to classify it that way.

Her face was so close to his, he had to look into her eyes. The hardest part of this whole ordeal was the effort it took him to keep from kissing her...because that would have been a really stupid thing to do under these circumstances.

As he fought that internal tug-of-war, Cara drew back suddenly, possibly only then realizing the position she was in. She pushed him away and scrambled to her feet. Looking down at him, she said in a quavering tone, "Don't tell them about this."

Rafe got to his feet. "Tell them what?"

"Swear," she said.

Didn't she know it was too late to hide her show of rebelliousness? As of a few seconds ago, they already had company. Of course she would have noted that, so what, exactly, was she asking of him?

"They know you're out here. It wouldn't be wise to

forget that you are a special guest," he said. "I have already mentioned our responsibilities regarding your safety. You do understand that going against what's asked of you doesn't win you any points?"

"It was something I had to do," Cara said.

"And it was terribly dangerous."

"Dangerous for my father. Not for me."

Her remark dropped a big black net over the conversation, stifling anything Rafe could think of to say. He didn't know what to make of her words as he ventured a glance over his shoulder at the park.

"This is where it happened," she explained. Her shaking hadn't eased, and not much of her color had returned. "This is where my father nearly lost his life."

Rafe's gaze drifted back to her. "How do you know?"

"My mother told me."

"When?"

"Minutes ago."

Rafe rubbed his forehead, trying hard to follow what she was saying. "You didn't have a cell phone. No place to hide one. How could she tell you that?"

"She called me to this place in another way."

Could he believe her? Rafe wasn't sure. There were so many odd and questionable things about Cara Kirk-Killion, he didn't know where to begin to catch a glimpse of the full picture.

She was a complex creature and way out of his league, but did that lessen his desire to kiss her?

No.

He was hot, energized and on edge. He also knew exactly how far he had to move to again enfold her in his arms. His attention kept returning to her face and the sensual mouth that had trembled with vulnerability a moment ago. Though no trace was left of the tears he had wiped from her cheek, those tears had been there for a reason. When she had first opened her eyes, they'd contained a silent plea for support.

So…no. The desire to hold Cara and kiss away whatever had shaken her was strong, even though part of her allure could be a trick. She could have been using her wiles to attract him.

Yet what she had gone through had seemed real to her. He had seen that in her eyes.

Confusion over this dilemma drove him to silence. Cara moved first. She pointed a slender finger at the darkness they both had the ability to see into.

"This is the place," she repeated. "I now know why my father became what he is. I saw how it happened. I experienced that fight with the vampires as if I also took part in it. But I wasn't there when he was. I didn't run to help the brown Were fight off so many fangs. It was my mother who did that. She moved in to help. I saw all of this through her eyes."

"Because she called you here," Rafe said with a skepticism he couldn't hide.

Cara shook her head. "This place called to me with her voice. Violent acts leave residue on a place. This was a memory for me to access because I have that brown Were's blood in my veins. My father's blood. After the attack, my mother's spirit became tied to those vampires, not out of any choice she made, but because she was born special in ways that left her open to roaming demons."

Weird as it might have been, Rafe was starting to believe her. As a cop he sometimes experienced sensations tied to past events at certain locations. At least, he imagined he could. To see those past events firsthand was an entirely different matter, and a level of awareness well beyond his capabilities. However, who was to say that Cara didn't have those kinds of talents, and that she spoke the truth?

Meanwhile, they were taking too much time outside the wall. He wasn't exactly sure how many minutes had actually gone by, but it had been long enough for the pack to find them. Others were close now, and closing in. The night had become pressurized due to his packmates' imminent arrival.

"How will we explain your quick exit if we don't mention what you saw?" Rafe asked.

"Will we have to?" Cara asked.

"Yes. They're coming now, as you well know, and are merely giving us some time to work this out. They will be watching us to see what we do next."

What she did then beat every single explanation Rafe could have thought up. She closed the few inches of distance separating them, stood on her toes, lifted her face… and pressed her lips to his.

Chapter 9

She had meant to distract the pack that was observing from a short distance away, pretending she and Rafe had retreated from view for a few private moments alone. But something unexpected happened.

The second her lips met his, Cara felt another kind of shift taking place. Not a physical alteration. Something different, new and exciting.

Rafe's mouth was hot and unmoving. He had been as surprised by her forwardness as she was. The heat he radiated through this meeting of their lips flushed her face and throat. The charge created by touching him so intimately quickly spread to her chest, where her heart raced.

She had done this without thinking, and sensed that this latest move had been dictated by the spirits she harbored. What did she know of kisses, feelings, planned distractions and relationships? She'd had a vision that had shaken her and in the aftermath had wanted to share her wayward energy with someone. Rafe Landau just happened to be the easiest to reach.

Or so she told herself.

Beyond that, she had no idea what might come next. She had expected that this closeness would make her feel better, but she actually felt worse. Rafe Landau was pure electricity, and he was sending her bottled-up energy into overdrive. Scrambled images flashed in her mind like small bombs going off, all of them connected to the emotions she held in check. Vampires were cold. Werewolves were warm. Rafe Landau was volcanic.

The world around her dimmed as the sensations she was experiencing took over. Air shivered. The ground moved. This one little meeting of their mouths sent Cara's stomach into free fall and numbed every warning message her nervous system kicked up.

She had dared to get close to a being that was most like her in terms of species, and they were connecting. Here, so far from her home, she had seen her father mauled by bloodsuckers, and she had found comfort after that vision where it was least expected…in the arms of one of the Landaus, who were gatekeepers to a past she desperately needed to find.

For another second or two—mere blips in the scale of time—when Rafe's lips parted and his emotion caught up with the surprise, the kiss became a real one. As his breath became her breath and his hands slid around her waist, Cara imagined that she also might have become nothing more than an image projected onto this place— someone both experiencing this closeness firsthand and observing it from afar.

His heat was her heat. Rafe's breath was sweet and his mouth was sublime. His body felt extremely masculine and toned, and that new awareness seemed to cue something in her body that had been dormant.

More changes were growing inside her, rising to engulf her, and all of them were centered in her chest. Her heart beat furiously and in time with Rafe's. His strength became hers as if transferred by the meeting of their lips. Their bodies were trysting on a physical level, and she didn't know how to deal.

In the periphery of Cara's awareness, sounds rang out that she couldn't concentrate on or identify. Rafe's mouth was everything and her sole focus. He was the epicenter for needs she had never before accessed.

His thoughts whirled like cyclones in her mind as their connection continued to deepen. When their tongues tentatively touched, more inner fires sprang up to engulf her. He silently repeated her name, moving his lips over hers. It was like a song that got progressively louder. Like a tune she had heard somewhere in the past.

She was listening to the call of the wild. The sound of one wolf attending to another in a time of need. Male to female. Were to Were…except that her world had spun her beyond all that and into a category all of its own.

"Cara, I'm here."

She couldn't take any more input. Circuits were frying and their mouths were sealed together in a way that neither of them had the power to disconnect. Half-hearted phrases she had once used for her dream man, such as *Make him pay* were something she no longer wanted. Not now. Not yet. Maybe never.

The outside world finally intervened, interrupting these moments of sensual chaos. Voices other than her and Rafe's inner messages to each other became too prominent to ignore, and her companion's lips left hers. Rafe's blue eyes bored into hers as if he had also been drowning in emotion and regretted coming up for air.

"Rafe," someone called out. "This is folly. Come home now."

Her wits returned too slowly to have aided her if this were an enemy. Cara shook her head hard and broke eye contact with Rafe. She turned her head to refocus, feeling as if she were tipping off balance until her attention landed on the silver-haired alpha of the pack, and recent events quickly filled her mind.

This kiss had been a distraction meant to cover up a rebellious act and had turned into something more.

Beside her, Rafe called out, "She's okay. We're okay. We just took a little detour."

There was a sharpness to his voice that made Cara's nerves buzz. Surely Rafe's father had heard that edge? Still, Rafe hadn't lied about the detour. So would there be repercussions for ignoring his father's suggestions and for kissing the freak he was supposed to have been protecting?

Back in action and mentally armed, Cara sensed a new disturbance that might have explained the seriousness of Dylan Landau's tone. There were other Weres here, and they were easy to locate by scent, but there was an alternate presence not quite so easy to assess. A presence that wasn't willing to be detected.

Not a vampire.

Not a werewolf like Rafe or his father.

Cara now regretted being the cause of this latest round of troubles for Rafe and his family. But she knew for a fact that more trouble was on its way.

His father had sent up a silent warning that Rafe barely heard over the words of Cara's messaged apology.

"I didn't mean to bring this down on you, but it was an inevitable consequence of my coming here."

Bring what down on them? Danger? Lust?

Rafe took a sideways step, holding up a hand to signal Cara to wait while two members of his pack glided in behind his father. Danger was a signal that made all werewolves twitchy. These Weres were on high alert, their muscles corded.

Rafe looked to Cara for guidance. Who else might be out there in the dark, able to avoid his extraordinary gift of sight? He had become aware of this other presence by reading her mind, though her face showed no hint of anything out of the ordinary.

His father strode forward like a silver bullet—fast, purposeful, geared up for the task at hand, whatever that might be. "Foreign," his dad said to the small group that surrounded Cara. With a few sharp gestures, he encouraged everyone to move in the direction of the wall.

There was no reason to disobey that directive. His father rarely issued commands, so when he did, everyone listened. Nevertheless, Rafe got no real sense of what Cara believed could be out here spying on them. In all the time he had worn a badge, his radar for anomalies had been trained on human criminals and rogue Weres. Tonight, he had added vampires to that list, but he didn't catch their odor on the sultry incoming breeze.

They swiftly hustled forward in their small circle, with Cara quiet in the center of this man-wolf show of testosterone. His father had brought the gate guards, two big guys used to tackling problems head-on. Against an invisible foe, however, muscle would be useless. Even so, though Rafe didn't often regret leaving his gun locked in a safe in his apartment, he regretted it now. If nothing else, he could have waved the weapon around as an added incentive for unseen interlopers to back off.

They reached the wall in tight formation. Rafe's father held out his hand to help Cara over, but she shook her head. Finding grooves in the stone with her fingertips, she simply hoisted herself up and over the wall with ease.

Rafe went next. He was used to climbing this wall, having mastered the skill as a kid. The others followed. Although he'd been afraid that Cara would be long gone when they landed, she was there on the lawn. Quiet and oddly calm, she nodded her thanks to each Were in turn, and then paused to search Rafe's face.

"They're not coming here," she said. Her voice was steady. "Not tonight."

Then she walked toward the house as if nothing had happened. All eyes turned to Rafe for the explanation. Regretfully, he had only one.

Privacy was the word that came to his mind, and also the worst possible thing he could have said.

"Sheer lunacy," Dylan Landau countered, with a hard look at his son.

Had they seen the kiss? The intimacy he and Cara had shared?

Cara had asked him not to mention her vision. If he was trustworthy, he'd honor that request and dig deep for another way to smooth over this breach of etiquette with his father. For werewolves, lies were tough to maintain. Weres read Weres. There was no option here but to speak as much of the truth as he could, in spite of what his father and the others might think.

"I'm attracted to her." Rafe shrugged his shoulders.

"So I see," his father said. "Does that make you mindless and blind to your responsibilities?"

"Neither, actually. If I couldn't handle what might have been out there, Cara certainly could have."

His father dismissed the other Weres with a barked thank-you, which meant that Rafe was going to have a one-on-one with the alpha.

"Seriously?" his father said, turning back. "You'd put Cara at risk after she ignored the rules a second time in a single night?"

"I had no real choice but to follow her. Should I have let her go out there alone or taken the time to call for help?"

"Is that what you call protecting her, Rafe? Holding her like that?"

So, his father had seen the kiss...

Instead of following up with further objections, though, his father added, "I get it. It was that way for me when I met Dana. I was instantly attracted to her. But your mother, who was forbidden as a mate for me at the time, was human until she had a lesson from the bad wolf that changed her. While Cara is...more."

Rafe smiled warily, able to feel the lingering softness of Cara's mouth. He recalled that Cara had been segregated from others for all of her young life, and that what had happened in the park tonight might have been her first dip into the realm of adult pastimes.

The thought gave him a few seconds of pleasure before he responded to his father.

"We haven't imprinted, so you can skip the birds and the bees lecture. She's safe. We're here. End of story," he said.

"I hope that's true, Rafe. I haven't set eyes on Colton Killion for more years than I can count on both hands. He was a tough bastard before fate rose up to bite him, and I can only imagine what he's like now. Entrusting his daughter to us was a miracle in itself. How she fares here is up to us."

"Maybe," Rafe countered. "However, it's not that straightforward. Cara has a mind of her own. She is unlike us, yes, and I'm not convinced that she wants to be like us, or if she even could be if that was the purpose for this visit. Cara is merely tolerating us and is used to having more freedom. Who among us would like to be displaced or caged?"

"No one is caged. Cara can go home any time she decides to. This is an invitation, not a life sentence. It's our home, not a prison."

"I hope she sees it that way," Rafe said.

"Cara will see it like that if she has no reason to believe otherwise."

"And if she jumps the wall on occasion in order to assure herself that she's free?" Rafe asked.

His father had no answer for that and didn't try to make one up. Dylan Landau had built his reputation as a lawyer and, eventually, a federal judge on honesty and fairness. He had always played fair with his son, as well as the other Weres in the pack he had inherited from Rafe's grandfather. No one could say this alpha didn't try to understand all sides of an argument. And Dylan Landau was still, after all these years, deeply in love with his wife.

"Kissing her was the only way to stop Cara from whatever she was going to do out there," Rafe said.

His father nodded thoughtfully. "Be careful. That's all I ask."

Their little chat had gotten them nowhere, really, and both of them knew it.

"Dad. Why would a vampire come after one of us if the stories about their appetites are true?" Rafe asked.

"Like the one you met tonight?"

Rafe nodded. "What did it have to gain if our blood disgusts them?"

His father eyed him thoughtfully. "I suppose that it might have been to take you out of the picture."

"I wonder what picture that would be?"

They both looked at the house as if they could still see Cara walking up the steps.

Rafe spoke first. "Believing that would mean that the vampires somehow knew about my affiliation with this pack, and perhaps even that Cara was coming here."

"Yes. And I don't like the sound of that," his father said in a sober tone. "Or that fact that vampires have returned and dare to show themselves. It will bear looking into."

A heavy silence fell as they contemplated the ramifications of what had been said. Finally, his father smiled and clapped Rafe on the back. "Hungry?" Without waiting for an answer, he led the way to the house. The house that felt different to Rafe now that Cara Kirk-Killion was here, stirring to life so many of its secrets.

Chapter 10

Cara stood by a window, fighting the need to go back out there, beyond the wall, to find more of her mother's memories and the elusive presence that had disturbed her.

At the moment, there were only three wolves in the house with her. No army. No bolted doors. Rafe and his father were on the lawn by the steps, deep in conversation. Here in a house where privileged werewolves lived and so many others came and went, sensing anything beyond the werewolf presence was impossible. Cara had to shelve her curiosity about that wall and what lay beyond it for the time being and try to get along when small aches plagued her from the way she was clenching her teeth.

The house was grand in spite of what Rafe's mother had said, and too large for Cara's simpler taste. There were rooms and doorways everywhere. The expansive salon she stood in had high ceilings and a polished wood fireplace. Pictures lined the walls. Each piece of furniture looked as though it had been placed with care. This was in direct contrast to her home, which was a sprawling cabin filled with rough-hewn furniture, surrounded by trees and reached by way of a seldom-used dirt road.

But her mother and father had both been guests here in the past, so Cara didn't feel completely isolated from them. It was possible that their spirits and memories remained in these hallways, as they had in the park. If that were the case, she would find them.

"Would you like to see your room before having something to eat?" Rafe's mother asked from an open doorway.

"Yes. Thank you," Cara replied, not used to being civil with strangers, no matter who they were.

"Hang tight, then. I'll just be a minute," Dana Delmonico Landau said before disappearing into the room beyond.

The offer to stay in the room her mother had used was another example of how these Weres seemed to know a lot about her parents, while she was at a disadvantage, knowing nothing about this pack. *Well, almost nothing,* Cara silently amended as she ran a fingertip over her lips. Some things about Rafe Landau were clear, and most of that information was as disturbing as everything else.

Though strong and capable, Rafe had not pressured her to behave. He had gone along with her without complaint when he could have turned things around. Would he honor her request to keep what she had seen in the park to himself, as well as the fact that she could wolf up without the help of a full moon?

Her treacherous body hadn't lost the sparks their intimacy had ignited and wanted her to return to Rafe now. Cara crossed her arms over her chest to hide the ongoing thud of each heartbeat as her thoughts stayed on Rafe.

When he turned and followed his father toward the house, she backed away from the window.

"Okay," Dana said from somewhere behind her. "If you'll follow me, I'll take you up. Your things are already in the room, having arrived before you did."

This could have been a small dig about Cara's earlier MIA status, though the tone didn't seem accusatory.

"If you'd prefer to have a tray in your room, that can be managed," Rafe's mother offered. "Just tell me what you want to do, and what would make you the most comfortable for your first night away from home."

"Tray, I think," Cara said gratefully, and Dana waved her toward the stairs.

"You knew her?" Cara asked as they climbed higher into the house, thinking more of her family than of food. "You knew Rosalind?"

"Not really. I loaned her some clothes once when she needed them," Dana said.

Cara wondered if this was another allusion to the fact that she was in a similar circumstance, dressed only in Rafe's torn shirt.

"I left my clothes near the ocean," she said.

"That's where you met the vampire?" Dana asked without looking back from the step above.

"Yes. There."

"Sensing vampires is a talent that comes in handy. Things could have been easier around here in the past if more of us had that capability," her hostess remarked.

"You've fought them before?"

"Oh, yes. And I'm lucky to be here to say so."

They reached a landing on the second floor and kept going to another set of stairs that led to a compact space high above the yard. Cara saw only one door here, which led to a small room. After so many years had passed, the small space somehow still carried a diluted version of Rosalind Kirk's floral scent.

Behind Dana's back, Cara finally smiled.

"The room hasn't been used in a while," Rafe's mother said. "We haven't had guests in years."

"It's fine for me."

Compact and spare, the room contained only a bed, a dresser and a chair. The ceiling slanted toward a window that someone had already opened to let the night air in. Her bag was on the floor.

Leaning against the doorjamb, Dana said, "Your mother jumped from that window once. No one knows how she accomplished that without breaking a bone."

Cara moved to the window to look out, noting the distance to the yard below.

"I hope you'll use the door while you're here, Cara," Dana said. She was smiling. "The bathroom is behind the curtain beside the closet."

Cara nodded.

"Now, about dinner," Dana said. "I'll get that tray and be back in no time."

"Thank you," Cara replied, though she was tuned in to the view of the yard and picturing her mother leaping three stories to freedom. Why Rosalind had taken such an action was the question that plagued her.

Rafe couldn't wait to see Cara and didn't appreciate how that thought kept taking precedence over others. He hesitated on the porch as his father went inside before he backtracked to the yard.

Taking his time, trying to remain calm, Rafe walked to the side of the house. It had only been occupied by his mother and father for the last ten years, though they had visited his grandparents here often before then. He knew which room was Cara's and that she would be there. That room, high under the eaves, was another part of the Kirk-Killion legend. Out of all rooms in the house, Cara would be the most comfortable there, when everyone else avoided the space.

He found the window he sought—Cara was framed in it. She hadn't changed her clothes. The fact that she still wore his shirt gave him unexpected pangs of pleasure. This was a category of female he had never expected to find. Cara was seductive, secretive, part animal and extraordinarily beautiful. He wanted not only to protect her, but to possess her.

And it was a good thing he hadn't imparted that piece of information to his father.

Can't have her, his mind argued. *I know better.*

Nice try, his mind kicked back. But the reminders weren't working. Rafe had a hard time convincing himself that he didn't really need to see her again so soon.

They hadn't had time to get to know each other. Their conversations had been sparse and their meetings filled with strange activity. Despite all that, Rafe felt as if he knew Cara on a level way beyond normal and that the extremes of their emotional connection bypassed any need for further details.

This thing between them, whether wrong or right, remained inexplicable. Maybe it was a case of animal magnetism at its best. Surely it was a hell of a lot more than lust at first sight.

"Are you all right?" he called out to her.

"She jumped from here," Cara said.

"Rosalind? Yes. So the story goes."

"Does the story say why she did that?"

"I don't suppose anyone would know the reason, except for your mother," Rafe said.

"We didn't sit around telling stories. My parents aren't legends to me."

"How did you pass the time out there?" Rafe knew he was pressing his luck, and he didn't actually expect Cara to reply. Plus, they were speaking loudly enough for anyone around to hear.

"We hunted," she said.

"For food?"

"For monsters."

Rafe blinked slowly to hide the fact that he should have seen that one coming. "Were there a lot of monsters?"

"An endless supply," she replied.

"Did anyone help?"

"Now and then, but it was a task for us in the end."

When Cara shook her head, her jet-black hair, dry now and sleek, ruffled in the breeze that also moved the curtains beside her. The desire to catch hold of those shiny tendrils drilled at Rafe's insides and caused him to take a few backward steps.

He heard another familiar voice through the open window and watched Cara turn her head. She then turned back.

"Dinner?" he asked.

After nodding, Cara left the window. Moments later, she was beside him on the lawn.

Rafe flinched with surprise.

She maintained a distance of several feet between them this time and seemed to be waiting for him to say something. Rafe rallied with a casual remark. "Maybe you can show me how to do that teleporting trick while you're here. Other officers on the force would be envious."

"It's a family secret," she said.

Rafe thought her tone was light, as if she might be teasing him. The fact that she could dig up some lightness, with everything going on, seemed like a good sign and provided him with more insight into the Cara he wanted to know.

He willed himself not to look at the bare legs she didn't seem at all self-conscious about. And that was hard. He was a male, after all, and it was a toss-up where to actually keep his focus, since all parts of the female standing in front of him were worthy of attention. He had to constantly remind himself that she was off-limits and that she would leave soon, in spite of those wicked inner flames and the desire to take her in his arms.

"Are we alone?" she asked, training her gaze on him. Her big green eyes were alight with excitement.

"No," he replied. "I think you know that without me having to tell you."

"Can we walk? Will they stop us this time?"

"That depends on the direction we go."

"Near to the wall."

"It wouldn't be a good idea," Rafe said.

"Just near to it. Not over it."

He waited for Cara to say more.

"Not over it," she repeated.

He nodded. "We can do that."

"Go ahead and say what you're thinking," she suggested.

"I might be arrested if I did."

The remark appeared to throw her. Dark hair curtained the sides of Cara's face when she tilted her head questioningly, so that she appeared to have been swathed in reams of black silk.

"Never mind," Rafe said. "Let's walk."

"I expected you to ask me to promise to behave myself," she said. "Why haven't you?"

"I don't recall how many times I broke that kind of

promise," he said. "I'll just trust you and leave it at that. Okay?"

She nodded.

Rafe balled both hands to keep from reaching for her, wishing she had put on a damn pair of pants and that she didn't look so immensely appealing. Both man and wolf were twitching with appreciation for the opportunity to be with Cara again. After her little excursion to the beach not more than a couple of hours ago, and a little wall-hopping after that, watchful eyes truly would be on them at all times.

He didn't like being observed. However, his father's trust might have slipped somewhat where Rafe's dealings with Cara were concerned, and with good reason…because as soon as they were out of direct light, and with others watching them or not, he planned on kissing Cara again. Anyone who protested that could go to hell.

Eyes like green fire met his, as though Cara had read that last thought, as well as the thoughts preceding it. Feeling as though he had been caught in a tractor beam, Rafe had a sudden sensation of falling through space.

Chapter 11

Within the chaos taking Cara over, two things stood out. The first was the idea of making it beyond the Landaus' wall as soon as the chance presented itself. The second was an almost dire need for more intimacy with Rafe. Right then, both desires carried equal weight.

In the open, with the grass under her feet and Rafe beside her, the hope of running away began to wither. So far, no one had mistreated her or allowed the rumors about her family to dictate the terms of her confinement. All in all, the Landaus had gone out of their way to make her feel welcome and as though she was just another potential packmate.

Once they got wind of Rafe's budding feelings for her, however, all that might change. If given a choice, Rafe would have to stand with his pack. It was useless to imagine otherwise, or that she and Rafe could develop a true friendship within these massive stone barriers. She had never had a friend. Had never needed one until now, though already Rafe felt like so much more than that to her.

With his scent in her lungs and his eyes following each move she made, Cara wished things could have been different. That she hadn't been born a creature whose segregation was necessary in order to protect outsiders from feeling the wrath of the monsters that regularly appeared at her family's gates.

Did friendship involve subjecting each other to danger? What if this thing with Rafe went well past the definition of that term?

Dealing with isolation was a lesson she had been taught early on, and it made good sense in the long run. If Miami's population knew nothing about the existence of werewolves and vampires, what would they think about demons? What would they think about a creature like her, who was a conglomeration of all those things?

She was the main attraction for monsters, just as her mother had been. Dark recognized dark, and inheriting the spirit of a Banshee meant she carried death's breath inside her in spite of the fact that housing this Banshee had been the result of a good deed done by that ancient spirit in her mother's family's past.

Tonight's vision in the park had shown Cara that her mother had used the dark spirit to save her future mate, in a daring replay of the incident in the dark spirit's ancient past that had tied the Banshee to Cara's ancestors. What this also insinuated was that the Banshee's purpose could somehow be manipulated, and that the spirit could possibly be persuaded to help with a cause that was contrary to a Banshee's reason for existing. Or else maybe the Banshee now owed Cara's family for giving it a place to exist.

The problem was that the black breath, however it had

gotten inside her, attracted anomalies of all kinds. Her mother had lived with that same problem for many years before unknowingly passing it to her daughter. Darkness was part of Cara's birthright. In contrast, everything in Miami was colorful and blindingly bright.

The only saving grace for her predicament, as far as Cara saw, was having her father's pure Lycan blood as a stabilizing factor. With the added infusion of his worldly, humanized Lycan DNA, she was able to tolerate having a dark spirit trapped inside her. So far. But she had vowed never to have children of her own for fear of passing that spirit on and gifting a life like hers to anyone else.

"Do you want to talk?" Rafe asked, walking beside her.

"I'm not sure what there is to say," Cara replied.

"Is talking about yourself prohibited in the grand scheme of things?"

"My life might read like a nightmare to you."

"Sometimes sharing nightmares can dilute them," he suggested.

Cara wondered what he'd think if she told him about the dreams she'd had of him before she had met him, and what she had planned to do if she were to meet the male who had given her so many puzzles and helped to lure her from her home. What she hadn't considered back then was the reason for fate bringing them together, when surely there had to be one.

"I guess that's the reason behind me coming here," she said. "Diluting the nightmares and securing my future."

"I've thought about that, Cara. What if coming here is some kind of a test?"

Cara paused to encourage Rafe to explain that remark.

"You aren't your mother," he began. "Maybe the test is to see if all those monsters can track you here or whether you've given them the slip."

He hesitated thoughtfully before continuing. "It's also possible that those monsters you've met are tied to the energy surrounding your home, and not to you. Could your family be giving you the chance to find out if you can live in the world with the rest of us, instead of being banished from it?"

Those theories resonated for Cara. They were perfectly viable explanations for the decision her parents had made, though she just couldn't see how it would all end.

"Brandi—that's what the vampire on the beach called herself—wasn't after you. That's what you told me," Rafe went on. "If you're such a monster magnet, why was I her target? Once she saw you, wouldn't she have changed her plan?"

Cara shook her head. "She had your scent already, which means that you were marked. It can be difficult for a bloodsucker to veer off a mark. Next to impossible sometimes."

"Even after you appeared and were a much tastier treat?" he asked.

"That's the way they operate. If they come for my mother, they have no interest in me until they find out too late that she has given the dark spirit to her daughter. Some remnant of that spirit must still remain either inside or around my mother. Enough of it to temporarily deter the monsters."

"Dark spirit?" Rafe asked.

"Banshee. You do know what that is?"

He nodded. "But maybe dealing with the vampire on the beach was the first test, according to my theory, and you passed it. The vamp went after me, ignoring you entirely until you made yourself known."

He stopped there before saying in a lighter tone, "Hell, Cara. Maybe you're not so tasty after all. And maybe," he added slowly and with careful precision, "the true test of your presence here is to see if I'd be the one to bite."

Rafe's hand was on her shoulder. With a gentle tug, he turned her to face him. She didn't meet his eyes, needing a few seconds to think about what he had said and how to understand his latest remark. She and Rafe were alike in many ways, but not nearly enough alike to keep him from being hurt if his theories were wrong and the bad guys came after her here.

What she didn't mention was the idea that the vampire had been after Rafe to get him out of the way, having been alerted to her arrival and the Landaus' plans to host her as a guest. One Landau down would have meant fewer werewolves to deal with when the bloodsuckers came after her.

"Well," Rafe continued, "I guess I could be mistaken about you not being like a magnet, because you've been like catnip to me since I first laid eyes on you at the beach. How's that for a confession? So, I have to wonder if you're seducing me on purpose, and if so, what that purpose might be."

With a nice show of Were speed, he brought her within the circle of his arms. They were hip to hip. Their chests were touching, and their thighs. The intensity of Rafe's attention was like facing a whole nest of vampires at once and demanded that she look up. Feeling the sensual energy he radiated as her gaze traveled from his neck to the blue gleam of his eyes, Cara realized that Rafe Landau had misjudged things.

He was the magnet...and she had unknowingly been caught in his force field.

Unprepared for the cascade of emotions hitting her, Cara let Rafe's mouth hover inches from hers. She could no longer look at him. She couldn't breathe when he smelled so fine. She was used to monsters, not strong wolves who teased new emotions from her instead of the usual shape-shifts.

"You're being hasty in your conclusions," she pointed out.

"I know that. I just thought I'd better get all that out in the open."

"Are you always so honest?" she asked.

"No. Not always."

Candor was something Cara understood, though she didn't know what to do with his. Rafe Landau was a daredevil, and proving that here. He was also a rebel, dodging the limitations that had been imposed on him by his family and his pack. But he didn't know the full extent of what carrying around a Banshee's spirit meant, and that through her brief connection to him, she already perceived that death was coming…not for Rafe, but for someone close to this pack that she saw clearly in her mind and had not yet met.

"I have only an inkling of what you're capable of," he said softly in a voice that made Cara's insides ache with longing for a hazy kind of fulfillment that was still unknown to her. "But this is nice, at least for now, isn't it?" he asked. "I'm glad you're here. I hope you'll stay awhile. More than six days."

"I'm trouble, Rafe. More trouble than the politics of this visit are worth."

"I'm sorry you think so. Saddened, actually."

Cara's body knew what was coming when her mind hadn't fully grasped it. Everything he had said was a lead-in to his next move, and as Rafe's lips brushed hers, she closed her eyes.

Just this once I'll allow another round of closeness. And then I'll put a stop to whatever you're thinking.

That plan faded away as the fleeting touch of Rafe's lips added another layer to the tumultuous emotions already bringing her dangerously close to a precipice. That precipice was the only obstacle standing between her and all hell breaking loose in Miami. It was the dividing line between good and evil, as well as the one thing she had dreaded to encounter all along—a mate.

She could not think of fitting in when so many Weres could be hurt if she remained. She could not with good conscience do anything that would involve passing this dark spirit on. Therefore, she couldn't continue to pursue this relationship with Rafe, for whom she had quickly developed her own soft spot.

This Landau wolf might cause a hitch in her getaway plan and interfere with her ability to focus if things got more serious between them. There would be more danger. More hurt.

Stop the madness, her mind cautioned.

Do it now, or all will be lost.

She had never wished so hard or fervently that she had been born normal as she did right then.

Rafe felt prickling sensations in his muscles as he feathered his lips over Cara's. The back of his neck chilled in direct contrast to the white-hot currents he encountered each time he got near to her. So, what was this sudden chill all about?

He was an ass for daring to ignore the warnings his family had issued. In his defense, Cara's physical strength and the softness of her lips were a tough counter to those inner arguments. The others didn't know her the way he already liked to imagine he did. He and Cara shared a bond that, though hard to define, very much controlled his actions.

He couldn't have stopped what was coming if he had tried.

Her lips were warm and supple as he increased the pressure of the kiss. Her breath was hot. Cara's mouth was an inferno. This was no ice queen from the bayou. He was almost completely sure that no frigging Banshee looked at him through those half-closed green eyes.

And yet the chills persisted.

He backed off. With a careful finger, he tilted Cara's chin upward again so that he could see all of her beautiful face in the light from an outdoor lamp. The face he searched was perfectly molded into feminine perfection, and a little too pale. He couldn't imagine what it must be like to house any spirits other than a wolf.

She avoided his gaze by lowering her lashes. Nothing in her expression suggested coyness or that she might be ill prepared for the attentions of a male. Cara could easily have pushed him away, and didn't. She could have used some of her incredible speed to outdistance him, but she stayed.

"I wonder if you believe any part of what I've said," Rafe began, uncertain about trusting himself for the next few minutes after having come this far. "Or if it makes sense."

Warning signals were flashing madly in his mind. His head was filled with whispers. *Do not get closer to her. Back away, you fool.*

Spikes of flame hit him when he noticed how Cara's face whitened more, and the way her lashes kept her eyes hidden. She hadn't moved, and yet something behind all that pale, beautiful skin did, as if there was something coming alive beneath the surface.

"Cara?" His voice was hushed.

Only silence answered him. When Cara finally

opened her eyes, the deep green color he had hoped to see was gone.

The eyes looking back at him were now a dull, flat black.

Chapter 12

Death was calling.

The intensity of that call punched through Cara with the force of a battering ram. The spirit had risen unannounced, and it was necessary to distance herself from Rafe to hear what that spirit had to say.

Brittle thoughts took shape in her mind—hard, unrelenting, violent thoughts. She had to leave Rafe, get away before the spirit overtook her completely. The message was that someone was coming. Something was near. And there was going to be a loss of life.

Night crowded in. Internal wailing sounds echoed in Cara's mind, and she struggled to contain them. Clamping her teeth together proved useless. Her hands were shaking. Her head hurt and her jaw ached.

She shook her head at Rafe's expression over the suddenness of her rejection and bit her tongue to keep from showing him again that all the fuss and rumors about this

Kirk-Killion freak of nature were true. The need to free the Banshee's cry was a terrible burden.

Swaying slightly before widening her stance, Cara opened her mouth to try to speak, and no words came out. As her throat began to loosen, the sound that emerged traveled upward through her body from the depths of her soul. But it wasn't a dark spirit's cry that came out. It was a haunting wolf's howl that rolled on and on as if it had no end…because she had avoided the Banshee's appearance by calling upon her wolf for help.

In seconds, her howl was answered. One response came from the direction of the house. Another came from someplace beyond the wall and was followed by a third and a fourth. Weres had emerged from their hidey-holes, lured by the sound she had made. Not the kind of Weres that would be in human form tonight. These responses were the vocalizations of a few full-blooded Lycans able to shapeshift without the lure of the moon—creatures almost as rare as she was, since very few werewolves on Earth could perform that trick.

It seemed the Landaus had a few secrets of their own, besides the obvious ones. Lycans were rallying to her cry as they would have in the wild, and she hadn't meant for that to happen. She had just needed to outwit the dark spirit she carried within her, at least temporarily, so that Rafe wouldn't see it and change his mind.

Recruiting every wolf molecule in her body was what it took to overpower the Banshee, and Cara succeeded. But that spirit coated her insides like an internal mist. The ancient thing that predated the wolf species swirled near the base of her throat, soaking up the last of her wolf's cry.

The spirit had to announce a death. That was its sole purpose. It had veered from this purpose twice in the entirety of its long existence, and each of those mistakes had cost it dearly. This Banshee could no longer live on its own and was doomed by its past transgressions to exist inside a host tied to the family it had helped instead of hindered centuries ago.

Death was coming, though. No mistake.

It was coming here.

With a roar of protest, Cara tore off her shirt and dropped to her hands and knees, feeling the escalation of Rafe's tension without being able to do anything about it.

He had seen her as a vampire and was about to find out more of what she could do. More secrets were going to be exposed, and Cara saw no other way to manage the next few minutes than to become a creature that could outrace Rafe and his pack.

"Do not follow," she warned him over Were channels as her body began its downsize into a new shape. *"It's already too late."*

Rafe stumbled back as if he'd been struck by an invisible hand. *Holy hell...* The partial shape-shift he had witnessed earlier had been a convincing disguise, but Cara was now a wolf. A real one, on all fours in a full transformation, with a rippling coat of black fur that shone by lamplight like liquid onyx.

When Cara's head came up, her eyes again shone with green fire, but nothing else about her was familiar. She growled menacingly. Her whole body shook. When her eyes met his one last time, Rafe understood what she was telling him. Cara was inside that shape. She was in control of this shape-shift and had changed for a reason that made this shift important.

In the distance, resounding howls that would have scared the pants off anyone in the park rolled through the night. The sounds shook Rafe up. Cara's latest trick seemed like a dream. Like the stories about her mother, Cara could become a rare black wolf.

Christ. What could he say, except…

"Do what you have to, Cara. We'll deal later."

She wheeled around so quickly, Rafe barely saw her move. Like a streak of supernatural lightning, she took a run at the wall and hurdled it before his next full breath.

Rafe heard the pounding of each thundering heartbeat in his chest. He replayed all the warnings he'd had with regard to Cara, knowing he had ignored them all, believing that she could handle being here and eventually learn to assimilate with the pack. He saw now that the idea had been a mistake, and that Cara was beyond anything his pack could have tamed.

He just couldn't get a take on the real Cara, or how this had happened to her, which left him more determined than ever to find out. So he lit out after her for the second time tonight, not sure who he'd find behind the rest of those answering howls, but envying those Lycan bastards for the ability they had to get to Cara faster than he could.

He took aim at the wall and scrambled over it, glad he had put on his boots. Dropping down on the opposite side, he traced movement to the west by the trees where he had promised himself to have that second kiss with Cara.

It turned out to be a werewolf, suited up in jeans, missing a shirt and running on two legs that Rafe saw. He knew this guy and blew out a sigh of relief. At least one Lycan was accounted for. It was Jonas Dale, one of the strongest Lycans in Miami, who was also in law enforcement. Jonas had been trolling the park tonight with the intention of keeping people safe.

Behind Rafe came the soft thud of someone else landing. A quick turn brought him face-to-face with Cameron Mitchell. The fiftysomething detective wasn't Lycan and therefore not in an altered shape, though his muscles visibly quivered across his wiry frame.

"You heard it?" Rafe asked.

"You'd have to be deaf not to," Cameron replied. "Where is the she-wolf?"

"Chasing something. I have no idea what."

"The others who responded?"

"Jonas is the only one I saw."

The more time spent at a standstill, the greater the possibility of losing Cara, so Rafe spun around and raced off. Since he knew this park well, as most of his pack did, he had a good idea where to start his search. No self-respecting criminal would go near the public streets on the opposite edge of the park. Off to the east were darker patches of ground that provided better camouflage.

The only wolf who didn't know any of this was the one he needed to find. Rafe had to understand what Cara's latest shape-shift was about and whether he could reach her in time to help.

He ran like the wind with his packmate beside him, scanning the dark, avoiding the lighter places near the boulevards in the far distance. Nothing could throw him off the scent. With Cara's fragrance embedded in his lungs, he was soon able to pick up her trail.

Cameron swore between breaths. "I saw her from the porch. I did see that correctly? She can make herself into a…"

"Wolf," Rafe replied over one shoulder as he pulled slightly ahead of Cameron. "We've all heard the tales, so this shouldn't really have been a surprise."

He failed to mention that it had been a complete surprise to him.

"Yeah. Well, good luck with that attitude," Cameron said, rocketing into a higher pace that made Rafe dig in.

Cameron continued to mutter to himself. Between the obscenities and a few human growls, Rafe heard him say, "This is something I've got to see up close."

As they covered more ground, Cara's scent grew stronger. Just as Rafe had suspected, she was making for the next notoriously troubled spot in this damn park as if she had a nose for these things. He wondered if there actually was someone out here or if she had again been taken in by a vision of some kind.

The night had gone quiet. Each breath he took seemed labored when he wasn't the least bit winded. *"Have to reach you,"* he messaged to Cara. *"Please wait."*

Cameron said, "You expect her to listen?"

"No."

Cameron grunted a nonverbal response as they rounded a line of trees that threw long shadows from the partial moon overhead. The scent became more convoluted here with a breeze from the north. And there was something else—a new scent that again chilled the back of Rafe's neck. It was an odor that he didn't recognize, and it tangled with Cara's fragrance. Cameron had no such problem pegging it.

"Hunter." Cameron spit out the word with a vehemence that could only have come from firsthand knowledge.

Rafe's stomach turned over. His mind rebelled. There hadn't been hunters in this part of Miami for years, and the idiots who had trespassed in the area in the past had been lethal. Not only that, they had been led by Cameron's mate's father. Having gone through tough times like that, Cameron had to be furious about the possibility of a replay.

"Cara is wily," Rafe sent to his packmate. *"She will watch for this."*

"And if she is in wolf form, her pelt would be worth a

few million bucks on the black market," Cameron sent back. *"That kind of money would make a hunter real hungry."*

"It would also mean that someone else would have to know about her and her whereabouts."

Rafe's protective instincts spurred him on with new determination. He couldn't wrap his mind around the idea that hunters were what Cara had perceived. Surely she would understand that his pack could deal with any black-market lackey that came along hoping to make his fortune? Even then, however, there would have to have been a leak of information about her visit and what Cara was capable of. But how, when her many talents had been a complete mystery to the pack? Until now.

For a hunter, Cara would be the rarest of the rare, the catch of a lifetime if trapped while in wolf form. But she was used to fighting for her life and for freedom, and was no fool. Since she and her family battled vampires and demons on a regular basis, what chance did a human with a weapon have against power and knowledge like hers?

The familiar report of gunfire split the night, adding another surprise to an evening full of them. Guns were a bad sign of the times and something he had to deal with on a daily basis at his job. Here, with Cara out of reach and a Lycan or two taking up the chase, the dreaded idea of silver bullets fueled Rafe's anger...and the thought that though a pair of fangs might not do damage to the daughter of two legendary Weres, that damn metal could.

He had the scars to show for it, as did a couple of his packmates. Worse still was the glimmer of a memory of the well-aimed silver round that had taken down the only other female he might have dared to love, once upon a time, in his youth.

So it was a damn good thing he wasn't stupid enough to have immediately fallen for the she-wolf they were chasing, in case she turned out to be the kind of adrenaline junkie whose life would end long before he could solidify a relationship with her…if, in fact, that's what he wanted. And if, in fact, he had a choice in the matter.

Too late, his mind argued. *It's already too late.*

The look Cameron threw him after Rafe finished that thought had sympathy written all over it.

Chapter 13

Sifting through so many odors kept Cara occupied as she sped from shadow to shadow hunting for the one scent she sought.

"Wait," Rafe had urged from somewhere behind her, but she was onto something he couldn't be involved with. Vampires were bad enough. This new presence was outrageous.

She locked her thoughts behind an iron wall in her mind that was much more secure than the Landaus' protective pile of stones. Without the ability to read her, she'd be invisible to most Weres. In full wolf form, she could outrun all of them put together.

The park wasn't as large as she had been led to believe. Skirting the trees, Cara located the shadows she searched for and the abomination hidden in them. Using her exceptional vision to separate other forms of darkness from the night, Cara saw the demon that was cloaked as a human.

No disguise could mask the stink of a demon, and their cunningness was legendary. This one had been waiting, having lured her here with insightful foreknowledge of what her reaction to its presence would be.

She didn't give the abomination time to appreciate how well its lure had worked, or to pounce. A single leap took her to the monster with her teeth bared and her claws swiping.

The thing hissed like a vampire as her first blow landed and fought back with maniacal energy derived from an innate connection to the others of its kind. The energy of one of these demons was siphoned from the energy of many, no matter how separated they all were from each other.

Being in human form didn't slow its reflexes much, though Cara didn't allow the freak leeway to discard the layers of its temporary disguise. She snapped at the hell spawn's moving limbs, caught skin in her teeth and tore away a large chunk of its muscle while trying not to breathe in the fetid smells emanating from wounds that should have bled and didn't.

This creep was old, treacherous and used to fighting. It managed to catch hold of her muzzle with both of its bony hands as she wheeled, temporarily delaying the damage she dished out.

Cara shook it off with a fluid show of wolf flexibility that brought her snapping canines dangerously close to the demon's face. It got to her again by yanking on the fur covering her left shoulder. Using a viselike grip, the demon lifted her front end off the ground, causing a round of pain Cara didn't have time to process as she heard the snap of her right paw breaking.

Had it broken every bone in her body, she would have continued to fight.

You don't belong here and can't be allowed to stay.

No one who knew about demons could have afforded to let this one go so near to a densely populated pocket of civilization like Miami. If granted free rein, others would follow. They might already be here somewhere.

Cara closed the remaining inch of distance to the creature's face and snapped again. Demons had two vulnerable spots, whatever form they took. Since one of those spots was their face, Cara dug deeply into this demon's cheek with her wolf-sharp teeth.

The monster screeched in anger and flailed wildly in an effort to dislodge her. Cara hung on, her strength centered in her jaws, until she was able to free herself from its grip.

As the demon leaned back to begin its own shape-shift, Cara heard another sound that drowned out its screech—a sharp crack followed by a puff of air that sailed past her right ear.

A gunshot.

The demon flew backward as if it had been knocked off its feet. Cara lunged toward it to regain her advantage as the demon's human semblance further dissolved. What remained in its place was an ugly six-foot-tall mass of jellified flesh with a pair of dark red eyes and matching horns.

There was no mouth with which to bite because half of its face was gone, but she hadn't done all of that damage. The bullet had torn a hole in the demon's face a few millimeters from where her teeth had clung. Even then, the demon should have recovered. Their composition wasn't like a human's. Usually it took a lot more than one big hole to bring a demon down. Yet the monster dissipated in a puff of black smoke as if it had been composed of air rather than a thick coat of recently adopted flesh and bone.

The surprise of such an easy victory stole Cara's breath. She backpedaled, already whirling to search for the second intruder. What she found instead was a huge, half-furred-up werewolf skidding to a stop in front of her.

The Were's growl shook the ground. She had to look up to see this guy, who was the biggest werewolf she had ever seen. Male. Lycan. Fierce. Dangerous and furred up. His chest was broad. His legs were thick. Though he had a werewolf's enhanced musculature, his face retained many recognizable human characteristics, which meant that he also had been bred from an ancient wolf lineage from a time before wolf blood had taken a hold on human anatomy.

Her new companion stared briefly at the spot where the demon had stood. With an incredible display of pure-blooded Lycan speed, he then caught hold of her. But Cara wasn't afraid. This was not an enemy. One of the answering howls in the distance had been his, and he had come to her aid.

He wrapped his claws in her fur and dragged her closer to him. Her injured paw pulsed with pain. Her heart boomed as the Lycan's gaze swept over first her face and then her paws. He pounded his chest to show his good intentions and then lifted her up as though she weighed nothing. After settling her into his arms, he walked briskly toward the sound of more running.

"Cara!" Rafe's shout was weighted with anger and concern as he and another Were closed in.

She couldn't blame him for being angry but was glad nothing of that demon remained for the Landau pack to feast their eyes upon. This one time, she had gotten away with leaving most of the Landau Weres behind as she performed her mission. She had tried to save them from the onslaught of problems caused by her nature. Nevertheless, she hadn't killed that demon, and whoever had done the honors remained at large, a mystery.

"We heard shots. Were you hit? Are you okay?" Rafe demanded, eyeing the Lycan holding her.

His blatant concern brought Cara a degree of warmth that she couldn't have explained even if she'd had vocal cords. Through Were channels, she sent him a thought. *"I'm all right."*

She began her reverse shift, shaking off the wolf, making the Lycan holding her tilt back and forth in order to keep her in his arms. Once she'd discarded the wolf semblance, she sank against the unknown Lycan's massive chest, slightly out of breath.

"Jonas," Rafe said to the Lycan holding her, "hand her over. And thanks."

The big werewolf did as Rafe requested, then took off again, possibly to search for the party responsible for the gunfire that had downed the demon with a single, specialized, well-targeted bullet.

"I'll help him search," Rafe's packmate said. "If it's a werewolf hunter, the idiot is a piss-poor shot."

Rafe waited until both Weres had gone before looking directly at her. "If you keep this up, your invitation might be revoked. It's too dangerous letting you do whatever the hell you please. You do get that? Hell, Cara, I'll take you back myself."

Cara said breathlessly, "You have no idea what's out there clinging to the shadows."

"More memories?"

"Not his time."

"You're injured, and on my watch," he said in a tone that again said he had truly been worried about her, not for the sake of the trouble he might be in with both of their families, but because he honestly cared about what happened to her.

Another flush of heat crept into her face as Cara acknowledged his words.

"The hand will heal," she said, adding to herself, *and that demon won't come calling again.*

Rafe didn't look at her hand. His focus remained on her face. Cara felt the intensity of desire he was withholding. Rafe wanted to let his attention slip to her naked body. His pulse moved beneath the skin under his left ear.

Now that she was in his arms, her injured hand seemed like nothing compared to the ache she felt in other places. Deep inside her, a distant thrumming vibration was producing longings she was now beginning to comprehend. In spite of what had just transpired, and with the acknowledgment of demon presence in Miami, she wanted Rafe to look at her. She wanted to remain in his arms for a while longer.

As strong and independent as she had always been, Cara was caving on the idea of remaining close to Rafe Landau. There was no look of horror on his face about her latest shift. None of the feeling she had for Rafe had struck her while she lay in the other Lycan's arms. Only Rafe made her feel this way. She sensed a strong, rapidly forming bond. Their bodies were in sync on this, although their wishes went unspoken.

"We have to get you home," he finally said. "Some damn fool has a gun. Is that what you were after?"

Cara shook her head. "He found me."

"How did you break your bones?"

Cara supposed Rafe might understand about the demon if she answered him truthfully, but she didn't yet dare to do so.

"Let's get you home," he said, continuing to stand there, holding her, as if he didn't want the moment to end despite the possibility of more gunshots.

"Does it hurt badly?" he asked, shifting his focus to her hand.

"I've had worse."

Cara studied Rafe's handsome face, expecting to find clues as to what he might be expecting from her at this point. She had to accept the fact that she truly was inept at deciphering some of the expressions that crossed his face.

"My mother will help with your hand, though she's not as gentle as my grandmother was when it comes to healing injured limbs," he said. "I suppose I'll have to loan you another shirt."

Cara wasn't sure how to respond, so she didn't try. She was thankful that the demon hadn't found any of Rafe's friends tonight.

Finally, he moved.

"I can walk, Rafe. There's nothing wrong with my legs."

"Yes. I suppose you can. But you're naked. In my arms you're not so exposed."

He was lying about his motives. Rafe wanted to hold her.

"Being without clothes will bother the others?" she asked.

"Probably not half as much as it bothers me," he returned.

The thrumming inside her was growing stronger. Cara slid her gaze downward, past Rafe's lips, his chin, to the broad muscular chest covered by a T-shirt that stretched tight. She fought the urge to tear that T-shirt to pieces with her teeth and get at what lay beneath. She would have liked Rafe better with no barriers between them and his bronze skin exposed.

Maybe she had been too long in animal form tonight and these urges belonged to the wolf—to the more primal parts of herself that had never been explored. As if she had just awakened to the world of a mature female's physical needs, Cara smiled at Rafe…and then found herself pressed to the bark of a tree with his hard body tight up against hers.

"Damn it." His curse was a whisper of molten air on her forehead. "They won't like this. Won't appreciate it."

He swore again, then added, "But what the hell?"

Chapter 14

Rafe was ravenous, and he let his instincts take over as he leaned against Cara in a way that indicated how the idea of friendship had evolved into a new kind of madness.

It didn't take a specialist to tell him that the state he found himself in had to mean he and Cara had imprinted. He was acting contrary to every rule he had in place to govern his behavior in the world so far. Somehow, and after such a short acquaintance, their souls were making these decisions for them.

Cara was a seamless, flawless turn-on, and having her naked or half-naked most of the time didn't help his will-power. Unlike his human partners, she had torn through his defenses as if none of them existed.

Her lips were there for him to taste. Her breath was sweet when he did. Musky wolf scent perfumed the dark tangles of hair that Rafe ran his fingers through. He had a very real need to explore every inch of this magnificent she-wolf hybrid whom everyone else secretly feared.

With her thighs against his and her high, firm breasts against his chest, self-control was quickly becoming non-existent.

Cara appeared to be as stunned as he was by this latest act, though she didn't resist. He tasted the blistering-hot tang of passion coating the inside her mouth. She had closed her eyes.

He kissed her as if there wouldn't be another opportunity, as if they were the only two Weres in the world… devouring, taking, possessing Cara's mouth the way he wanted to possess her body, and as though he too had become possessed.

He wasn't gentle. Didn't take his time. Her tongue was malleable and an instant addiction. For now, Cara's mouth was everything. It was the connecting link between two souls that hadn't expected such a pairing.

Although tearing his clothes off was not an option, Rafe felt feverish and confined. He maintained the hope that he could handle this and that things actually wouldn't get out of hand. Danger remained each moment they stayed in the park. They would be expected back behind the walls. But as Cara's palm slipped up his back, the caress burned through his shirt with the heat of a falling star. When she tugged at the hem of his shirt in order to reach his skin, his body rippled with anticipation.

He broke the connection with her lips just far enough to speak. "You're new to this, and I'm taking advantage."

In response, Cara raked her nails across his lower back. The sting told Rafe that though Cara might not be as experienced as he was in dealing with sexual desires, she was also part animal when it came right down to it, and all animals instinctively knew what to do in a situation like this.

Her touch turned him on. Spurred him on. The pain was real, which meant that Cara also was real. She was neither wholly pleasure nor wholly pain, but both things rolled into one. To love her, to make love to her, would be at her partner's peril, but that was just the kind of challenge a werewolf lived for.

He kissed Cara again with a vengeance, and she met him halfway as her fingers moved over him as if seeking a deeper connection. How could he tell her that she had already gotten under his skin?

The brash devouring that seemed to go on forever left him unsatisfied. Rafe vowed not to take this seduction farther tonight and to give Cara a chance to learn and adapt to the ways of the pack—and in particular a male Were's physical urgings. Yet even that promise was fading.

Animals.

Yes, we are animals inside, Cara.

You and me.

His hand moved without conscious direction, running over the length of Cara's smooth right thigh. She gasped and growled again, and the sound made Rafe want her all the more. The possibility of imprinting with Cara made adhering to former promises seem impossible.

He slid his hand down her leg, cursing the action, knowing what he would find and also that reaching that place would lead him to a state of mindless, blissful oblivion.

He was almost there when the word *don't* lit up in his mind with the brilliance of a neon sign, followed closely by *can't*. Because, hell…he might be an animal in human guise, but he was also an animal who cared about the female in his arms and about what would happen to her if the imprinting sequence had truly begun. Mating with Cara would seal the deal for good. No out.

No exit. After imprinting, no other partner would do for either of them. Ever.

Did they truly want that when they knew so little about each other, and when so much was already at stake with Cara's visit here?

Do you realize what's happening, Cara? Are you seeing the larger picture?

He had to stop now, before it was too late. Before more of Cara's delicious heat corroded his sense of what was right.

Damn, that was hard.

Nearly impossible.

When he pulled back, she opened her eyes. He had no words to offer her that might explain the rashness of his decision to stop what he had started.

Rafe had no idea whether or not Cara got this, got that he had only halted due to his concern for her. Before he had taken his next breath, she had slipped from his grasp, melted back into full wolf form and was limping away on three legs without looking back.

Cara had sensed Rafe's reluctance to indulge in this intimate moment before he had stopped kissing her. She hadn't wanted to face him after that.

She couldn't afford to let him see how being close to him affected her, and how breathless she was. So she walked away from the beauty of their moment of passion, unclear about what would happen from here but not willing to change back to her human shape in order to speak of those things.

Rafe followed her, keeping a distance of a few steps between them. He said only one thing. "Let me carry you back. I can get you in without anyone seeing you. I've spent a lot of time there and know the place well. I can at least try to ward off the questions they will have."

Ignoring his suggestion made her feel better in spite of the fact that her paw hurt like hell. She was being stubborn, when shifting to human form would have taken her weight off the broken bone. Still, the discomfort of a fracture didn't last long for any werewolf, and was a minor thing for a Kirk-Killion. The same combination of wolf and vampire blood that made her so strong also allowed her to heal more rapidly than most Weres. She would never have survived this long if that hadn't been the case.

She stopped near the wall to look at it, expecting to see more Weres looking down at her from the top. No one was there.

"They trust me," Rafe said, coming up alongside. "They trust me to do the right thing."

Growling at him did no good. Rafe added, "Follow me, then, if I can't help you any other way."

He turned and began to walk along the base of the wall, pausing once to make sure she was trailing him.

"Being naked in your human form might be less intimidating to others than your current incarnation," he continued, speaking to her calmly, as if nothing had happened between them that should have caused her silence. "It's up to you, though."

She thought about biting him and decided against it. Uncertainty had muddled her thinking where Rafe Landau was concerned, and the only way to stave off these new sensations was to keep her wolf shape and her distance. The discomfort of her broken paw was preferable to the strange longing she had to mate tooth and nail with Rafe.

"There's a break in the wall near the guardhouse," he said. "It's a small one, but sufficient to get through if you know about it. When we reach the other side, we can skirt the house and use a rear door. Hopefully Cameron hasn't returned with news about the shooter. If he had, there would be plenty of activity, and I don't see evidence of that. And just so you know, Cameron won't tell them about you unless you want him to."

They found the break in the wall and Rafe ushered her through it, touching her only once as she slid past him by running a quick helping hand over her black coat. The heat in his hand, so like static, raised the fur on the back of her neck.

If Rafe thought it would be easier on the rest of the Weres to see her in human form, she owed her hosts that much. She would change back for them as soon as she reached the grass.

She didn't have that chance. Just five steps across the Landaus' yard, the game of hide-and-seek came to an end. Lights came on. An alarm set for Were ears went up. And her Landau hosts appeared like apparitions near the driveway wearing grim, worried expressions.

Rafe moved forward without hesitation. "Possible hunter out there," he said. "Cameron's searching."

Their eyes were on her.

"Cara injured a hand," Rafe said. "It should be looked after."

"Yes," Dana Delmonico Landau agreed, observing Cara. "Did that hunter hurt you?"

"No," Rafe replied for her.

"Another moment of privacy needed?" Rafe's father asked with a hint of warning in his tone.

"Someone or something has been luring Cara out there. I'm not sure what. She will have to tell us if she wants to," Rafe explained.

Dylan Landau searched the rim of the wall before returning his attention to her. "Maybe you'd like to tell us about that now, Cara, so that we can be better prepared if there's trouble. I don't like the sound of this or the news of a shooter, whether or not it's a hunter stalking the park. And I don't like the fact that someone else might know you're here when that's private pack business."

As Rafe's mother removed her jacket, she said to both of the men, "Why don't you head to the house? Cara and I will be along shortly. I'll just have a quick word with her."

When Rafe's gaze returned to Cara, his expression was as intense as his kisses had been. The rising heat was a continuous indicator of what he could do to her body. She could not have been hotter. Concentration was next to impossible with Rafe beside her, and her injured paw ached from the pressure she was putting on it in order to stand on all fours.

Rafe didn't argue with his mother, probably because he realized that she'd removed her jacket to cover Cara's nakedness after her next shape-shift. The Landaus seemed to be good at reading others and sharing.

Her wolf shape hadn't seemed to bother or surprise them. But the mention of hunters had unsettled everyone here. Surely they would send more of the pack after the hunter, but they had no idea they'd been so close to a real threat in the form of a demon, or just how much trouble having a Kirk-Killion here could bring.

She watched Rafe go.

"I haven't been taught the ins and outs of social graces, Rafe. I'm merely stumbling along, trying to find out how to deal." She sent the message to him on Were channels, hoping he'd understand.

Obviously she was taking too long to deal with her own

issues, because when Dana Delmonico Landau turned back to her, the older woman's tone had changed.

"Now," Dana said. "Why don't you get on with that shift and tell me what is really going on."

Chapter 15

Rafe's mother was going to interrogate Cara. You couldn't truly take the detective out of a person, even after they had left the force in order to be the mate of an important alpha. His mother was no exception. She was also kind and intuitive, though, especially gifted in reading thoughts and unspoken intentions.

Having been on the receiving end of these interrogations while he was growing up, Rafe didn't envy Cara. But he figured she could handle it, even without him there.

"Did you know about her abilities?" he asked his father as they climbed the steps leading to the front porch. "About how special her wolf is?"

"I assumed Cara might have inherited that talent," his father replied. "We had never seen anything like her mother. I was sure I'd never see anything like Rosalind again, and for a minute there, I thought I was back in the past."

"Rosalind was a black wolf? A real wolf? That wasn't just a rumor?"

"Oh, yes. She was terribly strong and unfailingly rebellious."

Rafe nodded. "That rings a bell."

His father rested a hand on the white-painted pillar. "You would have had to meet or see Rosalind to fully understand what all those combinations of spirits could do. What they were, and how they reacted. Nevertheless, Rosalind's rebelliousness and her strength ended up saving many Were lives in the end."

"Colton Killion's life among them. I believe Cara might have come here to find out about the past," Rafe said.

The remark earned him a thoughtful sideways glance.

Rafe went on. "I don't think Cara knows much about her family history or the part her parents played in Cara's current situation. It's normal for her to want to learn about her origins, isn't it, and why she is the way she is?"

"Do you believe it's our place to enlighten her?" his father countered.

"I do if she needs that information enough to have agreed to come here to find it despite her reluctance to do so."

His father paused near the front door. "What was calling to her out there?"

"I don't think it was a hunter she was after, but there were shots fired. After shifting, she got away too quickly for Cameron and me to keep up. Whatever it was that Cara found out there broke bones in her hand, and yet we didn't see any intruders near where we found her and she wasn't willing to speak of it."

His father searched the wall in the distance. "We heard that howl."

Rafe was sure he'd never forget the haunting sound Cara had made. "You sent Jonas?"

"Without you here, he is the fastest."

"And the only shifter around tonight who is able to manipulate the moon for his own purposes," Rafe added.

"There is that," his father agreed.

"You do know that Cara won't be a willing prisoner here or mindful of the rules?"

"I never would have expected anything else from the daughter of an exceptionally talented Lycan like Colton Killion, even if Rosalind hadn't been tossed into the mix."

Rafe followed his father's gaze. The wall seemed darker by moonlight and even taller from where he stood. Cara had gone over it as if it was no obstacle at all. He had now seen three of her transformations and wondered how many more of them might be in store.

He said, "Maybe you should tell Cara about her father, and what you know."

"That would be good," his father agreed, "if I knew where to start. Colton wasn't part of this pack. His family kept to themselves. His was a very old family line that was more powerful than most, and the Killions had no interest in being part of a pack. Their sole purpose was to fit into the world around them. They tried hard to do that."

Rafe turned, wanting to go to Cara but willing to give her the time to settle down after whatever encounter she'd had out there. Unanswered questions kept arising, chief among them: *If not another vampire, what made you run?*

He didn't ask that question of Cara over Were channels, though. The need to hop over the wall and have another look at the park was making him anxious. He wasn't used to leaving hard tasks to others and hoped Cameron would return soon with news. Barring that, he'd have to find out what the holdup was without letting Cara see him leave. She would try to follow.

"You'll have plenty of time to find out what she was after if tonight is any indication of what we can expect," his father said, noting Rafe's fisted hands with a nod of his head.

Rafe said, "You knew this going in, and the kind of trouble she could bring."

"Yes. I just didn't expect things to happen so soon."

"Neither did I," Rafe muttered beneath his breath.

His meaning was different from his father's, though. He hadn't expected to bond with anyone, let alone their guest, which was what was already happening. The desire to go to Cara was like another fist curled up inside his stomach. He could hardly stay away from her. He couldn't keep his gaze off her.

Chastising himself wasn't working, so he headed to the side of the house to find an out-of-sight spot to get over the damn wall. As confusing as the night had been, doing what he did best would put him back on track. Chasing the bad guys. Sweeping the park. Getting it done. He could forget Cara for a while.

"Rafe?"

He turned back.

"I've been through this before, son. Nothing is different about this, and we can handle it," his father said.

Anxious to get going, Rafe shifted his weight nervously from boot to boot. "I'll be back when there's something to tell you, and not before then."

"Cara will be all right here," his father promised.

Rafe nodded. "I'd have no doubts about that if in fact you could keep her here."

Cara was in good hands with this pack on guard. The

doubts he didn't mention were about himself and what he might do next if he didn't get the hell out of there.

Cara wasn't with him now, and yet it felt as if she were. Her taste was in his mouth. Her fragrance stuck to his skin. Each time he thought her name, the image accompanying it melted from one shape to another, just as Cara had done several times now.

Maybe the pack could handle a shifter like Cara on a temporary basis. The question was whether they could handle her for much longer than that.

I'm acting like a besotted fool…

"Later," he called out to his dad as he launched himself at the wall.

He dropped down on the other side, relieved to be free to pursue other things than the compulsion to mate with the only female on the planet who was off-limits to him.

"That's better," Dana remarked as Cara completed her shape-shift. "Now, if you'll put this jacket on, we can have a conversation. Are you good with that?"

Cara took the offered clothing that smelled nothing like the shirt Rafe had loaned her earlier that night. She was sorry she'd had to ditch the shirt in the park.

Dana was tall and wiry, with a more petite bone structure than her height suggested. Her hair, so like Rafe's, was brown, but curly. Her skin, also like Rafe's, was a smooth golden bronze. She had an ageless face and large eyes that took in everything around her. And all of her attention was on Cara.

"I'd like to know what made you go out there, against the suggestions we made for your protection," Dana said.

Blunt and to the point. Cara was used to this. Telling Dana part of the reason for her escape couldn't hurt. She didn't have to lie to her hostess.

"I heard a call," she said. "Something called my name."

She watched Dana process this. "Does anyone else know you're here in Miami?"

Cara shook her head. "No one any of us would like to meet or acknowledge. That doesn't mean certain beings can't find me if they're in tune with what's going on around them."

"Like the vampire at the beach?"

"The vampire was an accident. It hadn't gotten wind of me before I sensed its presence."

"And Rafe just happened to be there when you all met up?"

Withholding information that Rafe might find personal and sensitive wasn't lying, so Cara said, "Unlike the vampire, Rafe sensed my presence on the beach and found me first."

Rafe's mother took some time before speaking again. "I've fought vampires on several occasions. They pass along information on channels similar to ours. Could it have been one of them calling to you in the park?"

"No. Not a vampire."

Cara could tell Dana wasn't saying what she was thinking, though she had to know Cara could guess what that was. If not a vampire, then what kind of creature had detected Cara so soon? That's the question Rafe's mother would likely want to ask. And since Cara didn't want to lie outright, she had to evade the question before it was voiced.

"If you press me, I'd have to tell you things you might not want to hear," Cara warned.

"And if you withhold important information that could potentially harm this pack, you'd be responsible for whatever might happen," Dana countered.

"Not wanting anyone to be harmed on my behalf is one of the reasons I didn't want to come to Miami."

"Yet you ultimately agreed to come," Dana pointed out.

"I'm trying to make peace with my decision, which isn't so easy for someone like me now that I'm here and trouble has already begun."

Dana's scrutiny was like having a bright light turned Cara's way. "But you like Rafe," Dana said.

Cara needed a moment to process the remark. Was it a change of direction intended to trip her up?

"Yes. I like him," she replied. "Just as my family must have liked their hosts and the Weres here who fought beside them in the ghost war."

The term *ghost war* caused the she-wolf across from Cara to flinch. Dana said, "You're alluding to the fight near Fairview Hospital?"

Cara mentally filed away what Dana had said about a hospital. There had been a battle near a place called Fairview, and that was information she needed in order to piece together more of her family's history.

"I was alluding to the attack in the park that left my father a white wolf and introduced him to my mother."

"Ah, yes." Dana's tone was solemn. "If we listed each and every time we came up against creatures unlike us looking for a fight, that list would extend from here to the ocean and back several times."

"I'm only interested in one of those incidents," Cara said. "For now."

"Of course." Dana nodded. "I can tell you what I know, having been in the fight near Fairview, if that's what you want, but how about if we postpone that conversation for a while and get you inside? I don't like the way the wind has changed in the last few minutes."

Cara inhaled the night air. "Humans," she said.

"Well, that's a relief." Dana sighed and took a quick look down the driveway. "After all, we're just like them, as far as they are concerned. I used to be one of them, you know."

Cara did know that. The she-wolf across from her was the reason Rafe had a human scent mixed with Were. Dylan Landau had mated with a human who had been either accidentally scratched or bitten by the wrong kind of wolf, because no human would willingly defect from the known world to a much darker and more secretive one in the shadows.

Everyone had a story, it suddenly seemed to Cara. Though her story had to come first.

In spite of what Dana had said, Rafe's mother was showing outward signs of being concerned about the human scent that now permeated the air. She fixed her attention on the gate in the distance long enough for Cara to follow her line of sight, then looked at the wall.

"A hunter wouldn't come here, surely," Cara said.

"No hunter in his right mind would. But then, hunters are by their very definition morally off track."

"I didn't get a sense of humans in the park where we were," Cara noted.

"But you heard the shots?"

"Yes." One of those shots had sent that demon back to the hell it had sprung from, saving her the task.

Dana was looking at her when Cara turned back. She said in a tone reserved for sharing secrets, "How did you hurt your hand, Cara?"

Cara focused her senses outward in search of something to use as a diversionary tactic to avoid Dana's question. She found it.

"They have found your hunter," she said.

Dana stepped forward to see who might be approaching

by way of the manned front gate, but it was too far away to get a good look, even for Weres. She again glanced at the wall, sensing what Cara had. The human presence was strongest there.

"Human male," Cara explained. "Smells like metal and hatred."

What she didn't say was that it also smelled like death, and that the Banshee's stifled cry in the park had been reserved for whoever this was.

Dana turned to her. "Hatred has a scent?"

Cara pulled the borrowed jacket tighter around her and nodded. "It's like nothing else."

"Please go to the house and wait there, Cara. Will you do this one thing I'm asking?"

Deciding to honor the request, Cara headed for the house. Yes, she could do this one thing, because who the hell cared about hunters? Humans were no match for werewolves. Weres had three times their strength and five times human speed. If a handful of humans knew about the existence of werewolves without understanding those facts, then hunting werewolves had to be a doomed sport.

The real reason for going to the house, however, was Rafe. Avoiding him right now was a necessity for everyone concerned.

This had been a night full of surprises…

And it wasn't over yet.

By the time she reached the porch, her arms were tingling in a reaction reserved only for her. Rafe was still close. Though she couldn't see him, she had picked up on the beat of his heart as though hers had been jump-started. Her hands began to shake with anxious excitement over how she was able to differentiate Rafe's presence from the others' and perceive his approach so easily.

There was shouting near the wall, but Rafe's wasn't

among the raised voices. His scent had accompanied the smell of the human she had detected while standing with Dana on the lawn, though.

And now he was here again, moments later, on this side of the wall, Cara's senses screamed. Rafe was closing in as the attention of others was drawn elsewhere.

He was in front of her. Beside her. Pressing her against the brick with a replay of what had happened in the park, and with a body that was strong enough to steal her breath away.

He was looking at her, and she could not look away.

Rafe's blue eyes were bright. He wasn't smiling or willing to explain his actions. His lips brushed hers, creating sparks that lit up her insides. When his mouth covered hers with a hungry, almost angry devouring, it seemed to Cara as if no one else existed.

His kiss was very wicked in the way it tortured her. His body was unrelenting in the pressure it applied. Rafe's needs formed their own kind of power that wrestled with her former desire for independence. She was afraid that this time, she wouldn't so easily get away.

She was slipping, becoming someone she didn't recognize, and was aware of the moment her carefully guarded restraint started to go.

For someone like her, losing control was never a good thing.

Chapter 16

Seconds.

They had mere seconds to break the rules this pack had set in place and be together.

Rafe hadn't planned to behave like a madman, but he wasn't completely surprised by the impulsive forwardness of his actions. He had reached Cara here without the usual argument with himself. Nor had she offered any.

It was now pretty damn clear they were going to be together for long periods of time no matter what anyone could have expected. Detective Rafe Landau had been cuffed to this incredibly beautiful hybrid without a key to extricate himself. Did that make him weak, or merely smitten?

Too late to decide...

Already, he was caught in an inexplicable undertow of feeling, though in the periphery Rafe heard the voices that were getting closer. He was needed at the wall and wasn't there. If he and Cara were discovered in a wayward embrace, it would prove to be worse for her. The pack might send her home if they were to comprehend the rapid evolution of the bond forming between two unsuspecting souls.

Cara's breathing came in rasps when their lips parted, and he fared no better. She was waiting for his eyes to find hers, and she shook her head when they did. It was possible that Cara, who hadn't seemed frightened of anything since he had met her, might be afraid of him.

"There can be no shape-shifting your way out of this one," he whispered to her. "We just have to be sure about what this is."

"Is insanity the conclusion you've come to?" she asked.

"Yes, possibly. Probably, in fact. But does that realization change things?"

"It means I can't stay."

"Doesn't it also mean that you can't get away?"

"Watch me," she said.

Rafe took a step back to allow Cara to test the truth of her reply. She didn't accept the challenge.

"You should tell me now if you've made this happen," Rafe continued. "Is this a trick that you wield?"

She was all eyes and lips and velvet-smooth skin. He wanted to drink in that beauty. Now that he had gotten that kiss out of his system, a replay was first on his agenda. However, the voices at the wall were now almost right on top of them.

There was to be no next kiss or further closeness. The stolen seconds had been used up, and the world was again encroaching.

After the voices, a sudden hush made the absence of sound seem sinister. Rafe's duty to his family and his pack made him turn. Behind him, Cara said, "Death has come," in a soft, knowing tone that instantly cooled him.

Hell. How did she know? How could she?

Troubled by a long list of seemingly impossible theories about Cara and tonight's events in the park, not to mention her latest announcement, Rafe left her. He hustled back to the wall, feeling her heated gaze follow.

Death had come. Yes. And it had struck while Cara was in the park. Since Cara was also part Banshee, he wondered if her howl had been for this poor human being they had found, and if she had covered up her knowledge of that death with a timely, wolfish shape-shift.

Hurling himself over the wall, Rafe found that his father, Cameron and his mother had gathered there. They were all quietly staring at the lifeless body lying at their feet.

This was not a Were they looked at, and no one Rafe recognized. Still, the shock of Cara's prediction about the body he and Cameron had found left Rafe uneasy.

"This could be our hunter," he said to the others.

"I believe so as well," Cameron agreed. "There's a smell of metal on him, though we found no weapon."

"Did you…?" his father started to ask.

"We found him this way," Rafe said.

"Cause of death?" Rafe's father asked.

Cameron said, "Looks like his spine has been severed. The poor bastard didn't have a chance of surviving that."

Rafe didn't have to glance over his shoulder to know that Cara would be watching. She might have had foreknowledge of this death, but she could not have had a hand in it. The time lapse between hearing the gunshot tonight and finding Cara with Jonas had been no longer than a minute at most. He had accompanied her here himself. So who else had been out there?

Going into full cop mode, Rafe reasoned that only two things he knew of could have severed this man's spine.

"Has to be either a strong werewolf's claws or a chain saw," he said. "What about Jonas?"

"Never," his father replied. "Jonas would not harm a human like this, and we all know it."

"I meant, has there been word from him yet about this?" Rafe clarified.

His father shook his head.

"So, who did it?" Rafe's mother asked. "Jonas isn't the only Lycan in the world with a gift enabling him to change tonight and do this kind of damage to an intruder wishing us harm."

"After handing your houseguest over to us, Jonas was long gone," Cameron said. "While Rafe went east, I followed Jonas to the west. It was on our return that I met up again with Rafe and we found this guy."

"There might have been two hunters, and Jonas went after the other guy, leaving this one to us," Rafe added.

"You found him here, where he lies?" his mother asked.

"Yes, but my guess would be he was dumped here," Rafe said.

"I agree," Cameron chimed in.

"Well, if this guy was a wolf hunter, it would seem that someone did us a favor, though it was a particularly grisly one," Rafe's mother remarked.

"And it would also suggest that he didn't know anything about Weres," Rafe said. "Unless, of course, this guy and his friend had gotten wind of Jonas prowling the park all wolfed up. But how would any human know about that when very few Weres do?"

"Jonas often prowls that park," Cameron reminded them. "Maybe one of these guys saw him and hatched a plan."

"Or else someone besides a nasty vampire or two knew about Cara's arrival," Rafe's father suggested.

All eyes turned to the alpha.

"No one else could know about Cara," Rafe countered. "Hell, only a select few know about us."

"So why would a wolf hunter be in this park tonight or be dumped at the foot of our wall?" Rafe's mother asked. "Maybe we're wrong about this guy being a hunter. Perhaps he was just an idiot with bad intentions, shooting at the wrong person out there who then retaliated."

"A person with the ability to sever his spine?" Rafe said.

"It seems that we have more investigating to do," Rafe's father concluded. "And we just happen to be good at that."

Cameron nodded. "I'll call it in and let the PD try to reason this one out. Determining the cause of his injuries will keep everyone busy. But finding him so close to the wall means we will be involved."

Rafe's father nodded. "We'll have to be doubly on guard with so many others snooping around."

His comment had mainly been meant for Cara. Had she heard it?

Rafe still felt her attention on him and didn't mention anything about the possibility that Cara's howl had covered up a Banshee's warning to the others. Especially after seeing her in full wolf form, everyone knew what Cara was capable of. He didn't need to fill in the details. His take was still that she had shape-shifted in the park so as not to scare either him or Cameron by presenting a part of herself she preferred to keep hidden.

Death has come, she had said.

"You wouldn't have liked it," she messaged to him now after gaining access to thoughts he hadn't protected from her. *"You wouldn't have understood what the spirit inside me does."*

Rafe didn't want to ask the next question, but he did anyway.

"Did you have anything to do with this guy's death?"

Her reply was immediate. *"It's a hellish injury inflicted by a monster. But I also smell wolf around it. The Banshee can't kill. She merely predicts death and calls death to its mark."*

"Merely?" he messaged back.

The lips he had kissed would have uttered those words of explanation aloud if Cara had been there beside him. Cara's hidden entity was a death caller, so Cara also had a kind of forced relationship with death. It was no surprise how well this would go down with a species like vampires.

What it also could imply, however, was that through the spirit she carried around, Cara might be able to predict the time and place of the death of everyone standing here. This realization should have turned him away. The barest hint of the idea should have made him rethink his connection to her.

As if that was actually possible.

"Rafe."

His mother brought him out of thought.

"Is it too late to say I'm sorry?" she asked.

Cara didn't require the help of Weres in law enforcement to find the answers about the body at foot of their wall. She could get those details if she was allowed more time in the park. But in order to get that time, she needed Rafe's understanding. She'd have to explain more to him about herself, and that would be more discomforting than a few broken bones.

The injury had become little more than a nagging ache that any wolf could have handled. By tomorrow, she'd regain some use of her hand. Dana would see to bandaging the injury soon. Rafe's mother would also come looking for Cara about her missed meal, avoiding any inquiry about the body at the wall in favor of treating a guest with kindness and respect.

The party near the wall began to disperse. Cara supposed all of them realized she was there, observing them from her perch on a shadowed section of that wall, though they let that slide.

Only the strongest and smartest Weres had successful and long-lived wolf packs. The silver-haired alpha of this pack took the wall as if it was a minor hurdle. Dana followed him. Cameron headed off across the park, speaking on a cell phone. When the other three were gone, Rafe said, "You can come out now."

Cara walked toward him along the top of the wall with the agility of a cat rather than a wolf.

"Do you know who did this?" he asked, looking up at her.

"No."

"But you knew it would happen?"

"Yes."

She gave Rafe time to absorb her answer. He then said, "Are there going to be any more surprises before the next sunrise?"

An expression of wary relief crossed Rafe's handsome features when she didn't answer.

"I'm going to be called in to investigate this body," he said. "Other cops will arrive in force any minute now. Can you hear the sirens? If any part of this was the work of a Were, the humans on the force can't be allowed to figure that out. If this guy was a human on a bender with a gun, they'll have to hunt for the missing weapon, as well as the blood an injury like this should normally have left behind."

He hesitated before continuing. "Did vampires have anything to do with the lack of blood at the scene, Cara? Did they get to this guy after he was injured? If he was dumped here, who brought him? All those questions need to be answered to start the ball rolling."

"Vampires got to him," she said. "I can smell their presence as well."

Rafe didn't like that news. "Damn it. Monsters and wolves and vampires, all at once, would muddy things up. This was an act of brutality against a human, and we don't condone such things."

"What do you do when the hunters come?"

"In the past, we turned them in."

"And when they talked about the existence of werewolves?"

"They were declared certifiably insane."

Cara supposed that might be true. "We can find the weapon this human used if we look."

Rafe shook his head. "What you need to do is get out of sight before everyone arrives."

The wail of the sirens he had mentioned became louder, and was in some ways similar to the Banshee's cry. Cara decided to share that thought.

"Sirens also mean that someone has died, or could be about to die, right? In that case, death is only a possibility. I don't have the option of offering a way out for the victims my spirit attaches to. When the Banshee cries, death answers."

She took a breath and continued. "Only one dark spirit has ever dared to try to change that outcome, and that spirit was doomed to reside within the living body of my relatives. After my mother's turn at playing host, she passed that spirit along to me."

"I'd like to know more about that, and about what you feel," Rafe said earnestly. "I can't begin to imagine what it's like." He swore under his breath and waved a hand at the park. "There are deaths all over a city like Miami. Can you see all of them, or only a few?"

Because he honestly wanted to know the answer to that question, Cara obliged. "Through the spirit, I can see the deaths of those closest to me."

Rafe looked at the body on the ground. "Then this guy got close? He could have been the shooter?"

"Yes. But…"

Rafe's gaze came back to her. "But?"

"He wasn't the one who got closest to me out there."

He stared at her as if not knowing what to make of that. He didn't know about the demon or the other presence she had sensed on the sidelines. Perhaps that mysterious second person had been the killer Rafe's pack would seek. She could help Rafe in one small way if she broke the rules that had been imposed on her, and on her family before that. She could give him a heads-up and face the consequences if there were to be any.

"You won't find the next body for a while," she said. "But there will be one."

The fact that there was to be another death and he now knew about it made Rafe's head swim. His next question was a no-brainer. "Who, Cara? Who is going to die?"

"I don't know," she replied. "It's not information meant for me. Telling is cheating, don't you see?"

He didn't actually see that at all, but there was no time to delve deeper into spirits and curses. The sirens had ceased. Officers parked along the boulevard would now have entered the park. The ground shook slightly with the effort the officers were making to get to the scene.

"Go, Cara," Rafe directed. "Go now."

He was happy to see that she heeded his request so he could face the oncoming investigators. These were guys he knew. Guys he worked with. Besides himself and Cameron, there were three more Weres disguised as human cops and detectives in this area, and Rafe hoped at least one of them would be on duty and know whose wall this was.

Still, he also figured that Cara wouldn't go far. Not only that, but she was withholding information that was pertinent to this case. Any cop worth his salt could have picked up on that.

"I'll see you later," he said aloud with a glance at the house. "Count on it."

Chapter 17

It wasn't Dana waiting for her this time. The silver-haired alpha stood on the porch.

"Tell me about what happened," Dylan Landau said calmly. "Dana said someone called to you from out there tonight. Who was it? What was it about?"

Did she owe this alpha the truth in payment for the help the Landaus had given her family in the past?

"Demon," she said.

Creases appeared on Dylan Landau's forehead. He hadn't really been expecting that kind of a reply. His tone changed to one of concern. "Can you explain?"

Dana interrupted, emerging from the open doorway. "About that injured hand?"

No one here had been fooled by her sudden appearance. Dana wasn't going to be left out of these discussions.

"There hasn't been a demon sighting near here, as far as I know," Dylan said.

"Demons are everywhere and rarely show themselves unless they want something," Cara explained. "This one looked like a human and smelled like cooked flesh."

Her description was graphic enough to cause a temporary silence on the porch before Dana said, "Actually, we have seen them."

The alpha looked to his wife.

"In those older times, when Rosalind called them out of hiding," Dana said.

"Why would it call you, Cara? How did it know you're here?" Dylan asked.

"It's possible that rumors spread after tonight's vampire event at the beach," Cara replied. "This demon could have sensed my vibration the way Weres sense disturbances in the areas they frequent. It was waiting for me out there."

"It knew your name?" That question was from Dana.

Cara shook her head. "It called to a dark spirit, and I showed up. That spirit is chained to my soul. Where it goes, I go."

She doubted whether either of these Weres could comprehend the complexity of spirits and vibrations. For them, even vampires were a nuisance of the past. Banshees and demons would be on another level.

"So this demon knows about what's hidden inside you?" Dana asked.

"Everything composed of darkness knows that about me," Cara replied.

Dana said, "Could the demon have killed the human in the park?"

"The demon that called to me was killed by a bullet that might have been meant for me. Maybe I was your hunter's target, and he missed."

"In which case the demon couldn't have killed the man we found," Dylan surmised.

"Unless there were two hunters out there tonight, as Cameron and Jonas thought, and only one of them got away," Dana said.

Dylan looked at Cara. "Perhaps the best thing to do, for your safety, would be to take you home. Then again, if there are demons around, it's possible that only you could recognize their presence from far enough away that we could do something about it. If you stay here, you can help."

Dylan Landau had given her an out by suggesting she could go home. All she had to do was say the word and that big black car would pull up, ready to whisk her away. Hadn't that been her wish from the start? However, there were now reasons to stay. The past had to be put in order.

And then there was Rafe.

"Do you want to go home, Cara?" Dana asked.

"No. But it has been long day. I'd like to rest."

"One more thing," Dylan said before she reached the door.

Cara easily anticipated what he would say next.

"It would be wise not to let Rafe be the deciding factor in what direction your next few days take," Dylan said. "I think you know why."

She repeated the word she had thought to herself earlier. "I've never had a friend. Rafe is the first."

That wasn't actually a lie. But already, Rafe was so much more than that.

Tired, hungry, Cara followed Dana upstairs to her room. Dana had a tray that contained an assortment of food and a mug of aromatic, rapidly cooling liquid for her to drink.

For all of that, Cara felt grateful.

Real fatigue didn't set in until she had been left alone in the room her mother had used so long ago. Though Dana also had brought up a bag of medical supplies and quickly bandaged her hand before leaving, intuition told Cara she wasn't going to be alone for long.

She could almost imagine what Rafe's upbringing must have been like in a mostly normal Were family that was so different from hers. Was she wrong to envy Rafe for that?

It was after midnight and the room was warm in spite of the open window. A soft breeze did nothing to alleviate the stifling weight of Miami's humidity. Cara sat on the sill with the mug of tepid tea. At home, she and her father would have been hunting until dawn if a demon had dared to set foot on Kirk-Killion land. They'd be scouting for more of them until the sun came up.

Here, Rafe and other city law-enforcement officers would take care of the surface mess associated with the body they had found. Even after sunup, however, they'd be in the dark in the search for an intruder able to sever a human spine.

As part of both investigating teams, Rafe would have a long night ahead. Like Rafe, she wasn't used to resting until a task was done. But she had to leave this to others for now. In a city as large as Miami, there could be hundreds of demons. Each shadowy street might hide a nest of hungry vampires.

Cara studied the area from her perch at the window. There were lights on the other side of the wall, and more raised voices. Those disturbances alone would keep lurking demons and human hunters away. Light had always been the bane of monsters while being a relief to everyone else. Instead of having her father watch over things, the Landau pack would take on that task.

With new memories of her own, she turned to stare at the room where ghosts of the past still lingered, hoping for once that thoughts of Rafe Landau might chase those ghosts away.

* * *

All of the big boys in law enforcement were there eyeing each other as forensics techs surveyed the scene. There was plenty of muttering among them. Four Weres, two in uniform and the others in jeans, studied the scene with blank cop faces, though their thoughts came to Rafe like shouts.

"Looks like we have a new problem."

"We'll need to gather the packs and get to the source of this mess."

"Has to have been a wolf. Who else could manage something like this?"

"These forensics bastards will have a field day and get nowhere."

"We'll have to make sure they get nowhere."

"We have to beat them to the place where this guy was killed and see for ourselves what turns up."

No one had seen anything like this before, and anxiety made them tense. Too many secrets were at stake if a Were had a hand in this gruesome deed. Packs thrived on the stories about the past, so the Weres here were thinking of the time when their Elders fought off whole armies of nasty things that went bump in the night.

It was important that they found the spot where this guy had been murdered, and Rafe knew how. He knew who could easily lead them there, though he was loath to suggest such a thing. Two of these cops were pack and two weren't. No one outside the extended Landau family had been privy to Cara's visit for reasons that now had been made abundantly clear to Rafe.

Someone was after Cara. Someone, possibly with a gun, planned to hurt her, and the best way to do that was to lure her into the open without backup.

Who would die next, as the damn Banshee had predicted? And when? Death's next victim could be anyone here, but he couldn't announce that fact to those standing around him.

Without the others knowing of Cara's visit and her many talents, predicting another dead body might turn up would incriminate whoever mentioned it when that turned out to be the truth.

Rafe was suddenly very tired of secrets.

News trucks were already circling on the street in the distance. TV personalities would be salivating for gory details worthy of morning headlines. Every cop on the force was familiar with the sound of those engines and what they meant. Tonight, due to the body's close proximity to Judge Landau's estate, the news vultures would be held back, at least for a while.

When his father appeared, each of the officers present nodded to the judge. He spoke to them calmly. "Those of us behind this wall will go on record as volunteers to help with this investigation in any way we can. The sooner justice is served, the better we can all rest."

There would be no rest, of course, not until this crime was solved, one way or another. With sunrise several hours off, members of the Landau pack would race through this park in search of details before anyone else got around to it. If a wolf was involved in this heinous act of violence, Weres would deal with it. Self-policing was the only way to handle problems pertaining to the existence of werewolves.

And if vampires had messed with the scene, as Cara had confirmed, Were secrets in the area were going to be sorely threatened. Smack in the middle of this dilemma was an unpredictable hybrid she-wolf who had not learned how to play well with others. Still, her help might be the key to solving the case.

Rafe's father wore a worried expression that ran counter to his usual calm outward demeanor. Things had gotten messy since Cara's arrival, and his father was showing the strain. Tonight had offered a concentrated sample of what they could probably expect as long as she remained in Miami.

Rafe had to be especially careful about messaging his father on Were channels, but he had more to say. *"If you were Cara, and not yet grounded in a new city or a new pack, would you choose to go or stay?"*

Cara might have heard that, of course. Though he had been cautious, her ability to tap into thought systems came to her as easily as hurdling eight-foot stone walls. Cara was indeed special. So he had to wonder if the reason she had been kept in seclusion was due to the danger that followed in her wake—or because she was the danger.

She had proved to him in one night that she had more secrets than the rest of them put together...

But just when he thought things were hard enough to figure out, he picked a word from his father's mind that set his hair on end.

That word was *demon*.

Chapter 18

She'd paced for so long, Cara was afraid she had worn down the carpet. But the lights beyond the wall had dimmed at last, and some of the people had finally dispersed.

It was time to find out if that demon she had encountered had friends, and if one of those hell spawns had murdered a human.

By the looks of things around here and the Landaus' reaction to tonight's events, this pack must have avoided real trouble for some time. She couldn't imagine a long stretch without the kind of problems that followed her around.

Her parents must have realized that by sending her to the Landaus' she might crave the kind of lives others led. So why send her here? Why put these Weres through a night like tonight when more of the same was a given?

Cara stood at the window her mother had long ago jumped from. She had no clue as to what might have precipitated that leap. Rosalind could have either been running away from something, or to something. That piece of the puzzle was unsolved.

"I'm ready to see this part of the picture," Cara muttered with a hand on the sill. The sensation of sharing the room with ghosts of the past had grown stronger. The sharp sting in her mouth was also a part of that.

Needle-sharp incisors pricked her lower lip. Cara wiped her fingers across her mouth, and they came away with tiny droplets of blood. Dark blood. With no vampires present. This was the second time tonight she had altered her appearance without the proper motivation. She spun toward the bed with her senses sparking. On the bed was a filmy, reclining figure.

"Rosalind," it whispered to her.

Dazed, Cara hit the wall next to the window with her shoulder as something blew past her with a speed that was little more than a time slip of barely disturbed air. A second ghostly apparition appeared beside her and gracefully leaped onto the sill, where it paused in a knee-bending crouch.

As Cara stared, more details about this apparition filled in. It was a young female dressed in a glossy black shirt that swirled to stillness as she settled on the sill. The ghostly spirit remained there for a moment more, outlined by the night beyond, long black hair billowing in a nonexistent breeze.

The female glanced at the bed, wiped a hand across her mouth and held up two bloodstained fingers as if to show them to whoever was in the room with her. She uttered a sob of fear and disgust. And then the apparition turned back to the window, pushed off both feet…and jumped.

Cara stood there, frozen beside the window, feeling like she was the one who had jumped. But she hadn't moved, and there was no one on the bed. She had fangs, like the female apparition, and blood on her fingers…didn't she? Or had the blood been someone else's burden?

Her mother's burden?

A knock at the door shook her, but she ignored it. She'd just received another vision of an event from the past, as if it had answered her request for enlightenment. The ghost at the window had been Rosalind. The figure on the bed must have been her father.

Cara leaned out the window with a sense that time had been suspended. The knocking sounds at the door grew louder and were a distraction she didn't need. Whatever had happened in this room to her parents remained a mystery that she would have to decipher later when the distractions ceased.

The door opened without her invitation. A deep voice said, "Can we talk?"

Rafe's powerful presence chased away all remnants of the room's former occupants and replaced her chills with familiar warmth. But she couldn't go to him or try to explain what had happened here with a mouthful of fangs.

Avoiding the directness of his gaze, Cara covered her mouth and reined in a shudder, not sure how she was going to get out of this.

Rafe didn't cross the threshold into Cara's room. Her appearance was a warning to stay where he was.

Her face had again lost color. Her dark glinting stare was trained on the window, as if something had happened there.

Clearly, she wasn't all right.

Why?

He scanned the room to make sure she was alone, rechecking each corner twice. After that, all he could manage to say was her name.

"Cara?"

Her silence wasn't necessarily anything to worry about. The way she covered her mouth might have been, though. She was hiding something from him.

"Hey," he finally said. "I came to tell you that I will take you home in the morning if you still want to go."

She continued to stare at the window, and that made him curious. She hadn't dropped her hand from her mouth. He had to get her to talk so that he could see what he was dealing with.

"Are you Cara?" he asked, hoping nothing of her dark side would start wailing. "Is Cara here?"

He was afraid to crowd her by advancing. Putting her in this room might not have been such a good idea after all. She'd probably find no real comfort sharing a space that had long ago been occupied by other spirits in various states of distress.

Why hadn't anyone here considered that?

Why hadn't he?

Cara was haunted and in need of help she wouldn't ask for. At the moment, she was wan and lifeless. Maybe remaining in Miami was going to harm her in ways none of his family could detect.

Worried, Rafe said, "I'll take you home right now. You can gather your things and I'll get a car."

She took one small step toward him as if drawn by the firmness of his tone. Rafe kept his eyes on her. When she again glanced toward the window, anxiousness over what she was thinking made him consider blocking her path to it.

"Tell me," he said. "Tell me what happened here."

Cara blinked slowly, as if shaking off the spell she had

been under. She dropped the hand that had covered her mouth and looked at him.

"You might go through this all the time and be used to surprises, but it looks to me like you might have had a different kind of shock here. Am I right about that?" he asked.

There were shadows beneath Cara's eyes that he hadn't noticed previously. Her green eyes had a dark cast. To be honest, Rafe had had enough uncomfortable silence to last him a lifetime, so he walked toward her with his hands in his pockets to make reaching for her impossible. Cara, however she looked and no matter how haunted she was, remained an ongoing temptation for him. He had to accept that.

"Taking you home won't solve the problems that are haunting you, but it might be a healthier option," he said.

Cara shook her head.

Rafe persisted. "If you're going to stay, I need to understand what's going on so I can help. Please let me in."

She spoke at last, repeating what she'd said earlier. "I came here to find the past."

That's when Rafe saw the fangs.

He hid the anxiety this caused him. "You're finding part of that past in this room?" he asked, wanting very badly to hold Cara. "What did you see?"

Speaking slowly, as if she hadn't yet shaken off her recent shock, Cara said, "I don't think my mother knew she could be like the vampires before coming here. I think she found that out in this room, and the revelation frightened her."

Rafe waited for her to go on, sensing she would. Cara was wild-eyed. Her body was rigid. She had to get this out.

"My father almost died by fang, and my mother had developed a pair. Think how that might have gone down with my father, Rafe, if his lover started to look like a vampire."

He tried to comprehend the meaning of what she had just told him, and spoke carefully. "You've connected with another moment in your mother's past?"

She nodded. "Those fangs might have been the reason she jumped from this window. She needed to hide them from him."

He was catching on to the importance of that. "Rosalind fled because she developed a new talent for growing fangs? Was there a vampire in this room to instigate such a change?"

Cara's voice lowered. "No. That's the significance of this memory. She had changed on her own. She had grown a pair of fangs for the first time, possibly because my father had so much vampire venom in his system and she was near to him here."

Rafe waited, not sure what to say. What Cara said made sense in a Kirk-Killion kind of way that he wasn't up on.

"My father was here also," Cara continued. "He was looking at her, and there was blood on her lips from dealing with those fangs."

"Your father was here?" Rafe asked.

She nodded. "He was on that bed."

"Do you think she bit him?"

"I think she was afraid to be around him when the fangs appeared. She was shocked and afraid of what my father would think after he had been so brutally attacked by the kind of being she was starting to become."

Rafe's insides twisted with the reminder that this visit to Miami hadn't been good for Cara. She couldn't have been paler. He felt her tension from two feet away.

As far as he could see, finding out about her parents' past wasn't making Cara feel better. It was only making things worse. If she wanted family history so damn badly, why hadn't she asked her parents to shed some light on the past? She was so brave in facing monsters, it seemed absurd that she couldn't face her parents for some answers.

"So Rosalind had discovered a new shape-shift and was terrified," he said.

"Yes," Cara replied breathlessly.

"What does that have to do with you? Why was discovering that such a shock?"

"She didn't understand how it could have happened, I think. Maybe she believed she could no longer control the shape-shifts in the way she had always believed she could."

"And that might lead to hurting your father? Hurting others?"

Cara's eyes grew wider. "Something sinister had taken place. In becoming like them, it would mean that vampires had some degree of kinship with her, and that she had become something else again, other than the previous merging of wolf and Banshee."

Cara took a step toward Rafe. "I think maybe she didn't actually know about the Banshee until then."

A light in Rafe's mind clicked on. He suddenly understood why Rosalind's jump from the window had been so important to Cara's understanding of the past. Rosalind had been a rare black wolf before the attack on Colton, but afterward, as a result of the part she had played in rescuing him, Cara's mother had learned that she housed another entity, along with more abilities that she could have dreamed of.

Speaking was a chore for him after that surprising streak of enlightenment. Cara had just located the moment that her mother's life, and hers, had been forever changed.

"Do you want to leave?" he asked, cautiously gauging Cara's emotional state. "Do you need to? You don't have to be a tortured guest here where so many ghosts roam. Get your things or leave them, and come with me."

"I'm not going home. Not yet," she argued. "I have to see this through."

"See what through, Cara?"

"There is more to come. I wasn't just sent here to try to assimilate. I'm here for another reason. I'm sure of it."

"I won't take you home if you're not ready for that, but this room is no longer an option. We can go to my place. We can find out how many vampires will catch on to our bait-and-switch routine."

The darkness faded from Cara's eyes as though it had simply drained away. Was that because he cared about her and had offered some comfort?

The premonition and shared memory stuff should have scared him off, but a detective who was also a werewolf couldn't admit to being so easily intimidated. For better or worse, they were now a couple and he had to see this through. He had to help her, protect her, in whatever kind of situation arose next.

"What happens to you also happens to me by proxy, Cara. Together, we're stronger. You just have to tell me what we're facing, and why, so that I can prepare."

She nodded again. "I don't know what's next, but I'm going to find out."

Rafe closed his eyes briefly to assimilate all of this. Imprinting could be a bitch or a boon, but it had rules.

No exit.

No detours.

Nowhere to run.

And damn it, he had no intention of trying to get out of this relationship, even if that were possible. As difficult as tonight had been—dilated eyes, wolf shapes, vampires, dead bodies and Banshees—he was in for the count. He was all hers, whoever and whatever Cara really was beneath all that black-haired beauty. This just wasn't the time or the place to tell her so.

She was moving toward the door. The idea of leaving the estate where she should have been safe from the rest of the outside world had been tempting to Cara. He took her bag from her. When they exited the room, he closed the door to seal off those damn ghosts.

They headed down the staircase. The house was quieter than it should have been, given the chaos surrounding the discovery of that body by the wall. Abducting their guest wasn't going to sit well with his folks, but Rafe had an argument ready in case he and Cara were caught making a quick exit.

He had gone over most of the possible consequences of taking Cara away. Rafe understood that he'd be breaking trust between the Landaus and the Kirk-Killions, and that he might be leaving the way open for more danger. Removing Cara, shielding her from so many watchful eyes, just seemed the right thing to do, if not for Cara's sanity, then for his.

She might find a few moments' peace in a smaller space that her parents had never seen or occupied. If they had to stake every damn vampire that found her, so be it.

They made it down all flights of stairs and halfway across the entrance hall before someone got in the way of their reaching the front door.

"Going somewhere?" his mother asked.

Chapter 19

The strange thing, Cara discovered as she studied her hostess, was that Dana Delmonico Landau wasn't half as put out as she appeared to be. Beneath the stern exterior lay a palpable aura of understanding that led Cara to believe a getaway might have been expected, at least by one member of this pack.

"Too many unwelcome newcomers know she's here," Rafe said. "It's too damn dangerous for Cara to stay right now."

Dana studied her son for a long moment before turning an inquisitive gaze on Cara. "Nothing can get past those walls out there, Cara. That, I can promise."

Though Rafe nodded in agreement, he said, "What about what's in this house?"

Dana didn't quite get what Rafe was saying. "No one here would hurt Cara."

"That's where you're wrong," Rafe countered. "Who's

to say that ghosts can't cause their own kind of damage to someone who is open to them?"

"Ghosts?" Dana echoed.

Rafe nodded. "Who is to say what can and can't hurt someone so unlike the rest of us?"

It was the first time Rafe had actually addressed the differences between them. With him, her inner wolf wanted dominance. The she-wolf wanted to reach out to Rafe, but the darker aspects of her soul were getting in the way.

"So you'll sign on as Cara's sole guardian?" Dana asked Rafe.

"For a night or two. Then we'll return," he answered.

Dana again looked to her. "You're okay with this, Cara?"

Cara nodded.

Dana gave them both a last once-over before stepping away from the door. "He won't like this," she said.

"I'm sure you can help with that," Rafe replied. "And you know where we'll be."

"So will those bloodsuckers, most likely."

"I hope not," Rafe said, and Cara saw that some of the strength of his will had been inherited from his mother.

The standoff was over. Rafe had chosen to be her champion, although he had no real notion yet of what he had signed on for. Did that make him a hero, or merely misguided in his affections?

A delicious warmth overcame Cara when Rafe took her hand. He liked to touch her and wasn't afraid. Slinging her bag over his shoulder, Rafe nodded to his mother and tossed Cara a quick look that said *Here we go*.

Leaving his father's house might have seemed like a stupid move to some, but it was based on solid reasoning. If vampires were like bloodhounds on a scent, Cara's lingering fragrance in and around the estate would occupy those bloodsuckers' cravings for some time. By taking her away, Rafe hoped Cara might have a brief respite from all that before they tracked her again. The bonus in all this was having Cara to himself.

He didn't dare lead her through the park or anywhere else on foot. With monster deflection in mind and a plan to try to leave no trail for others to follow, Rafe headed for the garage.

There were six cars parked there for him to choose from. He picked a small silver sedan that would blend in well with other cars on the road.

After opening the passenger door for Cara, he climbed behind the wheel to find the keys conveniently dangling from the ignition. The engine turned over with a soft roar, and they headed out. At the front gate, the guards waved him through, and then he and Cara were on their own.

"I wonder if you realize how powerful this thing is between us," he said.

Cara's gaze slid to him. She said, "Yes."

"If this location change doesn't work, we'll try something else to avoid the monsters," Rafe explained.

"You live near the water, and water can divert them," Cara said.

"Water?"

"It's what kept that vampire from seeing me on the beach. Salt water is a purifier," she said. "The smell distracts vampires by hampering their sensitivity to things around them. They hate it. Avoid it."

He said, "You're serious?"

Green eyes gleamed when they turned his way. Cara had just given him another lesson in a course titled Vampires 101.

Those green eyes of hers did more than that, though.

The seductive quality of her gaze produced enough heat to ease his tenseness. He began to relax as his mind retrieved images of him and Cara in the park, backed up against a tree, and how badly he had wanted to kiss her.

He wanted that same thing now.

"I have never been alone with a wolf like you," she confessed.

"I consider that a point in my favor," Rafe returned lightly. "It will be okay. You can rest and I'll stand guard."

"Do you understand why I wasn't allowed to be with others, Rafe?"

Several reasons came to mind, most of them having to do with her parents and the many forms she could take, but Rafe didn't say so.

"I've never been safe for anyone to be around. And I've certainly never been with someone willing to break down the barriers that have been erected for their own good," she said.

"Is that what I'm doing? Breaking barriers?"

"Yes."

"I'm willing to take my chances and see where this leads," Rafe said.

"Maybe that wasn't your choice, and our attraction is being guided by invisible hands," she suggested.

"Whose hands would those be?"

"Your parents'. My parents'. The imprinting phenomenon you keep thinking about could be derived from chance, or fate."

"Maybe all of those things combined," Rafe said.

"You believe that?"

Rafe nodded.

"I can read your thoughts, you know," Cara confessed.

"So, what am I thinking now?"

"You want to kiss me," she said.

Of course he did. Having Cara next to him drastically threatened his vow to not take advantage of her while she was in his care.

"It really is too late to fight the truth, and too late to question how we got this close so quickly," Rafe said. "It doesn't actually matter how, does it? Only that it happened. You do get that, Cara?"

He pulled the car to a curb near enough to his building for them to get to it quickly. Cara's only response to his remarks was a slow blink of those mesmerizing emerald eyes.

He turned off the engine and faced her. "From what I've witnessed, you fight for the right side, just as your parents did. You want to stamp out the evil that comes your way, and that objective makes you dangerous only to the bad guys."

Cara shook her head. "The spirit inside me is harder to control than anything you could imagine. She twists me into shapes I see only in my mind, and her hold on my soul doesn't diminish over time. That's where she resides, Rafe. In my soul."

She took a breath before continuing. "There's no option for releasing that spirit and no way to predict what she might do if I let down my guard. Vampires and demons want that spirit released. Death is their accomplice. If they can't have that spirit, then they will make do with the body sheltering it. Guess who that is."

"I thought the Banshee's deal was to predict oncoming death, and only that. Are you saying my understanding is wrong?"

"Wrong, yes, because of what happened all those years ago."

"How wrong?"

"The dark spirit can never be freed," Cara said.

Rafe thought that over. "You said freed. Does that mean you could release it if you wanted to, or if you found a way?"

"We made a pact to protect her, and that pact can't be broken."

"Who agreed to such a thing?" he asked. "Did they understand the consequences of such a vow?"

"My ancestors knew very well what they had agreed to. Those were the ancestors this spirit helped. If it wasn't for her help, I wouldn't be here. My mother wouldn't be here. My family's bloodline wouldn't exist."

"It's a her?" he said.

"The Banshee is a female spirit, or the closest thing to it. She can only exist within a female host."

Cara's explanation shed more light on things. She was bound to this dark spirit because of a blood vow by a family member in her past. This might mean that she could conceivably get rid of that spirit if she had a mind to, and instead she chose to honor that ancient pact.

Rafe nodded in understanding. "You said that instead of calling death to someone in your family, this spirit saved a life, and in doing so, went against its purpose for existing."

Cara nodded. "And we agreed to save the spirit, in turn."

"By passing it along in your family from soul to soul, which in essence hides it," Rafe said.

"That was the deal, yes."

"Yet other creatures seem to be able to find you and the Banshee with relative ease."

"And so some of us have become her protectors. We keep her safe."

He hadn't considered that line of reasoning, and it came as a surprise. Cara wasn't just unlucky to be inhabited by the dark spirit she spoke of. She was its guardian.

Or was she its jailer?

He didn't have a clear picture of what would happen if Cara were to release the spirit. The whole thing sounded ominous and inconceivable. It was no wonder that Cara had tried to keep the Banshee from appearing by shape-shifting away from it. Like his task of protecting the people of Miami, Cara was looking out for the spirit and had no choice in the matter.

"What would happen if you didn't adhere to that old vow?" he asked.

"Dark forces would come to deal with us all for that past transgression, and for harboring her."

Hell, that sounded bad. It also sounded like supernatural payback.

They were parked and couldn't afford to linger in the open, though Rafe wanted to remain close to Cara. He was beginning to comprehend the direness of Cara's position and the little effect he could have on something so serious.

She had said dark forces would come after them.

Damn it. All this made his job as a cop seem like a cakewalk. Because would anyone have liked the sound of that?

Chapter 20

No shock registered on the handsome face of the Were facing her. Cara found the whole idea of sharing confidences strangely intimate. Like their kiss in the park, talking things over with Rafe was also a new experience for her. By accepting Rafe as a confidant, she was allowing him a fair amount of power in their relationship. How he might direct that power was the question.

She was tired. Sleep had always been difficult, and it would be a luxury tonight if she managed to close her eyes. Things at home had been straightforward. All that mattered was living day by day to fight creatures that sought to limit her freedom. That wasn't so simple when others became involved with her story, and when Rafe had so quickly found a way to earn her trust.

He opened her car door for her but didn't offer a hand. His reluctance to touch her wasn't born of fear. It was a compassionate attempt to give her time to process what they meant to each other.

He gestured for her to precede him toward his apartment building. Their arms brushed when she did, and that slightest of sensations again set her senses ablaze.

"Cara?" The tender quality of Rafe's voice amplified her body's sudden buildup of heat. She couldn't let down her guard, but she was better prepared for ghosts and demons than the delicious distraction Rafe Landau posed.

The adrenaline surge that hit her now was similar to fight-or-flight syndrome. Yet Rafe wasn't the enemy. She couldn't take her eyes from him, and her body tingled all over. He had caused her to question the future and had made it clear he would have preferred to have her all to himself, with no dark spirit standing in the way of their union. Rafe was ingrained in her thoughts now and was therefore haunting her, still.

"The beach isn't safe tonight," he warned. "Too many people might be out, enjoying a late-night rendezvous, which could potentially bring more trouble if there do happen to be any vampires around. We should stay inside until dawn. I'd be willing to bet that sunrise can't be too far off."

He was avoiding the next question he probably wanted to ask her by circling the conversation back to the vampires. Still, she knew what Rafe might be thinking after telling him more details about the Banshee.

"I can't release the dark spirit, Rafe. I can't ever do that, and it would be useless to suggest such a thing."

He said, "I do understand about promises and vows, Cara."

As they reached the stairs that led to his apartment, she said, "This means I can never be free in the way you might wish me to be."

"Maybe you're wrong about what I wish," he returned,

pausing on the stairs to look at the beach. Thankfully, he changed the subject. "Is anyone out there?"

"No one that should concern us at the moment."

Rafe sighed with relief and used a key to unlock his front door. Then he waited for her to precede him inside. A light switch near the door illuminated the room with a wash of soft ambient light. It was easy for Cara to like what she saw.

The space was relatively small and not crowded with furniture. The flooring was a cool gray tile. Closed shutters on two front windows blocked out the night and the view. Rafe's furniture consisted of a leather couch with a small table beside it and a pair of fabric-covered chairs. Three interior doors led to other rooms. One of those would be his bedroom.

She turned her attention to the wall of glass that led to the balcony where she had first seen Rafe and the trouble he was in. Only a faint trace of the vampire he'd brought here remained. Most of Rafe's surroundings smelled like him.

The apartment was the exact opposite of the luxurious Landau estate, and it suited Rafe's personality. Free of pack rules and onlookers, Rafe could be his own man here.

Ocean sounds pervaded the room. Though the glass doors were closed, the rhythmical lull of waves washing onto the shore created a backdrop of comforting sounds that Cara welcomed.

"Home sweet home, small and simple," he said, watching her.

"This is more like my home," she told him. "Minus the trimmings."

"Hell. I have trimmings?"

Cara resisted the smile she felt tugging at the corners of her mouth.

"I'd like to hear more about where you live," he said, dropping her bag and crossing to the windows to make sure the shutters were closed tight. He pointed to one of the interior doors. "The bedroom is over there. Bathroom is to the right, and the kitchen is opposite. I don't suppose you ate whatever my mother fixed for you tonight, which was probably a good thing. She was a great cop. As a cook, she's not quite so special."

He waited a few beats before adding with a lazy smile, "You do eat normal food?"

The teasing was supposed to put her at ease, and worked. Rafe wanted her to like his home enough to feel comfortable. Everything he had done tonight had been for her, and she was learning a lot about Rafe Landau in bits and pieces.

"Do you have tea?" she asked, because he was waiting for her to speak.

"Sure. How about something terribly fast food–like to go with it?"

"Anything would be nice, as long as there's a lot of it," Cara replied.

When he offered her a dazzling, contagious smile, Cara couldn't quite recall the last time she had let herself enjoy a moment like this, however brief it might turn out to be.

This sense of having encountered unexpected happiness wasn't going to last, of course, because that would have been asking too much. She and Rafe weren't people with typical needs and wants. And they had too many secrets left that hadn't, out of necessity, been shared.

Dressed in her own clothes, Rafe's houseguest was no less seductive than she had been in his shirt and not much else. Cara seemed to prefer black—a black shirt and loose black pants. She had dared to kick off her boots, which might have meant that she would stay put for a while.

She had sleepy eyes. Now and then, her dark lashes lowered over them. She sat on the sofa with both hands folded in her lap as if she were a prim and proper schoolgirl instead of one of the world's most dangerous creatures. She had already removed the bandage on her hand.

Rafe noticed how frequently her gaze returned to the glass doors. She probably yearned for the water he had first found her near, but they both knew it would be a bad idea to let her go. Impossible, really. The goal was to evade vampires, not to send them an invitation.

It was 5:00 a.m. when he finally looked at the clock. Only a couple hours of seclusion were left, and then Cara could swim to her heart's delight while he found a way to finagle another day off from work—an especially difficult request with the investigation of that body underway. Harboring a sexy hybrid werewolf in need of a guardian wouldn't cut it as an excuse with his human boss.

He was curious about that body, though, and how deeply it might be wrapped up in Cara's business. Had it been deposited near the wall as a warning for the pack harboring Cara? Could the damage to that human have been caused by the same creature that had gotten close enough to Cara to break a few bones in her hands? The thought of that made him sick.

He hadn't kissed Cara again. True to his own personal promise, he hadn't gone near her, though waning willpower kept him riveted to the chair by the front door.

She had eaten a sandwich and drunk four cups of tea. Neither of them had slept, because who could have on a night filled with so many dark deeds?

Cara didn't talk or offer any more confidences. She didn't request a shower or look around the other rooms.

Her gaze connected with his every few minutes, inviting him to get out of the chair, but he refrained from acting on his instincts. The result of ignoring all those feelings and physical desires for closeness was a thickening of the atmosphere that made the room seem even smaller than it was.

Though the coffee in his mug had gone cold, Rafe drank it.

Guilt was also part of his new dilemma. The pack would have discovered more details about that murder in the hours before dawn, and he should have been there with them. He would have been there if he had left Cara in his family's care, but again, that hadn't been a choice.

His wish to keep her in his sight was strong enough to override other necessities. That's the way the imprinting process worked. Though still in the early stage, the compulsion to mate with Cara took precedence over most other things. Until they fully mated—on a bed or elsewhere, with him settled between Cara's thighs—every waking thought revolved around personal needs that both of them were pretending to ignore. Cara also felt these needs. He saw it in her big green eyes.

Since tone of voice and sharing confidences were other components of seduction, they didn't speak. Prolonged eye contact had to be avoided.

When golden streaks of sunlight finally filtered into the room, Rafe got up to stretch his legs. After removing his shirt and his boots, he took Cara by the hand and led her to the door. He preceded her down the steps and across the sidewalk that bordered the sand. There, he pulled her around so that she had to look at him.

"Freedom at last," he said. "But that also means no getting naked in the daylight, so we'll have to make do in our pants."

He wanted nothing more than to get Cara naked, and cautiously guarded that thought. The call for him to get to work would come any time now. Sun worshipers from the hotel and surrounding buildings would soon hit the beach, and his moment alone with Cara would be lost. Until then, they could relax their vigilance. Monsters didn't roam when the sun came out.

Cara was all his.

The sand felt warm on his feet and already reflected the sunlight. Cara dug in with her bare toes as she turned toward the water. She removed her shirt and tossed it aside, but kept her pants on as she broke into a run.

Rafe followed her, leaving a few feet of distance between them. When Cara reached the water, she didn't hesitate to wade in. He caught the item she tossed to him as he followed her into the surf. It was her pants.

Everything after that happened in slow motion.

Cara turned around in waist-deep water. Across the lapping silvery foam, she gave him a wide-eyed stare.

"Oh, no, you don't," Rafe said, his warning muted by the crash of the next wave. Damn it, he had misjudged the freedom he had just offered to her, and what Cara would do with it. He had believed she was on the same page.

The back of his neck prickled as he waded in after her. But it was too late. In a repeat of the night before, and in spite of events that had taken place between then and now, Cara was suddenly gone. She just vanished.

Knowing that it was futile to go after her, he nevertheless had to try. Rafe moved into deeper water and swam in a direction parallel to the shore. Strong strokes took him halfway up the beach, where there was no sign of the female he had promised to protect.

He had let her go, and there would be consequences,

though the worst of it was the way he felt. "Cara…" he messaged to her. "Don't do this."

The only response he got was the steady drumming of the waves and the irregular beat of his heart.

He couldn't wait all day for the runaway to show up. An hour had passed since he had lost Cara, and he needed to retrieve his cell phone and get down to other business. He'd have to also confess to his family about having lost her in broad daylight. And really, where would a naked woman go? How far would she get?

Rafe walked back to his apartment, dropped Cara's clothes beside his on the floor in the bathroom and stepped into the shower, not sure what was worse…thinking about Cara out there, or in here—as a runaway, or as his lover. He tried not to imagine her sleek body turning to him, and the way he might have pressed her to the cool, wet tiles as he readied for the move he hadn't been able to get out of his mind since meeting her.

He could almost see the water dripping down her face, and the look in her eyes that told him she wanted the same thing. He could feel his hands on her, his mouth on her, his hardness entering her softness. It all felt so real, and so right, he wondered if this was a premonition of things to come or merely more wishful thinking, and if those two things had become inexplicably intertwined. The images and sensations were so vivid, so potent and realistic, he cut the damn shower short so he could again breathe properly and regain perspective.

Hell, this imprinting business was a bitch.

Soon he was fully dressed, armed with his gun and his badge and ready to roll. He left his front door unlocked in case Cara returned and headed for the street, wishing that his only problem in the next half hour was the ribbing he'd get from other cops if they saw him driving his father's luxury car.

It turned out he didn't have to worry about that. Cameron had beaten him there and was leaning casually against the silver sedan at the curb.

"Thought you might need some help," the Were said, adding with a wry grin, "with the car."

Chapter 21

The Were who had captured a piece of her heart in so short a time didn't return to his apartment before the sun went down. Cara's boundless need for freedom, even from her new feelings for Rafe, continued to resonate in every cell in her body.

At sunset, most of the humans on the beach had dispersed. Despite the few people still around, Cara finally left the water, figuring the others who saw her were so skimpily clad themselves, they might simply let it go. And there was no evidence of vampires flooding the area. The salt water would have covered her tracks if there had been a fanged scout or two.

Rafe had left the door unlocked. Her open bag was on the table where she had left it that morning. Damp clothes, Rafe's and hers, had been hung up on a rack to dry.

She had trouble in the shower that not only smelled like Rafe, but reflected happier things related to his life.

His thoughts seemed to linger there. Those thoughts made her blush.

Dressed in dry clothes, Cara walked from room to room studying the details. Rafe was neat. Several framed photos of his family lined one hallway. There was a television set and a radio in the bedroom. She ran a hand over the mattress, feeling for hints of Rafe, though no one had slept in that bed last night.

She didn't have any family photos at home, or a refrigerator filled with things to eat. Although comfortable and snug, the Kirk-Killion cottage served up more basic fare. She hadn't felt any lack of comfort while growing up, or the necessity for company other than her mother's and father's until the dreams had started. Dreams that turned out to be of Rafe, and a life like his.

When a knock broke the silence, Cara whirled to face the door. Rafe had returned. He had known she would be here. Would he be angry? Upset about that morning?

"Are you decent?" he called out. And Cara let go of the breath she had been holding.

Rafe's familiar scent preceded him into the room like a separate being. Contrary to her misgivings about seeing him after her disappearance, Cara felt relief. She was sorry she had given him the slip. Rafe had become her mooring, her stabilizing rock in a new world, and he had been confident about her return.

Their gazes connected. Through that meeting of their eyes, their thoughts and hopes melded together. Rafe's expression showed his hunger and his need for more than just speaking to her, but he said, "Are you ready?" without acting on those needs or chastising her for the earlier defection.

"Yes," she replied, gleaning a picture of where Rafe

wanted to take her—the place that took precedence over their desires and what they both would rather have done.

Their wants were to be put on hold.

They were going back to the park.

She was to help him find a killer.

There were working streetlights surrounding the park on three sides, but not to the east, where gangs occasionally used the globes for target practice. The east side was where he took Cara.

Rafe parked his older SUV next to two unmanned police cruisers and Cameron's showy beige sports car. "Cops are in the west and Weres are everywhere else," he said to her. "The body we found near the wall has been taken to the morgue and the investigation is well underway."

Cara's eyes were clear and focused, he thought. A good sign. Still, he would have preferred to have been with her anywhere but here.

"There haven't been any other deaths today, such as the one that dark spirit predicted. Not yet, anyway. So now," he said, leaning back in the seat, "tell me about that gunshot. The one that came too close to you for comfort."

Cara replied quickly. "One shot."

"You're sure?"

She nodded. "Only one."

"Pistol or rifle?"

"He wasn't close."

"Rifle then, maybe. It came from which direction?"

After scanning the park through the windshield, Cara said, "Where it was the darkest."

"Figures. Can you show me where you were? Do you think you can find that place again?"

"Didn't the big Were named Jonas tell you?"

"Jonas has been inconsiderately MIA today, so it's up

to you, if you have anything to show me that can help with this investigation."

"You believe that whoever fired a shot at me could have had something to do with the death of the human?"

"I don't believe that. We have to start somewhere, however, and you encountered trouble near the same time that body was being mutilated. I wanted to take another look around without the rest of my police team here, since I'd have a hard time explaining about you or keeping you from getting mixed up in the investigation."

"Won't we be interfering?"

"That depends on how it turns out. If a Were had anything to do with that human's murder, it's our job to find him. If it was something else, well, we wouldn't want to cause a panic about that, would we?"

Cara and Rafe got out of the car and he rested a hand on the warm metal hood. In any other situation, he would have hurdled the car to get at her.

She looked at him soberly. "I didn't tell you everything."

"Yeah, I figured as much," Rafe said. "Better late than never is how the saying goes, so any light you can shed would help. Would you like to tell me what it is that you didn't mention?"

Rafe rounded the car slowly, careful to give Cara time to respond to his question.

"I'm sorry about today," she said.

All he could think to say was "Okay."

Her eyes narrowed on the park. "I don't think that bullet was meant for me, as you all supposed. I don't think it was a wolf hunter out there."

"Why do you think that?" Rafe asked.

"The bullet carried a strange scent."

Rafe drew in a breath, anticipating that Cara would

mention silver. He carried silver rounds in a hidden pocket on his belt because a bad werewolf was a danger to everyone, not just to humans.

"Can you describe the smell?" he asked.

"The bullet smelled like fire."

All right. He had not expected that.

"A wolf hunter would have used silver," he pointed out.

She nodded. "No hunter."

Rafe had to process what she had said. If Cara was right about the shooter not hunting Weres, what could the imbecile have been after, and with a bullet that Cara said smelled like fire? Cara, who was a kind of monster hunter herself, would be able to tell what kind of bullet had come anywhere near her.

Needing more thinking room, Rafe absently tugged at the collar of his shirt. It was important for them to find that bullet. Imperative, actually.

With a little luck, maybe they'd locate a casing on the ground or the damn bullet embedded in the trunk of a tree. It might not help to explain how the murder victim got a severed spine, but there was a chance that bullet could provide some kind of a clue that could give this investigation a kick in the right direction.

"Can you show me where it happened?" he asked Cara.

Cara gestured for him to follow her.

After the events of last night, walking in the dark, with Cara a few steps in front of him, kept Rafe on edge. Cara could drop to all fours at any moment and race away in the opposite direction if she had a mind to. He now knew that her MO was to run away from her feelings for him.

He could still hear the howl she'd made last night. The shock had stayed with him.

The park wasn't quiet tonight, either. Though the perimeter was blocked off by cops on foot and in squad cars, there was still plenty of noise. Muted music came from the boulevard. Sirens wailed in the distance and car horns honked. Those sounds dimmed as he and Cara strode deeper into the darkness with their inner radar humming.

His companion walked with an outward show of confidence he didn't feel. Cara exhibited no sign of having concerns about who or what might jump out of the shadows. After his close call with bloodsucking Brandi, he preferred to place his trust in Cara's expertise in the realm of the supernatural.

"Not far now," she said, as if she could have arrived at the spot they were looking for with her eyes shut.

They had to find something soon or turn back. They were nearing the southeastern portion of the grounds where crimes occurred on a weekly basis. The pack had taken to patrolling the area in nightly sweeps and would likely have been here soon after sundown, along with the cops. It wasn't much past that time now, but Rafe recognized the smell of trouble.

They were going to have company.

Any packmate out for a prolonged stroll would at least know about Cara's visit, so bumping into one would merely be an inconvenience. It was everyone else Rafe had to worry about. Humans pretty much all smelled alike, which made telling the difference between good guys and bad guys a toss-up until their behavior came to light. Bad guys tended to carry guns and knives, but the kind of trouble Rafe sensed smelled like...death.

They moved in silence over dry, trampled grass and beneath trees that didn't yet cast shadows. Overhead, the moon was partially covered by clouds. In five days Weres would come out from behind walls and shadows to howl at that moon. A park full of Miami's werewolves was probably the safest place around if anyone dared to come here to cause problems.

His attention had slipped. Ahead of him, Cara stopped suddenly and stood very still, driving Rafe's nerves to a state of red alert. His right hand went to his weapon and hovered there. He heard Cara whisper, "Company," as he got a whiff of what that company might be.

Cara placed a hand on his to keep him from drawing his gun and shook her head adamantly. She said the words no one wanted to hear in such a precariously dangerous situation.

"Won't do any good against this guy."

This wasn't a memory. What was happening was real because Rafe, beside her, had also picked up on the smell. He also noticed the way she had to speak around the sharp tips of her fangs, and warily glanced away.

"Damn it. Another one?" he asked.

The only questions she had now were how soon that bloodsucker would take to get to here and which one of them would tangle with it first.

Rafe was keyed up in a way that made her nerves dance. He was probably angry the search for the bullet had been interrupted and plagued by the reminder of how he'd been fooled by the ancient parasite he'd invited into his apartment yesterday.

He took a step and Cara matched it.

"Which one of us do you suppose looks like dinner?" he asked cynically.

"This is highly unusual," Cara explained. "Normally, vamps don't come after wolves unless there is no one else around."

"Either their tastes have evolved, or we're just lucky." Rafe glanced at her again. "If they don't usually like wolves, why would they bother to come around here, where there are so many of us? And why did they attack your father here, in this same park?"

"I think they attacked my father to rid the city of one of the oldest werewolf lines. They knew about the Lycans who could do them some major damage. Every wolf they took down would mean more freedom to prey upon Miami's population."

"Well, that plan didn't turn out so well, did it? Maybe this sucker won't overstep its bounds."

Cara wanted to tell Rafe that vampires had no bounds, but just then a tall skeletal form cloaked in black slid into the shadows between two trees...and her fangs began to throb.

Chapter 22

Rafe tried not to show the disgust he felt as he faced this animated corpse. The creature was painful to look at and hadn't bothered to hide its true semblance. Or so Rafe surmised, because nothing could have been worse than this guy.

Unlike the high-gloss version of the undead that Brandi had presented him with, this bloodsucker looked and smelled like it had recently crawled up from a grave. It had a white face and gray hair. Red-rimmed eyes glowered at him from a sunken face that was not much more than a conglomeration of exposed bone. There was barely enough flesh on its lips to hide the bloodsucker's long, pointed fangs. The way it stared was unnerving.

Cara, on the other hand, didn't seem surprised by the awful appearance of this gaunt apparition. Her vibe was calm as she waited for their visitor to make a move. For her, this was a regular occurrence.

Rafe broke the silence by muttering, "Where's a carved wooden stake when we need one?"

The vampire—a male, Rafe thought, but couldn't be sure—emitted a hissing noise through its fangs that was reminiscent of steam escaping from a vent. Rafe got the feeling the vamp was angry, and yet its face didn't reflect that. The creature didn't move. This guy was probably sizing them up and wondering if it could manage a twofer. Or maybe this ugly bastard hadn't expected to find two Weres in the park tonight and was therefore reassessing its options...as if it had any.

"Wait," Cara softly cautioned Rafe.

"Which of us is the target?" Rafe asked, ready to tear this creature apart with his bare hands if it showed any intention of going after Cara. Those bones looked brittle enough to snap without much force.

The vampire finally took a step, which was actually more like a glide, as if it wore skates beneath the rags covering its body.

That was creepy.

"You don't belong here," Cara said.

Rafe heard the warning in her tone. Her voice was like steel.

"What do you want?" she asked the creature.

Rafe clenched his fists when it replied in a hollow voice that sounded like it had originated in an echo chamber.

"Information."

"We are not friends or allies," Cara said.

"Yet we are sometimes like cousins, are we not?" the vampire returned, showing more wit than Rafe would have imagined possible given the bastard's tattered state.

"Not even close," Cara said.

The vampire pointed a bony finger at her. Rafe leaned

forward ready to act. "The dark is strong in you, wolf girl," the vampire remarked.

Rafe wondered if Cara wore her darkness like a special perfume only other hybrids could smell. Vampires, it seemed to him, were another kind of hybrid. They weren't completely one thing or another—not completely dead, or they couldn't be walking around, and not fully alive, either—which made them creatures able to somehow bridge the gap between life and death.

Did they like being in limbo and feasting on the life force of others? This wasn't the time or place to ask that question. Rafe avoided looking at Cara to see how she had reacted to the vampire's remark. It would have been suicidal to shift his attention from the creature in front of them after seeing how fast his fanged date had moved.

"What do you want?" Cara asked again.

"Life," the vamp replied.

"Then you've come to the wrong place," she said.

The creature dropped its hand. "And yet you have so much of it. So much life. Surely you can spare some of it for a cousin in need."

"You can't bite me," Cara said. "I think you already know that."

Rafe resisted the urge to glance sideways at her. This was news to him. If vampires couldn't bite Cara, how in hell did they assume they'd be able to get at what her body kept hidden inside?

"She is mine to carry," Cara said.

"Perhaps she would like true darkness for a change," the vamp suggested. "Could it be that you have carried this burden long enough? Perhaps the spirit longs for freedom after all this time."

So that was it. The vampire wanted to become the Banshee's new host. But according to Cara, that kind of transference couldn't happen, and she'd never allow it even if it was possible.

"I do not own the spirit," Cara said. "She is not mine to give away. Nor would I try. My family owes her a debt of honor. The Banshee must remain with us, and it is my place to guard her."

The vampire's eyes darkened considerably. "I am sorry to hear that."

"Why?" Rafe broke in. "Why are you sorry to hear that?"

He didn't like the way the red-rimmed eyes turned to him.

"I am old. Blood no longer sustains me," the dark-eyed sucker replied.

Rafe didn't really want to know what that meant. Chatting with this vampire was disconcerting enough. Finding out that vampires—at least some of them—retained their wits and could speak in proper sentences was worrisome. The questions pummeling him now were crucial ones about what this bloodsucker would do next. Would Cara, who hated the breed that had sent her father into exile and plagued her current existence, let this one go?

There were rustling sounds from the west that brought Rafe a wary moment of relief. A new scent filled the air. Weres were coming. They would see this creature, and if the vampire valued what was left of its pitiful existence, it would have to flee.

He watched the vampire turn to look in the direction of the noise. In the moonlight, Rafe caught the gleam of exposed fangs between Cara's full lips. If the vamp stayed, Cara's fangs would also stay, and the Weres searching the park would see them. But the dilemma of outing Cara seemed trivial against the prospect of his friends in a face-off with an ancient bloodsucker that looked like death itself.

As the sounds got closer, Rafe's tension escalated to a higher pulse-pounding frequency. What would happen? Would this creature do something to save itself?

He didn't have to wait long to find out. The bony parasite nodded to Cara as if acknowledging defeat, then spun around with almost subliminal speed…and vanished.

Rafe kept his focus on the spot where it had stood, not at all sure why the fanged creep had retreated so easily without a fight. Cara seemed to know the answer, but she didn't offer an explanation.

She shook her head hard, as if she could rid herself of the fangs that way. Whereas she hadn't given any hint of concern over meeting the vampire, she now buzzed with nervousness over the possibility of meeting the approaching Weres.

To vampires she was no freak, only an adversary.

Right at that moment, Rafe wasn't so sure about her ability to fit in with the pack, either. The fangs had not retracted, and he hurt for her. With her. The fierceness of his need to protect Cara kicked in so swiftly, he had little time to think about anything else.

The others were almost here, and each passing second made Cara more anxious. She was as white as a sheet.

"It will be okay," Rafe said, moving closer to her. "Touch me, Cara. Let me hold you."

There were other things he didn't say. Couldn't confess.

"Touch me." Not for the sake of the lust I feel, or my need to possess you, body and soul… "Touching me will bring out your wolf."

She let him slip his right arm around her and met his eyes when he demanded it. And as easily as that, with no more words spoken, and as his eyes bored into hers, her razor-sharp incisors disappeared and a hint of color crept back into her cheeks.

* * *

Cara tasted blood, and it was her own. She had bitten down hard on her lower lip when Rafe touched her, mindful of what he was doing, and why. But she had also heard the thoughts that had preceded his willingness to help her—thoughts about lust and possession that again ignited sparks of desire deep inside her.

If they had been alone…

If no one had been coming…

She would have acted on those desires.

They way Rafe made her feel was exciting. She was comforted by the knowledge that though he saw what she was capable of, the son of Miami's alpha wanted her anyway. They were connected by a thread that had stretched tightly between souls. She had no further doubts about this connection or what it might mean, and the remark Rafe had made the night before reappeared in her mind now like a haunting refrain.

Maybe the true test of your presence here is to see if I'd be the one to bite.

Was there a possibility that her parents had sent her to Miami to meet her mate and Rafe had been part of the plan all along?

Who would dare to concoct such a bond when she didn't resemble the rest of the Weres and would never fit in? What kind of parents did Rafe have if they had agreed to such a thing?

She was missing something. They all were. But she couldn't afford to be any more distracted than she already was. The vampire they had faced wasn't alone. Very old bloodsuckers seldom traveled solo, and this vamp had likely walked the earth for centuries. Older even than the term ancient, it had confessed to be nearing a state of nonexistence. Maybe there had been no fight left in it, no real strength, other than a short list of last needs.

"There are more of them," she said to Rafe. "We have to prepare."

Rafe frowned. "More vampires?"

"That one was a master. A leader, and the head of a nest. Others fight for him and do his bidding. The loss of control over his body means nothing when he commands his own fanged army."

"When he snaps his fingers, how many will come?"

"I'm not certain," she confessed.

"Does that bastard believe it can take the spirit from you by force if you refuse to relinquish it?"

Cara shook her head. "It will try to kill everyone and everything around me so that I might change my mind about giving up the Banshee."

"It will go after those it perceives to be the weakest first?" Rafe mused.

She closed her eyes. "Yes. Then they will go after the pack the way they went after my father, hoping to eliminate werewolves one by one."

Rafe ran a hand over his eyes as if that could erase the image of the fanged monster they'd just encountered. "Run away," he said to Cara. "Get behind the wall. We can handle this."

She shook her head stubbornly.

"Why did you let this vampire go if it was so dangerous?"

"I let it go because…" Her reply faded as Cara sensed Were presence that was so strong and vibrant, it undermined what she had been about to say. Along with that vibration came a faint sense of familiarity.

She turned, and Rafe turned with her. The three Weres who appeared didn't reek of the kind of power she had detected in the periphery. They didn't cause the air to change or the night to shiver the way the other more elusive presence had.

Again, she heard her name whispered and looked to Rafe, whose lips didn't move. She tuned in to Rafe's thoughts and found them directed to his packmates and the need to catch the vampire.

There was no time to tell him that she had let the vampire go because she was beginning to see a pattern in the things taking place, and that this vampire might yet have a part to play in her future. As sickening as that thought was, it had taken root.

"Vampire," Rafe said when Cameron and two other Weres Cara hadn't yet met drew up beside them. "And it has friends."

All eyes landed on her before drifting off to check out the surrounding area. Cara had no idea if any of these Weres had ever seen or even believed in the fanged hordes that existed in their city. For them, this was going to be a wake-up call.

"Five," she said, inhaling deeply, sure now about the tally. "There are five of them, moving like a bad wind."

Chapter 23

Rafe watched Cara's eyes glaze over as she stared into the distance. She seemed to have retreated into a space only she could access, where sight and scent and hearing provided her with foreknowledge of what might appear in the next few minutes.

There was no time to waste. Nor was there a need to guess what these creatures wanted, since the pasty-faced master of this little oncoming group had been quite clear about that.

The ancient bloodsucker wanted to get its talons on the dark spirit Cara harbored, believing the spirit could prolong its existence, such as that existence was. If blood no longer bolstered it, surely a Banshee could. And if a vampire played host to such a powerful darkness, there was no way to calculate the kind of damage it could inflict.

It was imperative that the sucker never got close to Cara again.

"Cara, go," he said. "You've done your share of fighting here."

She ignored him, just as Rafe feared she might. This was what Cara did, what she had been bred for. Fighting was the price she paid for being born a Kirk-Killion.

"Rafe," Cameron called from beyond the closest trees. "Are you coming?"

This time, he and Cara would fight together. Beside him, she was gathering herself and her energy. If anyone looked more closely, they might have seen the glow of all her talents coming together for a singular purpose.

God…he wanted her. Badly.

One look passed between them before they both took steps toward the oncoming red tide…and it was the only look that could have counted.

The night stank of death and bad intentions. Cara wasn't the only one who noticed. Rafe and Cameron had been joined by the two other Weres she had seen before while behind the Landau walls. Theirs was a formidable group, but only she could change shape tonight to call up more strength and power.

Against five wolfed-up werewolves, five vampire fledglings wouldn't have stood a chance. But werewolves in human shape, though fast and dexterous, didn't have same kind of speed these bloodsuckers had. Cara wasn't sure what was going to happen. She silently promised these Weres that she would fight for them with every last ounce of her strength.

The first wave of attack brought three fanged creatures. One after the other, the emaciated, white-faced, skeletal apparitions appeared. Silent. Ghastly. Deadly.

Cameron hit the first one head-on. Rafe leaped toward the second. She took the third, backed by the two large

Were guards who'd probably also been instructed to keep her safe, when it was actually going to be the other way around.

Sounds of their struggles echoed in the dark. If these vampires assumed darkness was on their side, they had another think coming. Werewolf sight was as legendary as the stories about the moon that ruled their changes, and each Were here carried a weapon—a bone-handled, silver-bladed knife that could stop a vampire if placed correctly, though the best way to seal a vampire's fate for good was to sever its head from its body.

She had something better, something besides the fangs and the claws that had appeared simultaneously to combine two very different parts of herself. She had an intimate knowledge of vampire behavior that was a fast pass into their messy, often jumbled thoughts. Cara used that now.

"Two more are coming," she shouted to the others.

The push was on to make sure these three were out of commission by the time the next two arrived. The Landau Weres were fighting fiercely, bravely, honorably. She pressed past Rafe and turned to stand back to back with him. The fanged invader Rafe was fighting was large but might not have had as much at stake in the fight as these Weres did. She prayed this would give the werewolves an edge.

"Throat," she shouted to Rafe, who swore vehemently as he repeatedly blocked the vampire's almost subliminally quick fang strikes. "Or heart."

"I thought these suckers were heartless," he tossed back with a grunt as his vampire opponent's fangs got a little too close to Rafe's face.

"Their bodies don't know that. You have to make them see it."

Cara slashed at her attacker and caught hold of it with

her claws. She felt its hunger and its need to follow a directive. That, too, was necessary information. These beasts were here because their master demanded it. They would never have attacked a group of Weres otherwise.

The other approaching vamps hadn't yet joined in. They were now waiting on the sidelines for the Weres to weaken with fatigue. Through the sounds of fighting, Cara heard their jaws snapping.

Rafe's Weres fought to the best of their abilities and were still standing, but no one had turned the tide or gained the advantage after several long minutes. These vamps had speed and the Weres had strength, but how long would that strength last?

Something had to be done, and she had to do it. The solution might shock Rafe and the others, and yet there was only one way open to her for getting rid of these emaciated parasites.

She called on her wolf, demanding that it listen to her and take shape in spite of the fangs in her mouth. Since she still had claws, part of her wolf was already in evidence. All that was needed was for her to tip the balance.

She had done this before to avoid the wail of the Banshee, and now she demanded the extra burst of power her wolf would provide. There was a chance the dark spirit would feel the extremes of this shift and use the energy for her own benefit, so caution was needed to avoid the death caller.

Shifting was always dangerous for that reason, and she had undergone too many shape-shifts in the past two days. Still, she had to try.

Wolf…

Come.

Now!

The wolf particles in her bloodstream responded to her

command with a flare of molten heat that seared her veins. An image of the shape she needed to find flashed in Cara's mind. Not the animal with four legs this time, but another one that shocked her system with a combined jolt of power and pain that was like being pinned by a silver dart.

The sound of her bones cracking made Rafe turn his head. The shudders of her muscles reshaping brought a slow hiss from her throat. Cara swayed and shook off a brief round of dizziness, but stood her ground. She clamped her teeth together as her heart rate accelerated and the werewolf, half human, half wolf, hot-blooded and feral, soared into existence.

One more strike with her powerful claws was all it took for her to dust the vampire beside her. Rafe, still slashing at his nemesis, shoved his vampire away to look at her.

Maybe it was his expression, or the way he blinked back his surprise, that sent her shape-shift spiraling into another direction than the one she had intended. And maybe it was the way his vampire attacker's red-lined black eyes caught hers that caused the rift between her intended shift and what actually took place.

Her wolf sucked back into itself with a reversal that was so swift and unexpected, Cara's lungs were squeezed. More dizziness hit with a whirl of vertigo that nearly sent her to her knees as the wolf she had called upon suddenly devolved, leaving the space it was supposed to have occupied open for another shape.

And there was nothing she could do about it.

Shock had no place on a battlefield, so Rafe had to swallow his. But his skin chilled so fast, his teeth began to chatter as the temperature around him dropped considerably. The speed of these vampires trumped anything he had ever seen.

A chill wind assailed him from behind. His shirt, damp with the sweat of his exertion, turned to ice. He couldn't turn to find the source of this latest phenomenon, didn't dare, although he figured it was related to Cara, and that he wasn't going to like it.

Even the vampires recognized the change in the atmosphere. Their efforts slowed. They stopped moving as the icy wind blew through the area like the touchdown of a tornado.

Shrieks went up from fanged mouths. Something sticky hit Rafe in the face, and he didn't take the time to find out what it was. A shout went up from Cameron, followed by another from one of the guards. Rafe's hands had frozen in a raised position and he left them there, unable to comprehend what was going on and why the vampires had stopped fighting.

For a long, seemingly endless moment, Rafe thought he might have died here in the park and was about to bridge the gap to wherever his next stop might be. Time had slowed further, dragging the movement surrounding him along with it. Turning his head again took real effort. Breathing was tough. He finally managed to glance behind him, looking for Cara in the last place where she had been standing.

He saw nothing at first because, hell…it wasn't winter and this was Miami, and yet snow was falling, tiny foul-smelling gray snowflakes that drifted down to cover his shoulders.

But these weren't snowflakes. The disgusting flurry of ashy particles was all that remained of the vampires.

There wasn't one damn vampire left. And by the expressions on the faces of his packmates, they were as stunned as he was.

Cameron said, "They're gone. All of them."

Panic struck Rafe square in the chest. He spun around on his heels and called out, "Cara?"

The silence that met him seemed unnatural after all the grunting and shrieks. Darkness hovered over the area like a big black cloud. There was no glint of moonlight.

Rafe strained to focus his enhanced sight. "Why don't you answer?"

His chest hurt. His head throbbed. Rafe's packmates, gathered around him, were staring at something above them. He had never been as afraid of anything as he was right then, when his gaze rose to the lowest branch of the tree beside him.

And damn it...that fear was warranted.

Chapter 24

Cara was there, though unrecognizable. Rafe felt her presence in the tree without having to look. What had happened to the vampires was also suddenly clear.

Cara had beaten them at their own game.

The sight of her latest incarnation rendered him speechless. Cara's shape had altered again, and she might have gone too far this time. She had become a dark entity that was difficult to look at. There was hardly a visible outline, because the area around it wavered like a desert mirage. It looked like a mistake or as if some kind of ancient process had taken over. One thing was certain, though: Cara had killed those vampires by allowing the dark spirit inside her its freedom.

The Banshee facing them was terrifying. With each passing second, parts of its countenance flickered and changed, as if none of them could stick permanently. He saw the flash of a face that was beautiful beyond belief.

Following that was a skeletal mask that made his insides roil. Then came the face of a wolf. And after that, the features of an unfamiliar female.

Black hair, so like Cara's and almost invisible in the night, flew in the swirls of a nonexistent breeze, each tendril seeming to have a life of its own. The black clothes Cara had worn became a gauzy dark cloud of moving shadows. The only light spot in this vision was the pallor of the face that finally settled into place. Most of Cara's features were there and recognizable, possibly because the spirit couldn't entirely separate itself from its host.

Cara was there, but she wasn't looking back at him. She had done the unthinkable by letting the Banshee out for some air. Was this how she had taken on the vampires? Had she channeled the spirit's power in order to aid his packmates?

Would she be able to tuck that spirit back where it belonged if she wanted to? The Banshee was an entity that ate souls for breakfast. Rafe hoped this one couldn't see into his soul to locate the fears forming there.

"Can you come back, Cara?" he messaged to her.

The Banshee's silver-eyed gaze made him uncomfortable. This spirit was female, Cara had said, though it seemed so much more than any one thing. She could no doubt track the anxiety present in all of the Weres here without having to turn her head. Crouched on that branch, the apparition, a physical melding of Cara and the Banshee, most resembled a vampire queen ready to pounce.

"I know what you are and who you are," Rafe said. "I'd like to speak to Cara."

Rafe's packmates had been stunned to silence. Up to this point, only Cameron had witnessed the kinds of things Cara could do. And hell, a wolf was nothing compared to this.

The dark spirit again flickered in and out of focus as if it was more of an idea or a dream than anything truly corporeal. Rafe didn't know much about the Banshee other than the few things Cara had told him. Did it understand that he and Cara had forged a connection?

He was seeing for the first time what lived inside Cara, and it was disturbing. One of the most dangerous and feared entities on earth was looking at him through Cara's eyes. This was what Cara had been protecting.

What few details he had learned about the dark spirit hardly prepared him for this moment. Cara's ancestors must have understood the ramifications of agreeing to house this creature. Was their decision worth the sacrifice? And were there more Banshees in the world to take up the task of shouting about death? Could there only have been one of them to begin with?

The spirit's pale eyes fixed on him in a way that told Rafe his thoughts were transparent. He wondered if it shared Cara's feelings, and if the entity had also shared their kiss. It was possible this Banshee knew him as intimately as Cara did, but what would it do with that information?

Rafe said, "If you were the one who vanquished those bloodsuckers, let me be the first to offer thanks."

The eyes truly were silver, a werewolf's bane. The gaze that pinned him was cold.

Christ! What was normal about Cara giving this thing sanctuary, or about what this entity could do to her if it got tired of hiding?

"How long do you propose to stay?" he dared to ask.

His question drew wary glances from his packmates, who were frozen in place.

"According to Cara, you must remain hidden. That was part of the deal you made with her ancestors."

He has letting his packmates hear things they should not have been privy to, but this wasn't the time to worry about it. He had to find Cara in all that darkness.

"Isn't it dangerous for you to appear to anyone, including us, though we appreciate your help and your trust in appearing now?"

Still no response. Rafe had no idea if the dark spirit could talk or speak through Cara. Anxiousness lowered his voice.

"We'd like to take Cara to safety. She's supposed to be in our care. My care. I take that seriously."

The idea bordered on being ludicrous, Rafe had to admit. Cara had just wiped five vampires off the surface of the planet in seconds and obviously had used a boost from whatever special kind of power this dark entity possessed. She might owe that spirit for help with this skirmish. Conversely, the Banshee might owe Cara for its current home.

None of this made his goal of protecting Cara any less urgent. Banshees might be powerful and utterly inhuman, yet Cara was in there, listening. The body concealed beneath that black cloud belonged to her.

It was an inopportune time for reflection, but Rafe wondered who Cara might have been without all of the tricks and talents and vows. He couldn't picture what her smile would be like, or her laugh. He couldn't see her as a kid, doing things that occupied most youngsters. Maybe Cara missed what she'd never had.

Those thoughts made him want to yank that Banshee out of the tree and demand Cara's return…and to hell with the consequences.

Speaking in Cara's voice, the thing in the tree said, "I wouldn't try it, wolf. Trust me on that."

* * *

Cara felt her own spirit rising through the fog that had taken her over. Free again to speak and to breathe, she fought off the icy sensations associated with the Banshee and waited for the dark spirit to retreat, fully aware that it didn't have to. After getting a taste of long-awaited freedom, the spirit she housed was taking her time to withdraw.

Rafe was watching her closely to see when she would surface. His body hummed with anxious energy. He had dared to address death's right hand and so far had gotten away with it.

She had never been almost completely overtaken by this spirit, and that was her fault. By piling energy on top of energy, she had created a gap that the Banshee had used to take form.

She was the only one here to realize that the dark spirit had allowed Rafe to address her only out of curiosity. Maybe the Banshee picked up on Rafe's need to protect Cara, which also meant he would be protecting the spirit she housed, though it was the deadliest entity around and they all knew this.

She felt nothing of the spirit's hold on her now. For the time being, after sharing its power in the fight with the vampires, the Banshee had simply and willingly gone back inside. All that was left of the icy chill that was the spirit's calling card was a harsh dryness in Cara's throat.

Rafe thanked you, and I thank you, Cara silently said as she jumped from the branch to land solidly on both feet.

The Weres were quick to form a circle around her despite what they'd witnessed, though they didn't get too close. Could she blame them? Nor did they pose any of the questions that had to be running through their minds. Cara appreciated the moments of silence that followed the

Banshee's big reveal. She didn't hear the word freak reso-
nating in any of their minds.

"Okay," Rafe said without taking her in his arms the
way she knew he wanted to. "Time to go. Are you good
with that, Cara? Are we in the clear?"

His packmates again looked to him.

"We haven't completed the search," Cara said, sure that
none of these Weres would want anything more to do with
the park tonight.

"We'll get you back first," Rafe said.

"Then you'll go out again without me?"

"Don't you agree that would be for the best?"

Rafe followed his remark with another more personal
question, even though they had company. "Was this unusual?"

She replied, "Yes."

Rafe was tense, but not twitchy like his packmates. He
had what it took to be an alpha wolf, with the necessary
outward calmness and candor to back up his courage when
the time came for him to inherit the job from his father.
His stance was easy when his insides were tight. His face
wasn't bloodless or rigid with fear after she had shown
him her most terrifying aspect.

He was paving the way for his packmates to accept
her. Rafe Landau was slated for big things, not just bab-
ysitting a hybrid who would never be truly accepted in
Were society.

He was perfect in every way. The hardness of his body
alone chased away any doubts she had, and kept her rooted
in place when in the past she would have run away from
any and all emotion.

The level of her desire to be with another Were was
new, exciting and nearly as overwhelming as the Banshee's takeover. However, she couldn't rush into Rafe's

arms with others looking on. The Weres surrounding him didn't need any more surprises.

"So, okay. The bastards are gone and no one will weep for them," he said, tearing his gaze from her to address everyone in the circle. "We'll go back now and let the others in on what's happening in this damn park."

He didn't touch her when she walked past him, though he raised a hand as if he would. His packmates closed around her, forming a barrier of muscle that prevented her from getting closer to Rafe. They were protecting her from monsters, and keeping Rafe from her.

"It will be all right, Cara. I see what this is, and I'm not afraid to face it" was the only message Rafe sent her.

Deep inside Cara, the dark spirit moved.

The spirit feels what I feel, she should have answered. *As long as she is part of me, she knows all*. But that information was too scary to share.

"You take me, you take it all, Rafe," she messaged to him. *"You do get that?"*

The look he gave her sent her doubts scurrying.

Chapter 25

Cara was taunting him with her closeness. Recovering from the dark spirit's appearance, she would need comfort when they got back to the house. Hell, strong as he was, he also needed comfort after this.

The damn Banshee might have been trying to scare him off, to keep from sharing Cara with anyone else, but his craving for closeness with her was insane. He had to hold on and pretend to be detached when his heart was revving and his body ached for Cara in places too numerous to mention.

If love were to find a place in Cara's heart, would that displace her internal parasitic spirit?

His father had warned him not to indulge in fantasies regarding their guest, yet it was too damn late. His world had narrowed down to Cara, and his view of things had changed. She was the central focus, the epicenter of the emotions he now struggled to keep in check.

He realized that with Cara headlining every thought that popped into his mind, he'd be no good to anyone in the search for a killer. Cara was causing a rift in his sense of duty. That was a first. Meanwhile, there was an ancient vampire on the loose that had been bold enough to confront them in Were territory. While his mind was filled with anticipation about making love to Cara, who could predict what other kinds of atrocities lurked in the shadows, wanting a piece of her?

He'd take her to his parents and hope they could exert some control over her rebellious ways. He needed to rejoin the search party. Keeping the Were world safe was paramount, and a hell of a lot more important than his love life.

So why didn't he actually believe that?

"I can help." Cara's voice was soft and earnest.

"There's too much at stake to keep you out in the open," he said.

Each time her eyes met his, he seemed to lose his place in reality. Cara was dangerous, all right. Most of all, she was dangerous for him.

"Home," he said in a tone that encouraged everyone to pick up their pace.

Minutes later, the wall and the lights beyond it came into view. Several cops combed the area, sniffing for missed clues. He recognized all of them from afar and had to change direction to avoid their attention and keep Cara out of sight.

His little pack moved in a symbiotic manner without the need for communication. Once they had cleared the wall and were again near pack headquarters, he turned to Cameron.

"Can you make sure Cara goes inside and take her to my mother?"

Cameron nodded. Cara didn't react. Her eyes were hidden beneath her long lashes, and Rafe felt colder without those eyes on him. He'd be sorry to let Cara go, but he could do this. He would temporarily break the chains binding them, get to the bottom of what the mysterious killer wanted and figure out if the target was Cara.

I can let you go, for now...

That unsent message repeated on a loop inside his head. He couldn't say the words aloud, because he had never been a very good liar.

Cara went with Cameron when she could have refused. Rafe couldn't imagine someone actually making this Kirk-Killion do anything she didn't want to do. Cara was a supernatural force to be reckoned with.

Was he afraid of her abilities? No. If no more creatures were to come after Cara and her life could become more or less normal, could they be happy?

"I'll be back before sunrise," he said.

She didn't stop to acknowledge him, and seemed willing to follow his instructions. She didn't fool him, though. Cara's apparent willingness to listen could be a ruse designed to throw them all off her real objectives. Like her mother, would she leap from that damn window the first chance she got?

Hell, wolf spelled backward was flow...and Cara was nothing if not flexible. In retreat, she gave nothing away about possibly having a secret agenda. He detected no deception in the way she had acquiesced to his request. But Rafe felt the pull she had on his system and wondered if there truly was going to be any way to escape whatever the future with Cara might bring.

"You coming?" he said to the other Weres gathered around him. "Shall we hunt for the killer that threatens to expose us?"

"I'd say that's only one of many new problems," one of the guards remarked.

His father approached, his voice overlapping the guard's. "I just got back from a fruitless search." After taking in the serious expressions of their faces, he added, "What happened out there?"

"More bloodsuckers on a rampage," Rafe said and left it at that.

The guards also remained silent about what had actually taken place. Even though the hierarchy here was nothing like in some other packs, Landau wolves didn't have to worry about retribution from their alpha for speaking their minds or telling the truth as they saw it. Every opinion was taken into consideration by Dylan Landau. But in all likelihood these guys were still questioning themselves about what they had seen tonight.

Rafe's father turned toward the wall.

"The park is still crawling with cops," Rafe reminded him.

"When did that stop us?" his father said over his shoulder.

Rafe didn't look at the house, or for the light in Cara's window. She'd be standing there, watching.

"Dana is there," his father said when Rafe caught up to him.

"Yes." The weight of Rafe's concern was obvious in his brief reply.

"We're not Cara's keepers, merely her hosts, Rafe."

"I understand that."

"One problem at a time is the way to go."

"Cara is at the center of all of them," Rafe said.

His father hadn't seen her all vamped up in that tree, or in Banshee mode, or as a wolf running on all fours. His father wasn't aware of how tightly his son's soul had meshed with hers, and that thoughts of Cara would take precedence until they had fully mated in body as well as in soul.

"We'll skip around to the east," Rafe said. "That's where we left off."

"Then let's get to it," the Landau alpha directed as he leaped onto the wall as agilely as if he was still a Were pup, and Rafe and the guards eagerly followed.

Cara sensed Dana outside her closed door, about to knock, and wasn't in the mood for conversation. She needed a rest and an energy reboot. Her shape-shifts were getting out of hand.

Rafe's theory about her being sent here to see if other creatures would follow or could sense her presence had been proven. Miami was a goddamn creaturefest.

That old vampire hadn't given up easily. The attack he had directed had called the Banshee she housed to the surface and revealed the dark spirit to some of Rafe's pack. It was possible the vampire had meant to do just that and hoped Rafe's packmates would be scared off so she could be singled out. She'd be on her own, without anyone at her back.

That hadn't happened. The old vamp would be furious.

"Do you mind if I take a minute?" she called out to Rafe's mother, stopping the knock before Dana's knuckles connected with the door. "I'll be down shortly."

"Sure," Dana said, with a hint of suspicion in her voice. "I'll wait in the front room with drinks."

Cara leaned against the windowsill. Drinks? They were to sip the hours away while Rafe and the Weres searched through shadows? When vampires and demons had trespassed in the world of men because of her?

She felt the rise of her own inner darkness and held it back. All forms of darkness fed the Banshee.

"It's what the monsters want," she muttered. "What they always have wanted. You."

Her borrowed bedroom was nice, but confining. The breeze coming from the open window stirred Cara's restlessness. Sleep was underrated. Drinks and conversation with her hostess would be torturous. The fact was that trouble had come here because of her, and she had to deal with it before any more deaths occurred.

She needed to see Rafe, and she also needed to stay away from him. She desired to share her secrets and her body with him while danger still posed a threat to everyone in their pack.

This kind of impossible craving was the very definition of the imprinting state. Rafe had warned her of this.

When she again sensed the presence at the door, Cara whirled toward it, thinking that Dana wasn't going to let up after all and might be blocking her exit. Still, she also sensed another presence nearby and turned back to the window.

"Rafe?"

Maybe she had wished too damn hard for this to happen. Maybe Rafe would have come to her now even if she hadn't silently called to him, because he wanted this as much as she did.

He should have been working with the search party. He had no right to be here, but he was.

And her heart was racing.

Sensing the need for stealth and secrecy, Rafe climbed up the side of the house by digging his boots and fingertips into the grooves in the brick. He had not meant to return again. Though he was needed elsewhere, he found himself back at the house and on his way to Cara as though he no longer had a mind of his own.

She was waiting for him, and backed away from the window as he reached the sill. She had expected him. Her heart was beating as furiously as his was.

His need for Cara didn't stop with eye contact. He had a ravenous craving for his mate, and Cara's eyes reflected that same hunger. Their needs were mutual. Cara's desires matched his.

"You must understand why they don't want this," she said with a note of sadness in her tone. "You can be hurt. All of you can be hurt. Those vampires are savages and won't stop coming. The demons you face will only get worse if I stay."

She paused for a breath before continuing. "Keeping the Banshee inside me is at times like swallowing shards of glass. Nothing equals the pain of having all that power and darkness inside me. But in the end, it is separate and belongs to someone else. I have no better explanation with which to warn you about me, Rafe. You have no idea what we've done."

"Too bad it's too late for me to have a choice in the matter, then," Rafe said. "I can't imagine what that must be like for you. What I see in front of me is the most beautiful and courageous she-wolf I've ever laid eyes on. Someone selfless enough to have taken on the burden that was handed to you. Someone who deserves to be loved."

She stared at him with her lips slightly parted. "I have more secrets."

Rafe slid off the sill to stand beside Cara. "Not everyone is afraid of you or those secrets, Cara. I'm not afraid."

He gave her no more time for arguments or protests. Talking wasn't going to satisfy their cravings for each other. Their wolves were directing how this was to go, and their souls were in accord. They had to imprint, mate, seal the deal, or these cravings would go on and on until they did. He was on fire, and having Cara in his arms was the only way to appease those needs.

Rafe backed her to into the corner and leaned in close. He pressed his lips to hers, hoping she would respond, and drank in her scent as if his sanity depended on it. Because it did.

When she sighed with a heated breath, he came undone. Fire became only the smallest part of the feelings that erupted inside him. Her name was being etched on his soul. Real closeness was what he hoped to find, a permanent connection that would last if they made it to that bed.

Shudders rocked him when she kissed him back. But they had done this before, and this time a kiss or two wouldn't be nearly enough.

Her fingers slipped into his hair. The only way they could have been closer was for him to be inside her...and there was no way to explain how much he wanted that.

She kissed him with fervor now—she was a swift learner with an appetite to rival his. Her skin was hot. Her slender hips ground against his. He was going to claim her as his mate, and his erection was proof of the necessity of their next step. This was what had to happen here with Cara, and no one could stop it. This had been the goal since they had first met.

With a smooth move that required little effort, Rafe had her on her back, on the bed. Looming over her, perched on his arms, he took the time to search Cara's flushed face.

Her eyes were dilated and still green. Her lips were a pale shade of pink that would never bruise beneath the weight of his passion, because Cara was above all a wolf. Their passion would take them to heights no one had ever seen. He would love her deeply, completely. And after that, he'd come back for more.

Rafe exhaled his next question in a breathless rush as the last few seconds of sanity ticked away. "You did lock the damn door?"

Chapter 26

Cara had no desire to answer Rafe's question, and he wouldn't have let her if she had. Instead he kissed her with a fury that sent her senses haywire. Whether they were safe or not amid the chaos going on outside the Landau estate, this room was going to be their personal haven, just as it had been for her parents.

Still, Cara was instantly aware of a tug on her senses that threatened to interfere in these moments of passion, and the tug was familiar. Her mother and father were crowding the room. Their presence rode on the crest of her emotions. Shutting them out would take more energy than she had and split her loyalties, but she inwardly protested the intrusion. *You did the same thing and survived. Let me have my chance.*

Rafe's hands were on her face. Her body was surrendering to his touch. He lay beside her on the mattress. They had too many clothes on for this mating thing to work. No one had explained about the birds and the bees when she was growing up. She had never seen her father touch her mother, though she had heard their lovemaking on many occasions when they assumed she wasn't around.

It was her turn now to find out what sex and closeness were all about. She was going to find out what being Rafe's mate would be like, and how this act might change the future.

Instincts took over as she curled into Rafe's heat, seeking to be bested by him, and only by him, willing to loosen her hold on her own strength and power. The sheer force of his hunger drove her deeper into the pillows. She tore at his clothes with both hands to get at the smooth skin beneath, and he did the same, reaching her bare stomach in a few mad seconds.

Cara gasped as he slid his hand upward to her breasts and stalled there, possibly expecting an argument she didn't make. He stroked her rib cage and ran his fingertips in small circles without landing in any one place. She strained toward him, offering herself, silently demanding that he comply with her wishes.

It was too much, and not nearly enough. She was determined to take whatever Rafe had to offer. Only in that way would she be able to think straight and get her priorities in order.

His touch, unlike his kisses, became suddenly tender. When his movements slowed to a controlled exploration of what lay under her shirt, Cara began to get a sense of the ecstasy that was to come.

She tugged at him with her hands and nipped at his mouth with her teeth in an unspoken, wolfish command for more. Biting turned Rafe on. He had her shirt over her head before her next breath. His lips left a trail of kisses along the base of her neck, and all Cara could think about was how sanity could be so overrated.

More heat filled her, soaking through every cell. It was the heat of a fever, like sinking into a tub of scalding water. But Rafe didn't focus his attentions on any one place, because time wasn't on their side.

Her pants joined her shirt in a pile on the floor, leaving her naked at last. Though Rafe had seen her this way before, his gaze swept over her longingly, as if he coveted each angle and curve and regretted not being able to linger in all of those places.

His hand moved downward over her hips and her belly, leaving fluttering muscles in its wake. Dipping his fingers between her thighs made her growl. The pressure of his fingers on her sensitive parts made her insides quake. When he found what he wanted there, the place so hidden and low on her body, his kisses stopped long enough for his eyes to again find hers.

"Don't think," he said roughly. "Go with it. Feel. Enjoy our bond. This is what matters, Cara. You have no idea how much. Let me prove that to you."

"And then what?" she asked.

"We go from there."

His fingers tested her willingness, her moistness, her waiting heat, before he stood up to remove his clothes and give her a first full look at the Were she was going to pledge herself to.

Rafe was incredibly well sculpted. He was masculine and beautifully built. His skin was bronze and mostly flawless, except for two small scars near his left shoulder that were evidence of an old fight. And he was magnificently hard.

He was hard for her.

He lowered himself to her slowly, so that she felt his

hardness pressing close. His eyes bored into hers as he eased himself into her with a slow, slick slide that robbed her of breath. Muffled cries erupted from her throat, not out of pain, but from her intense need for more of what Rafe had to offer.

She took hold of Rafe's hips and pulled him closer so that he slid farther inside her. Then she growled again, deep in her throat, and tried to hold on to both Rafe and her human shape when the animal inside her threatened to bloom.

Wildness rose in her as her wolf rushed upward to the surface, encouraged by the overwhelming sensations and the new emotions she was experiencing. She had never felt anything like this. Like him…

"Now!" she whispered, feeling the fierceness of her wolf. "Before it's too late."

His next plunge was deeper, and followed by a swift retreat. He then entered her again and again…with a rhythmical buildup of sweet and terrible speed that kept her entranced.

The extremes of the pleasure he gave her caused her body to seize. Waves of heat licked at her insides and that distant drumbeat she had sampled once before spiraled toward Rafe as if it had developed a special relationship with him.

When he stopped, she clawed at him with her fingertips. But he didn't move again, and didn't need to. Buried inside her, Rafe locked her to that beat until sparks flashed behind her eyes and internal fireworks went off…so many fireworks that Cara thought she might die of pleasure. Then he moved one more time…a perfect strike so deep that it seemed to have reached her soul…and Rafe Landau collided with her in the fury of that internal beat that only the two of them could share.

This was the wolf's mating dance, their union, and it sealed the bargain their souls had made without them.

Caught up in the rush, Cara threw her head back and arched off the bed. Rafe's arms were shaking. His eyes were closed. This time when she growled, Cara heard Rafe do the same. When she howled with her newly found satisfaction, Rafe's howl mingled with hers, echoing through the room.

But as the sounds of the culmination of their lovemaking faded and Cara lay breathless beneath Rafe on the bed with her self-defenses on hiatus, something else began to worry her.

The past had again interfered.

Without a word of warning or explanation, Cara slid out from beneath Rafe and reached for her clothes. Uttering just one more growl—of caution this time—she climbed onto the windowsill and crouched there.

Rafe was up quickly and moving toward her, his expression one of shock and surprise. But she didn't take that jump of escape she had been about to make. Instead, she was stopped by the shimmer of air that she had anticipated would gather around her.

Shapes began to form inside that moving shimmer—rippling images that told a story. Her mother and father had been in this room in the past, and they had mated on the bed where she and Rafe had lain together. Cara saw this clearly now, as if that act was taking place on the same rumpled sheets. Two naked bodies were joining. She heard them groaning with pleasure, and she couldn't make the image stop or go away.

Black hair spread across the pillow in the same way hers had. A muscular backside of pure white skin glowed in the light from the open window as the male drove in and out of the female beneath him with a fierceness that Cara had only moments before experienced with Rafe.

God…they were here. Her parents had taken over the space. Like them, she and Rafe had broken the rules set forth by their respective families by mating. Just like Rafe and her, Rosalind and Colton had thumbed their noses at what was forbidden and sealed their souls together.

The dreamlike images overlapped with Rafe's approach. Cara put a hand to her head to try to halt the whirling that went on and on, with those two commingling bodies centered on the mattress. She had to speak, break the connection to the past. Her voice cracked when she said, "Did we just do this, Rafe, or did I imagine it?"

He was beside her, tall, buff, naked and shining like a bronze star in the moonlight streaming through the open window she huddled in.

"Are you real?" she whispered. "Or are you, like them, a dream?"

Rafe's was the scent embedded in her lungs. His was the body she had shared hers with. Surely she knew this?

"I'm real. This was real. Are you all right. Cara? What are you seeing?"

She didn't stop to listen to him. Pleasure had pushed her over the edge of reason, and only her wolf could cope.

All ten claws sprang from her fingertips at once. The room filled with the sound of bones realigning. There was agony in this transition, possibly stemming from having experienced the heights of a pleasure that went beyond anything she had known mere seconds before. Or maybe the pain arrived like a silver-tipped arrow to her chest because she didn't really want to run from Rafe like this but felt that she had to.

Whatever the cause, the sharpness of her discomfort paused her transition halfway. She looked at Rafe, who was glorious and masculine, strong and caring, and cried out when moonlight hit her face. She roared with her wolf's throat, then turned away from her lover...and jumped.

"Damn it..." Rafe reached for Cara but found the space empty. Pressing himself to the sill, he stared at the drop to the ground below, swore several times more, then hurriedly retrieved his clothes.

Forgoing the door—and whoever would be in the house to question him—Rafe climbed out the window using the foot and handholds in the brick, the same way he had gotten in.

Had Cara not liked feeling vulnerable? Did she regret what they had done? She might not be afraid of vampires and other things that slithered through the night, but it was conceivable that she feared real closeness with another being, and therefore feared him.

That was a hell of a bad thing, given how much he wished for a repeat of what had occurred between them on that bed. Both man and wolf craved that. But her face...the look Cara had given him before she jumped had been...

"There is no escape, Cara," he whispered as his boots touched grass. "It's you and me from here on out, so I need to know what's going on."

He saw no one in the yard. No hint of Cara. Cameron and the other two Weres had been in the park, along with his father. Whether or not they had missed him didn't matter. Only finding Cara did. He had to find out why she had run, and what she had seen in that room that made her question their closeness.

Cara had to be assured that she was not a freak, and that she could be loved. That he loved her.

"It's all right," he messaged to her. *"We both can handle this. Just give me a chance to prove that."*

The three wolves who squatted on top of the wall at the end of the yard nodded to Rafe when he climbed up beside them.

"Did she come this way?" Rafe asked, searching the dark. "Did anyone come this way in the last few minutes?"

The answer was no, so Cara had somehow managed to avoid all these watchful eyes. Rafe landed lightly on the park side of the wall and set off in an easterly direction, not sure which Cara he'd find this time, if he found her at all. Full wolf? Half wolf? Vampire? Human? She was so many things.

Would she let him hold her? Let him take away the fears that made her feel unwelcome and separated from everyone else? He thought he had already done that.

"Cara…" he called out. "Please find me. Let me help you."

He heard sounds that his brain processed as trampling feet, headed his way. Vampires, he now knew, didn't make noise when they moved, so this was someone else. *See, Cara. I am learning.*

Two cops walked forward with their hands on their weapons, wary of meeting up with anyone in the dark after that body had been found.

"Landau," he called out to them. "Miami Metro."

"Detective Landau?" one of them asked.

"One and the same," Rafe said.

He recognized both of these guys when they got closer, though he didn't know their names. The taller of the two cops spoke first. "We've been over this park twice and found nothing other than a couple of people making out near the boulevard. There are three more officers sweeping the eastern portion. Our guess is that if there is something to be found out here, it will have to be in the daylight. Flashlights just don't cut it on a night like this."

The cop glanced over his shoulder. "You going out there anyway?"

Rafe nodded. "My team is somewhere in the east, running along the edge where the factories are. No doubt they will meet up with your guys, if they haven't already. I got a late start on this and have to join them."

The tall cop pointed to a spot beyond where Rafe stood and said, "That's your wall? Where the body was found?"

"My family's place. I don't live there."

The cops shared a glance that told Rafe they might be wondering what kind of privileges a detective coming from such a prominent family might have had. But that wasn't Rafe's concern. Beat cops and detectives didn't always get along, and the fact that these two might envy his background and his rank was no big surprise.

"Thanks for the sweep," Rafe said, passing them in a few easy strides. "It's my turn. See you boys later."

Though he wanted to sprint, Rafe waited until he was out of the cops' view. Once in the clear he took off, following the scent of wolf that wafted to him from the north, instead of the east, where it would have been expected.

Breathing in the scent, feeling his body respond with a shiver of pleasure, Rafe smiled. "Got you," he said, and changed direction.

Chapter 27

She didn't usually get winded, but Cara's breath came in gasps and flutters as she headed north. Her body shouldn't have hurt now that she was in the clear, and yet it did. Most of those leftover aches had nothing to do with shape-shifting or leaping from third-story windows, however. They were centered in the place where her and Rafe's bodies had connected. She still felt the flames.

With her claws, she swiped at the trees she passed as if marking her territory and staking a claim. In truth, this was her lover's land. He oversaw everything, and now he also owned her body. What about the portion of her soul that wasn't occupied by spirits? Would Rafe find space there, too?

He was following her, as she figured he would. He'd want to comfort her when she didn't deserve it. Seeing that memory of her father and mother in the room had spooked her. Her father's ghostly, colorless skin and her mother's inky-black hair spread across the sheets were big reminders that the two of them were a species apart from the Were world she was trespassing in at the moment.

Rafe was just a werewolf, and not even Lycan. He possessed no freakish traits other than a dire need to protect what wasn't protectable. While she…well, she was a Kirk-Killion and should have known better than to fall for a good guy.

"Cara. Let me help you."

The messages Rafe sent hurt her and made her want to let him catch up. She would have liked another session on the bed or anywhere else they could have conceived of. But if she kept her distance from Rafe, she might be able to get more insight on who desired her the most… Rafe, or the monsters.

She whirled when she heard Rafe speak to someone else and was again stabbed by jealousy. Cara clung to the bark of the tree beside her, needing to ground herself. Humans also roamed this park tonight, and she was in half-wolf stasis.

"You deserve better, Rafe. I'm sorry it's too late for you to have that chance," she whispered to herself.

The approach of a Were nearby made Cara turn her head. This wasn't Rafe. It was someone else whose vibration was familiar because of the Were's relation to her lover.

"Alpha," she said, dragging her claws from the bark.

Dylan Landau came toward her with a kind of grace only pure-blooded Lycans possessed. The alpha had found her when she hadn't wanted to be found. Possibly he could smell his son's essence, mixed with hers.

"There's no need to take this on by yourself," he said calmly, maintaining a polite distance of several feet.

"Isn't there?" Cara countered.

"We will find the culprit who harmed the human. We always do."

"The pack is strong," she agreed.

The way Dylan Landau was intently eyeing her reminded her of Rafe. It felt to her as if this alpha also had the ability to read things in her that very few others could.

"What's done is done," he said.

So, he knew what had happened in that attic room. She had feared that he might.

"Against your wishes and the wishes of my family," Cara returned.

"We had no preconceived notion about what might or might not have taken place when you two met," he said. "You're both strong individuals with your own minds."

"And yet if there was the slightest chance of an unanticipated connection developing between Rafe and me, why did you invite me here?" she asked.

"We invited you here to fulfill an old promise."

"What promise, exactly, is that?"

"Your father asked that you be allowed to assimilate with other Weres when your time came. I thought we told you this."

"My father left with my mother in order to keep the monsters away from your doorstep," Cara said.

Dylan Landau nodded. "Don't think we didn't realize and appreciate that at the time."

"Monsters are my middle name," Cara said. "I don't belong here any more than my parents did. I believe I have already proven that a few times over."

"Perhaps. But maybe they left for other reasons as well."

"Such as?"

"The desire to protect any offspring they might produce."

Cara stared at the alpha, who spoke again.

"None of the monsters that were left after that last fight at Fairview actually left Miami. They merely went deeper underground, showing themselves now and then by adding to the city's body count. Some of us had to make sure that they remained a secret. We have dealt with the problem as best we could."

Cara tucked her claws inside with a sting and a brief internal whisper. An idea formed in her mind that she wasn't sure she liked, and yet she had to mention it to the Were responsible for so many lives.

She said slowly, "Was I to come here to help with that? Dig up those monsters? Bring them out of hiding so they can be dealt with in a more effective manner?"

Cara breathed out before continuing. "Could that have been part of the reason you would honor an old promise by inviting someone like me here? We were to help each other? Each of us was to benefit by my visit in some way?"

"Yes," Dylan Landau said. "I suppose that was the gist of the plan."

"How do you feel about it now that your son is involved?"

"The only thing your connection with him proves is that your parents were right in the belief that you could assimilate and fit in here, with us."

She almost smiled. "You truly believe that?"

He nodded. "I do, and I am obviously not the only one who does."

The plan had been a good one, Cara agreed, until Rafe had found her on that beach. Who could possibly have expected the result of that one evening spent with him, away from all this?

Rafe was speaking to her now, messaging her along selective channels. But his father had more to say.

"Now that you know about old promises, what can we expect?"

She said, "I don't know." But she did know, of course. Her bond with Rafe was unbreakable—Rafe had told her. Theirs was a deep connection and would last forever.

Her gaze traveled upward to the alpha's handsome face—a face whose chiseled features Rafe shared. Other than Dylan's silver hair, the two of them could have been brothers.

It's too late, she thought again. *I can't live without Rafe, and it might kill us all if I try to live with him.*

"Cara?" Dylan's voice brought her back to the conversation. He was waiting for her decision when there was no decision to be made. None that she could have made, anyway. The only way to avoid the bond she and Rafe had formed was if one of them were to die, and she had no intention of letting that happen. So she had to make the best of things and do her part. She had to honor that old promise, no matter what.

"Rafe has a sadness tucked inside," she said. "I can feel it when I'm with him."

Dylan nodded again. "He once liked a woman who was killed by a monster none of us saw. Maybe you can understand why he wants to protect you."

"She-wolf?" Cara asked, knowing Dylan would follow her question.

"Human," Dylan replied.

"Then they could not have…"

"There was no real bond. There couldn't have been, you know."

Rafe had lost someone he had cared for, and that was the source of his fierce protectiveness for her. Weres didn't as a rule condone human-Were matings, but the alpha across from her couldn't have objected to his son's previous preference, since Dylan had also married a woman who had at one time been human. The difference was that Dana had already become a wolf when she and Dylan had met and bonded.

"Imprinting," Cara said, testing out the word.

"Hell of a thing," Dylan returned. "Wonderful when it happens to the right combination of souls."

Unless one half of that combination is like me. Cara didn't say that out loud. What she said was, "Yes. Hell of a thing."

"Shall we return? Go home?" he suggested. "There are humans in the park tonight, along with the wolves. Keeping you out of sight might prevent anything else from showing up unannounced."

She hadn't considered that, and should have. She didn't have the freedom to do as she pleased in Miami. Dylan was right to be wary.

"There are ghosts at the house," she confessed. "For me, whatever might show up out here is easier to manage."

Dylan raised an eyebrow in question.

"Though there might have been hunters here, as you tend to believe, and although a werewolf could have done the damage that human sustained, it seems like the work of a demon. And where there is one demon, there are always others. Many others."

"Demon." Dylan's tone darkened. A shadow crossed his face.

"That's the monster your shooter took down. A demon came for me and took a timely bullet that missed my head."

Dylan said, "Bullets are never timely, Cara. What you've said changes things dramatically."

"You didn't know about the demons?"

"No," Dylan said. "I did not."

"Do you still want to take me back, behind walls that would never be able to keep a demon out?" she asked.

Dylan Landau didn't immediately answer that question. His attention was torn by the sound of others approaching. Humans, by scent. The alpha gave her a look of warning and moved toward them.

Cara hung back until she heard Dylan's greeting. Then, seeing an opportunity to help with this investigation, which would in turn get this park back to normal for a limited time and perhaps help the pack accept her role as Rafe's mate, Cara melted into the shadows as if she was one of them…and slipped silently away.

Rafe saw his father talking to the cops. He would have closed the whole area off to everyone if he could have and afterward burned the damn park down. This place had been the bane of Weres for years and a death trap for humans who ignored the danger. It made every detective on the job wary, every damn night, and put werewolves in jeopardy each time a full moon came around.

He sensed that Cara had been near his father and wondered what he had missed. When he heard his father shout, Rafe's chills returned. Something was wrong, and he knew what had happened as surely as he knew his own name.

Cara had given his dad the slip. She hadn't just run away from him. She had fled from everyone.

"What the hell are you thinking?" he said aloud. He muscled up to his father when the cops disappeared, and said roughly, "What did you tell her?"

The alpha wasn't intimidated by his tone. "I told her it was okay, and about the old plan."

"What else?"

"Nothing we hadn't told her before."

Rafe rubbed a hand over his face. "We have to find her. I have to find her."

"There are more important things in need of our attention. Cara mentioned demons. Plural. Hell, as if vampires aren't bad enough."

If Cara had brought a demon out of its hole, they really did need to burn this place down.

"You might not realize what you're up against if you go after her," his father said.

"On the contrary, I have a pretty good idea about that," Rafe countered.

"Yes. I suppose you do," his father said.

"I'll help you find her," Cameron said from behind them.

"You're needed here, Cameron. You called in the body. They'll be asking you for more details and may take more statements," Rafe's father said. To Rafe, he added, "I'll come with you to search for Cara."

"No need. I know where she'd go."

"There are several reasons to worry about that," his father warned, deciphering Rafe's thought.

"So there are," Rafe muttered. As he spun around on his heels, Rafe repeated the phrase to himself. "So there damn well are."

Chapter 28

Cara remembered all the cars in the Landau garage and would have taken one if she knew how to drive. Then again, getting out of the Landau compound alone, with a borrowed car, would have been a nightmare. And she'd had one too many nightmares lately.

The body that had been dumped at the base of the Landaus' wall had been meant as a warning—not for the wolves inside those walls, but for her. It was a none-too-subtle reminder that though she had changed locations, there would be plenty of danger wherever she went unless she relinquished the dark spirit she housed.

She was a danger magnet. Coming to Miami and involving others in her trials had been a mistake. The plan that had been set in motion after all this time had been terribly shortsighted and flawed. She would never be like these Weres, even if she tried.

There would be more deaths. She had been warned

about the next one that would soon come. Would it turn out be another mutilated body? This one a Were?

Sooner or later, Rafe and his family would come under careful scrutiny. The Were species couldn't afford that kind of close attention. She owed this pack for adhering to promises their former alpha had made, and she owed them for at least trying to accept her. Everyone would be safer if she left Miami, but leaving was no longer an option. The thought of never seeing Rafe again made her sick.

Her only option was to stay in Miami and go renegade...sneaking away to fight the dirty battles on her own. She could warn the pack each time the Banshee wailed for someone near to them, even when that would be breaking another set of rules. Pack protected pack, and Rafe was now the central core of hers.

That acknowledgment didn't prevent the rumbles of inner protest against the current situation, though. Jumbled thoughts came and went, most of them about Rafe and about how, for a time on that bed, she had experienced what it must be like to feel normal. In Rafe's arms, she had experienced the sublime, and she could look forward to more of that if this pack survived the oncoming tide of monsters.

"Rafe. I'm not sorry we met. I can't be sorry about what we feel."

She sent that message to Rafe without meaning to. She had been thinking about him for too long and too hard. Their bond would ensure that he heard her. He would now know what she was doing and where she would go.

"Don't come after me. This is something I must do."

Would he see this latest defection as an act of selfishness? Or that she hadn't liked what happened in that attic room?

Rafe soon responded, *"I can be with you, help you. Wait for me. Let me do this. Give me a clue."*

Cara erected a mental wall and reinforced it with continued conscious effort. Then she cursed and backed it up with a growl that tickled her human throat.

How would she manage the distance, let alone getting to an unknown location, if she had to traverse the miles on foot? Daylight wasn't too far off. Sunlight would make shape-shifting out of the question. Shifting required darkness and had been born of the secrets darkness hid. She had to hurry, shift now, somehow find her way.

A breeze, warm and steamy, ruffled her hair. The scent of wolf the breeze carried offered no comfort now. She had to find a way out of the Landaus' gates without being seen. The dark spirit was urging her to get going, perhaps for reasons Cara didn't yet know anything about.

Out of a whole host of sounds going on around her, Cara picked out one as being significant. The slamming of a car door.

Footfalls, light but meaningful, became louder as they got closer to where Cara stood. A woman appeared, heading toward her on the driveway. No. Not a woman, really.

"I suppose you'll need a ride," Dana Delmonico Landau said, as if she had either been privy to everything that had happened so far—or possessed a set of talents that she usually kept hidden.

Rafe looked for the black SUV in the garage, feeling guilty about leaving the dirty work regarding the body and finding the killer to the others. But the car was gone. This was curious, since the SUV was seldom used by anyone except the Weres who were out with his father in the park at the moment.

He chose another car and slipped onto the warm leather

seat. He had to find Cara. He would bring her back and chain her to the house if necessary until he could get some things done without thinking about her.

It was likely that others had heard what had transpired between them on Were channels. He didn't care. Most of his pack had their own mates and would understand his dilemma with Cara. If she was right about the uprising of monsters in Miami, only she could help to locate and cull their numbers, and yet it was dangerous for her to do so. Having Cara here would benefit everyone, except maybe Cara.

She had closed down communication. He could no longer see her in his mind at present, which would make locating her a problem. Had she gone home? If so, was there a chance he might intercept her before she got there? How would she get away from Miami? Heaven only knew what Colton and Rosalind would think if she returned on her own. Or if he showed up unannounced looking for her.

Rafe waved at the guards at the gate as he drove up and stopped to ask, "Did you see Cara?"

A quick no in reply was all it took for the glimmer of an idea to form in his mind. Cara had not come this way on foot, and she wouldn't have gotten past the guards if she had. She was wily, however, and could have easily skirted the front gate.

Rafe stepped on the gas. Using the GPS, he plotted the secret location of the Kirk-Killions' home that his family had been allowed access to in order to bring Cara to Miami. That place was a couple of hours away. He'd have to find Cara somewhere between here and there.

Barely three miles from the estate, Rafe slowed the car to process another thought that had dropped into his mind. Was it a message? He'd heard a whisper. In that whisper was a name he recognized.

Hell, Cara hadn't gone home. The name he had heard was a place wrapped up in the legends that formed his pack's history.

Fairview.

He made a U-turn and drove at breakneck speed for a few more miles with an eye out for the old sign that had been left standing after the psychiatric hospital had supposedly closed down—*supposedly* being the operative word.

Every Were in Miami knew of this place and that it was where humans freshly inducted into the moon's cult were taken, if they were lucky, to go through their first bone-shattering transition from human to werewolf. Although Fairview's windows now appeared to be dark and the gates were padlocked, there was plenty of activity behind those old brick walls that went undetected by all except for the wounded humans Fairview's conscientious staff served.

It wasn't far to that place. A slight detour only, and one Rafe had to take in case Cara had been the one to guide him there.

Cara sat back on the seat, staring out the half-open window. "This isn't the way home," she said.

"You weren't really thinking of going home tonight, were you?" Dana replied.

Cara gave her a brief glance. "No."

"I thought you might like to see the spot that's been on your mind," Dana said. "I can always turn around if I was wrong about that."

Cara gave her hostess another sideways glance.

"Do you have any idea where that might be?" Dana asked.

There was only one more place tied to the memories of her parents' past left to see in Miami. Dana had mentioned it earlier. After everything that had happened since then, this trip was to be a fitting finale to her quest for the truth. And Rafe's mother had picked up on that.

"Fairview," Cara said.

"It's only a few miles from us," Dana explained.

Cara studied the landscape intently. Because Dana seemed to understand what was going on, Cara asked what was on her mind. "Was there a reason a fight with the vampires took place there instead of in the park?"

"No one knows that for sure, other than your parents. I tend to think that Rosalind led the vampires here because it was far enough from the city to allow her to do what she wanted to do."

"Which was what?" Cara asked.

"Fight them, once and for all. Prove her dominance over them."

A shiver of apprehension iced Cara's neck when she heard that word. *Dominance.* Out of the corner of her eye, she caught sight of a sign that had long since fallen into disrepair and now hung from its hinges. It would have directed people to the Fairview Hospital Psychiatric Clinic when the hospital was up and running.

She felt an even deeper chill when they turned down a long, dark driveway. Tingling sensations accompanied a new premonition. Something was about to happen here that went beyond her objective of taking a quick look around.

She leaned forward on the seat. Everything outside the car's window had once again become dreamlike, as if she was seeing the landscape through the tight weave of a net. Her sight was limited, but smells came through.

"Wolf," she said.

Dana nodded. "Wolves have always been a part of the history of this place, and still are. One of our packmates runs Fairview now, the same as long ago when part of it was open to the public."

"Wolves and humans mixed there?"

"They were kept segregated, of course. No one on the outside ever knew what went on in some of those corridors."

"It's still open?" Cara asked.

"Jenna James runs Fairview now, and she is very good at what she does."

Cara said thoughtfully, "Wolf scent could have been what helped to draw the vampires to the area."

"That certainly could have been a part of why they appeared back then," Dana agreed.

Cara turned to her. "But you don't really believe that was the case?"

"I tend to believe it was Rosalind who purposefully drew them here for a reason of her own, and that she was merely aided by the darker aspects of this place. I think she planned this in order to keep others away."

If that was true, and Dana was right about her mother's motives for coming here, Rosalind had cared about the lives of others and had chosen this place for its remote location. She might have taken into consideration that wolves injured in a fight could have been treated at this hospital.

She was beginning to fill in the blanks of her family's past. She had seen what had happened to her father in the park. She had seen her parents making love in the attic room. Now she was going to find out the rest. The puzzle was about to be solved.

The long driveway to Fairview was partially overgrown with grass and knee-high weeds. There were no lights. As the car wound through a dense stand of trees, the moon ducked behind a cloud.

When the outline of a building came into view in the

headlights, Cara put a hand on her chest to try to ease her racing heartbeats. As Dana pulled up to an old chain-link fence and stopped the car, Cara's hand flew to the door handle.

"Wait," Dana cautioned. "Someone else is here."

Cara already knew that, though, and also that the past was about to come alive in a way that could affect them all.

Chapter 29

Rafe drove up to the chain-link fence surrounding the hospital and parked the car. Fairview had a forgotten, forlorn look that was deceiving, and appeared to have been abandoned for years.

Grass had overtaken whole stretches of the circular driveway. The fence drooped in places, and moss crept up the brick near the base of the steps leading to the front door, presenting onlookers with a broody atmosphere that ghost hunters might have liked to explore. Yet Fairview wasn't empty or abandoned, and anyone trespassing here would get a decent shock if they somehow managed to get inside.

He saw no one. Heard nothing. The quiet was so convincing, he almost believed what that boarded-up exterior suggested, when he knew better. Nevertheless, he had to wonder why Cara would want to come here, if in fact she would.

He got out of the car and took several deep breaths. Then he scanned the area for hints of life beyond the faint scent of wolves that only another wolf would have noticed.

His visits to Fairview were rare and made him uneasy. He seldom set foot here unless called upon to investigate any incident caused by a wolf biting a human. There were several such cases each year, and all of them required the good guys of their species to go after the bad guys afterward to track down those toothy bastards.

Things had been fairly quiet in that arena lately, and now the danger had escalated to include another kind of bite. All of a sudden, the current pack had vampires to worry about. There was no help for humans punctured by fangs, and no private hospitals like this one to take in the undead. Only the cold slabs of city morgues could host a new vampire's temporary stay.

With the back of his neck prickling, Rafe walked toward the padlocked gate. There was something here... but what?

What was he supposed to find?

There was no sign of Cara, but the hum of an engine on the driveway made him turn around. The needling sensations at the base of his neck tripled as he waited to find out if the whisper he heard had been legitimate and if Cara had sent it.

When the SUV rounded a corner, Rafe breathed a sigh of relief. It was the missing vehicle from his family's garage. If his father and others with access to the garage had been scouring the park, who was driving that SUV?

Two headlights coming his way made the night temporarily brighter. Rafe waited by the gate on the opposite side of the building until the car pulled up and the passenger door opened. Cara got out. Following closely behind her was the surprise of the night.

"What are you doing here?" his mother said.

The only sound left after that was the unusual pounding of his heart.

Cara froze when she saw Rafe. She attempted to hide how grateful she was to see him, because there was a downside to meeting him like this, here. Emotions she had tried to leave behind rolled over her. Unable to think of anything to say, she turned to Dana, who stood on her left.

"I suppose he has a right to be here and to share this," Dana said.

"Share what?" Rafe asked, sounding as confused as Cara was.

"Her family's past," Dana said.

Cara realized by observing the way Rafe looked at his mother that he was in the dark about why he was here and might have been following a hunch as to where she would turn up next.

"The bond between you is obvious," Dana went on. "Maybe it's a good thing you're here."

Cara finally spoke up and said to Dana, "You can't possibly find that kind of bond acceptable."

Dana wasn't intimidated by the intensity of Cara's gaze or her frankness. "Why wouldn't we accept it?" Dana said. "Why do you suppose you were sent here, if not to become one of us?"

Rafe stepped closer…close enough for Cara to feel that familiar flush of warmth he gave her and to remember the exquisite seductiveness of his body stretched out on top of hers in that attic room. Her own memories were now of deep, drowning kisses, and how Rafe's scent could chase away thoughts of the bad things in her life.

"This is the place," Cara said.

The set of Rafe's jaw told her he was trying to ignore

the compulsion to look around him. For Rafe, what had happed here was part of his pack's dark history.

"What do you want to find here?" he asked her. "More of your mother's memories? Further trauma that might make you feel worse than you already do?"

Rafe was probably wondering if her feelings for him might be nothing more than a chapter in her family's lingering past. If she might have gone to bed with him only because she thought she was dreaming, or reliving something that had happened long ago between her parents.

You're wrong, Cara wanted to tell him, though she wasn't completely sure about that, either.

"My family's memories could be coloring everything," she said in answer to the questions Rafe hadn't voiced. "I have to find out what is here for me, and if I can let the past go once I understand it."

Rafe's blue eyes searched her face in a caressing way that was the equivalent of having his hands feather over her body. He wasn't going to stop her from finding what was here. Maybe he wouldn't offer another protest.

"Trust me," he said. "What we did in that room had nothing to do with Colton and Rosalind. You can forget about that. You were there. I was there. We did what we did because we wanted to, and because we had to. Your discoveries about them and their affection for each other can't cause you to love me any more or less than you do. Neither can someone else's memories or words sway my feelings for you."

She wanted to believe him. She honestly did. The strange thing was how quickly the imprinting state had taken them over. This was only her second day in Miami, though it felt like she'd been here much longer. Did anyone really know how the mating game could happen so fast, or tie two Weres together so strongly?

Rafe faced his mother. "Did Cara ask you to bring her here?"

"No," Cara said. "Dana merely offered me a ride."

"I thought you ran back toward your home," Rafe said. "I thought you had gone."

Cara shook her head. "It's not over. This is where things in Miami ended for my parents and their life of seclusion began. What happened here was the final battle with the vampires. Something secretive must have been disclosed here that I'm meant to see."

As she had in the park, Cara sensed in the hospital's grounds the remnants of that battle tugging at her. Anger and death lingered in places where lives were lost. She had mentioned that to Rafe earlier, and he could choose to believe it or not.

She didn't look past the fence, already feeling Fairview's chill. The air surrounding the old building was thick and difficult to breathe. No one with an ounce of sensitivity would have been comfortable here.

"Seeing what happened near this place might make me better understand my fears," she said, thinking out loud and avoiding Rafe's gaze.

"What fears?" Rafe asked.

She couldn't hide things from him now, but she didn't want to tell Rafe everything. He hadn't shared the horrors she had seen growing up. Rafe belonged to a pack that supported his species and offered backup in a crisis.

How can you love a monster killer who is also a monster herself?

"No," Rafe objected, having either tuned in to or guessed what she was thinking. "You have to realize by now that you aren't a monster, and neither were Colton or Rosalind. How could you even think such a thing when theirs was the ultimate sacrifice? They gave up our kind of freedom for another one that they believed would suit them better. They offered the same kind of freedom to you before extending the choice of something else."

Cara glanced up, drawn to the tender adamancy of his remarks.

His eyes bored into hers to help drill home a point as he said, "Your parents could have stayed here. No one turned them away. If what they left was so bad, why would they send you here? If they weren't wanted in Miami, why would they expect things to be different for you?"

Rafe's earnestness was as beautiful as his face. What his eyes told her was that he had fallen in love with her. After everything that had happened during their brief acquaintance, their souls had mingled in the way only Were souls could, and he loved her.

The pleasure of that made her sway on her feet. He steadied her with a firm hand that forced her to again meet his eyes.

Could he see that she was desperate to believe him? Was he able to read that in her face?

"This is the final piece of the puzzle," she repeated. "I have to see it in order to understand why my parents made the choices they made."

Rafe nodded reluctantly. His anxiousness surrounded him. But the net of her mother's memory had already dropped in front of her vision, and the process of dipping into the past had begun.

There was no way to stop what was coming, and Cara didn't want to. By finding what she needed here, there was a good chance she could let the past go and love Rafe back. When this was over, she might be able to throw herself into his arms.

At last, she might shed the tears she had held back for so long, and the anger she had harbored for the kind of life she and her family could have lived if things had gone differently and events in Miami had turned out well.

Fears.

There were just too damn many to count. And Rafe had added to them by concentrating, right now, on the word she feared most of all.

Love.

He loved her. It was true.

And she loved him back.

She was Lycan above all, he had said. And as the strongest and fiercest of the breed, Lycans were supposed to be the masters of their own destinies, not pawns to anyone else's.

"Then let's see what there is to see," Rafe said as he took her hand in his.

Blue light shone from his eyes, and that light grounded her. Cara sent the tentacles of her mind into the surrounding landscape and said, "Rosalind. Show me what happened here so that this can be over, once and for all. And so that I can make a choice for the direction my life is to go."

The musty green smell of uncut grass and old trees reached her before it changed to make way for the acrid odor of stale blood.

Cara turned her head…

No, it was someone else who turned to search for the origins of that smell. It was someone else who realized vampires were coming. Cara was experiencing this through someone else's well-tuned senses.

Ten claws and a set of extremely sharp fangs simultaneously altered her appearance. Shuddering with distaste, she set out toward the trees, not half as scared as she should have been when the fate of so many was at stake. Her teeth chattered. Her heartbeats soared.

This isn't me, Cara chanted inwardly, trying hard to remember that.

Focusing on the area beside an old dirt road where the trees were thickest, she put a hand to her chest, barely able to perceive the sting of the grooves her claws were digging. The word *No!* shattered the silence into a million pieces that left a bad taste in her mouth. Enemies were coming, and not just the vampires.

The dark thing inside her stirred, recognized what those odors meant. She felt the cold spiral of that spirit's ascent.

Cara clenched her teeth as if that could keep the sprit trapped inside. Again, though, it was Rosalind who did the teeth clenching. This was Rosalind's picture. Rosalind's answer to Cara's request to view the past. Cara was merely getting a ringside seat at the show.

Cara shook her head to deny what was happening. Rosalind did the same as the dark spirit began to seep through her pores, turning her hands and arms a glossy shade of black. The spirit forced Rosalind to open her mouth. A cry escaped as the Banshee took over with a terrible swiftness, and the wail went on and on, shaking the ground and the leaves in the trees. But this wail wasn't for her.

The first batch of bloodsuckers appeared in the field to her left. They wore rags, and those rags were bloody. Their gaunt faces were the color of dry bones. Black eyes sank into endlessly deep sockets. Their stink preceded them like a stale wind.

There had to be at least forty hungry, angry, soulless ghouls. And she alone would meet them. She was ready, and she waited for the crush that was to come. These monsters had hurt her lover, and she would make them pay for that.

Beside her, there was a sudden flash of white, as if the storm she had expected had come to ground in the form of a dazzling streak of lightning. That luminous streak sailed by her on two long legs, white hair and skin glowing like moonlight, and issuing growls that were as fierce as anything she had ever heard.

Colton had come. Ghost. Werewolf. Lover.

Her mate would fight by her side.

The white-furred werewolf tore through the vampires like a battering ram. Black blood and ash flew as he hacked his way through them with his claws active and jaws like a steel trap.

Rosalind ran toward him with her claws slashing and her legs moving to the rhythm of her heartbeats. She took one vampire down with a slice to its scrawny neck and another soon after that. A third bloodsucker tried its hardest to avoid her claws and her wrath and didn't succeed. Colton had cleared a path through the fang-snapping horde by circling to her right.

It wasn't until she reached Colton that she heard the sound of oncoming cars and realized what that meant.

The Landau pack had arrived.

More help had come.

The brush of a hand against her throat catapulted Rosalind into yet another shape, and her claws disappeared. With her fangs, she did more damage to the parasites now turning toward the group of Weres who were running toward them. Without a full moon to guide their ancient DNA, none of them could shape-shift into their strongest forms, but that didn't stop them. Ten werewolves joined the fight with silver-bladed knives and carved wooden stakes. Guns would have been easier, of course, but the sound would have carried.

More vampires went down. The scene, gray with a continuous flurry of ash, seemed surreal. Rosalind knew that Banshees didn't wail for the undead, and that vampires had no souls to call to death's door, but none of the Weres had fallen tonight, and still the dark spirit's cry again pushed upward through her to escape through her parted lips.

Blue sparks accompanied the ear-shattering wail. Hearing it, the handful of vampires left standing stopped fighting. In the periphery came the rustling sounds of demons gathering as if they had been invited to a party. Those sounds closed in.

The werewolves cut down the vampires, taking advantage of the suddenness of their frozen state. If they sensed demon presence, they didn't let on. Each dusted vampire was a point in their favor on the road to victory.

The pale faces of another enemy now formed a large circle around the fighting field, shining like small fires in the dark and reflecting the flames from which they had sprung.

When the werewolves stopped to acknowledge the newcomers, the fact that the worst was yet to come was reflected in the expressions of all the Landau pack.

And yet no one moved.

The demons stayed back.

Because the Banshee's wail hadn't been meant for any member of the pack. It had been meant for her.

That realization was the impetus for another shapeshift. As it began, all eyes turned to her. Waves of anxiousness ruffled through the crowd, affecting Weres and demons alike as they tracked her next transformation.

Her skin again became a glossy black before quickly fading to ivory. Her hair, now waist length, hung over half of her face like a shiny black curtain. Something wet trickled down her chin, and black blood stained the fist she raised to catch it.

Banshee.

But the transformation didn't stop there.

Her skin began to dry out. The ivory smoothness became yellowed and cracked as her shoulders hunched forward. From each of the grooves in her chest that she had made with her claws came tiny licks of red-orange flame. As her insides overheated, she blinked through eyes able to see right through the skin of the werewolves around her.

Demon.

Colton was there beside her, seemingly unafraid of this latest incarnation that even Rosalind feared. She was to die. The Banshee had wailed for her…but which incarnation had the Banshee perceived and chosen to call to death's door?

Was it going to be her, as Rosalind Kirk, or the hell spawn that had taken her over? Could the Banshee separate one soul from among so many facets of herself?

The thought that prevailed as she waited to find out was that she might never see Colton again. And in spite of that, she had to make sure he lived.

She lifted an arm and uttered a sound that brought the circle of surrounding demons forward. The reptilian creatures that owed fealty to hell came to her like moths to the flame, hustling forward without realizing they were going to be slaughtered and that she was not really a demon, after all. She just looked like one.

Spurred into action by the gruesome sight, the Weres attacked with force. Mesmerized as they were, the demons didn't know what hit them. And the Banshee, the dark and brutal entity she carried around, wailed again as the last vestiges of the demon in Rosalind died with them.

Within the chaos of bodies dropping and werewolves growling with humanlike throats, Colton was there, again in his human form, and he was speaking to her.

"One more shape-shift" was his request.

Rosalind saw the form of this shift in his mind, and

what he wanted from her now. He desired to see her in her own skin. He wanted to look into her eyes. When he reached out to her, she didn't back away.

Her gaze drifted to the werewolves who had fought so bravely. Dylan Landau was there, and beside him his mate, Dana Delmonico. There were others she recognized and couldn't name. All standing. Not looking too bad after their valiant fight.

When Colton took her hand, the next changes began. Glancing down, she saw that her hands and arms were again becoming thin and pale, and that there were no claws. Her lips closed easily because her fangs were gone. No bloodstain remained on her fist. Rosalind Kirk was back to face her lover. But her hair was no longer a deep midnight black. The tendrils covering her shoulders were snowy white—an exact match for Colton's hair.

She had taken on the ghost wolf's whiteness. They were now both ghosts of a sort, and would be feared by the Weres who had come to their aid…though those wolves would never have admitted it. They were Lycans whose systems had been compromised by fate, and by so many other things that lay beyond their control. For them, there was no going back. There was no normal, and never had been.

She and Colton would not find life easy after this night. The Landau pack had seen some of her many variations and would always be afraid of her, or at the very least, wary.

"We will go away," Colton said to appease her fears. "Away from staring eyes and the need to think of ourselves as freaks. We'll go someplace where in the future the monsters won't bother our friends. Do you know of such a place?"

Cara, stunned by all this, nodded along as Rosalind whispered in reply, "Home."

* * *

Cara staggered backward as the images she had seen and shared dissolved. She gaped at the spot where Rosalind and Colton had made that pledge.

Some of sickness that had been growing inside her eased, though not all of it was so easily dislodged by what she had just witnessed. Seeing her parents in action drilled deeper into her the fact of how different they had become and how dangerous they were. It was those differences, and the need to feel free, that had taken her parents away from Miami.

And she was like them.

Rafe, her beautiful lover whom she craved with every fiber of her being, would be alpha of the Landau pack someday...while she would always be eyed with distrust if she were to stay.

"You know," a voice said in her ear. Rafe's voice—deep, masculine and loaded with concern. "The worst trait I can think of is avoidance of a problem that can be solved over time. I don't believe there's a shape-shift for that."

Chapter 30

Cara was shaking. Rafe tightened his grip on her hand, not sure if he should gather her in his arms. There were hints of wildness in her wide-legged stance. Her eyes were glazed. Close enough to whisper to her, he hoped his voice might bring her fully back from wherever she had gone, and that she would believe every word he said.

"You know…the worst trait I can think of is avoidance of a problem that can be solved over time. I don't believe there's a shape-shift for that."

She didn't immediately respond. She didn't seem to see him. Rafe's heart rate sped as he searched for cracks in Cara's demeanor that might provide him with insight on what was happening to her. He had to admit to being shocked by the way she had looked minutes before. There was an added pressure in his chest over the way she looked now. But Cara hadn't gone anywhere. Only her mind had.

Her face had drained of color. Her black hair lay flat

against her slender body, hugging her curves. She seemed frailer, thinner. Inside his hand, her fingers curled into a fist.

"Come back to me," he whispered to her with the realization that Cara was not only the epitome of the concept of *wild*, but that she always would be. There was no way to tame her inner beasts.

"If you take me, you take it all," she had messaged to him, which now seemed to have been a long time ago.

Born to wildness, and reared on its taste, Cara would always be an enigma who kept her problems, like her Banshee, trapped inside. Who knew what she had seen out here? He hadn't been able to share that, but there was no doubt this had been a very real experience for her. Proof of that was in the rapid loop of expressions her face had undergone and the quakes that continued to rock her. Whatever she had seen had taken a toll.

She must have once again been taken over by Rosalind for a time. Cara had spoken to him of partaking in her mother's memories, but she hadn't confessed to actually becoming part of those memories. However, he knew that was what was happening. Hell, she had jumped from that window.

Her mother's memories had to be what Cara had found here, and what she had been searching for. Was it done now? Was her search for the past over?

Could they move on?

As for Rosalind…he didn't have to know what had transpired here in order to understand what Cara's mother had done in this place, and which monsters had been present at the time. That too was part of the legend and mystique of the Kirk-Killions.

Werewolves had fought vampires and demons in this

field, and had survived. Cara's mother had called them forth and then dealt with the problem they presented.

And now, Cara was so pale and distant.

"I'm here," he said, hoping to get through to her.

Rafe couldn't tear his attention from her for even a quick glance at his mother, who stood by the car. It was highly possibly that his mother had also taken part in that past skirmish. His father as well. This was another example of the tie binding Cara's parents and the Landau pack. They had fought together on more than one occasion, and in Fairview's front yard they had carved out a victory that had chased the monsters off Miami's streets for a very long time.

Like her mother, Cara—his lover, the she-wolf he had sealed himself to—was also an enticement for monsters. But his pack could handle that. He could handle that. If this was his future, then okay. He was all in.

I just want you...

"Think of what kind of a help you can be here," he said. "You can give us a bird's-eye view of anyone or anything intending to ring the doorbell. Housing a Banshee can allow us to see our own futures, if the spirit is willing to show us. Your talents can save lives here, and not just ours."

He had so much more to say. So many things to tell Cara.

"Maybe losing some freedom will be a sacrifice on your part, but I'm willing to help in any way that I can. I will be beside you."

No. Damn it, that wasn't what he wanted to tell her. Was this the time and the place for him to relay the rest? That for better or worse, they were a team forever?

"You are not alone, Cara. I think you know that."

She didn't meet his eyes. Her skin was almost transparent.

"What was once here is over and long gone. It's time to go. It's not safe to remain."

Heaven only knew what could happen if the vampires seeking her found them here in the open with no backup, and with Cara in a semi-catatonic state. He and his mother could put up a good fight if it came to that, but would Cara snap out of her stupor?

Cara leaned forward as if suddenly lulled by his voice. Her long lashes fluttered, creating shadows that contrasted with her skin. She took a big breath, and when her eyes reopened, they were once again a clear, vibrant green.

For now, her inner battle, whatever that had been, had been won.

He reached out to steady her, wanting desperately to kiss her trembling lips. God, how he wanted that. But this wasn't the right moment to indulge his feelings, so he laced their fingers together to reinforce their bond, determined to get through to her and to fix the fallout from a bad situation.

"In finding what you sought, does that make things better or clearer to you? Does it change things here in the present for you or for us?"

She blinked slowly as if finally wakening to the world around her. With another deep breath and in a wavering tone, Cara said, "It changes everything."

She could have meant what she said, though Rafe didn't believe it. Cara was still seeing things through a different lens and was being suffocated by what she had found.

Rafe's soul ached for her and the burden she carried. Hell, what was the life span of a spirit, anyway? Would it have a hold on Cara forever, or until she found a way to pass that spirit along to somebody else?

Was there a way for her to get rid of the Banshee and keep the promises her family had made so long ago?

"Cara, look at me."

Her eyes traveled upward with an agonizing slowness. They were haunted eyes, and thoughtful.

"Nothing changes. Do you hear me? Nothing," Rafe said.

His mother had moved up to stand behind him. Cara turned her gaze that way.

"We all have something that tries to drag us down now and then," his mother said. "The strength of our character is what defines us. You were born with that kind of strength, and that's what will move us forward from here."

"You were here, so you know how this goes," Cara observed.

"Yes," his mother conceded.

"Why did you offer to host someone like me?"

"Because of promises that were made a long time ago, and the necessary fulfillment of them."

"What promises?" Cara asked.

Rafe sensed some discomfort in his mother's reluctance to answer Cara's question, which made it imperative for him that she did. He said, "Yes. What promises?"

His mother finally replied, "That our packs would join forces again when the time arose for such a necessity."

Rafe swore under his breath. "You're talking about the return of those vampires?"

"Yes," his mother said. "Among other things."

Rafe turned that over in his mind. Bringing Cara here was some kind of payback for the aid the Landau pack had given to Rosalind and Colton a long time ago? Their daughter had been sent to Miami in order to flush the monsters out when and if they resurfaced in this city?

If that was true…

If that was true, Rafe thought with an appraising glance at his mother, then someone here had known about the return of the vampires and had not provided that information to the rest of the pack.

He zeroed in on his mother's practiced cop face, which seldom gave anything away, as the final piece of that idea struck him.

Someone who had known about that old promise had called it in, and Colton and Rosalind had sent their secret weapon in the war with monsters. Their only offspring. Their only daughter.

Cara.

So now you see...
Now you know.

She hadn't just been sent here to assimilate with other Weres, but to help them. Only she wielded the magic necessary for finding anomalies and beasts.

This was a wake-up call. That was the way Rafe was describing his sudden enlightenment in the thoughts he was telegraphing. Yet who among them could have anticipated that their packs would be joined together in other ways, or that she and Rafe would be mates?

He was looking at her. Trying to read her, in turn. Rafe was like a rock in this gathering storm, and so very brave to have gotten this far.

Things were in the open now, so there was no need for any of them to hide what they were thinking.

"So how many demons can we expect, Cara? One of them killed that human who was dumped near our wall, I believe," Dana said.

It was time to do her job. What she had been sent here for. There was no running from this kind of commitment. Still, Cara wondered if this was the reason Dana Delmo-

nico Landau had brought her to Fairview tonight. Dana had used a little added pressure to kick Cara's senses into overdrive.

"Only one demon came for me," Cara said. "A bullet took that one down."

"Not before his friends found out about you?" Dana pressed.

"They share thoughts the way we do. If that one found me, others will follow."

"Christ!" Rafe muttered.

"And the vampires?" Dana asked.

"There's a nest not far from the beach. Vampires don't travel far from their resting places, and that's where the first one appeared. The park shouldn't be part of their area, but that's where I met the second one and his friends."

"That's the vamp presence you detected around the body we found?" Rafe asked.

"Maybe," Cara replied.

Dana cut in. "Wanting what you keep hidden inside can't be the only reason these creatures have come above-ground."

Rafe responded with new insight. "Because whoever brought Cara here might have known of the monsters' return before calling the Kirk-Killions for a favor. Either that, or we have a psychic in our midst who can predict the future. It's possible that Cara isn't the inciting factor for vampires coming out of hiding after all and that her presence here is only coincidental with that."

Rafe tightened his hold on Cara's hand. She would have loved him for that alone when there were so many other reasons for her feelings.

"Our alpha seemed to be as surprised as we were by news of the vampires. If he knew about this, he has become a damn fine actor," he said.

Dana shook her head. "It wasn't your father who sensed vamp presence and started the ball rolling. I would have known about that."

"But the alpha would have initiated my invitation," Cara pointed out.

Dana was eyeing her thoughtfully. "Yes. Dylan sent the invitation, but it wasn't to confront a possible vampire invasion. It was so that…"

"Cara and I could meet and possibly form a friendship?" Rafe finished for his mother.

His grip on Cara's hand could have snapped a human's bones. She relished the minor twinge of leftover discomfort in that injured hand that told her some of her fears about winding up alone in this strange life would disappear if only Rafe continued to hang on.

Had she been promised to Rafe as a mate? Was that one of the promises Dana had mentioned, or had the fates she had blamed after first setting eyes on Rafe Landau been responsible for getting them together, meaning that most of this was pure coincidence?

"Our relationship aside," Rafe said, tensing slightly, "it would seem that there's another mystery to be solved here. Who butchered that body, and why?"

Though the question needed an answer, he quickly circled back to the former subject. "Wasn't it a long shot that Cara and I would imprint?"

Dana didn't shirk the question. "I suppose. However, Colton and Rosalind were willing to take that chance if it eventually led to you being mated." Dana looked to Cara as she went on. "Because if it worked out, Cara would be freed from the burden she carries."

Cara's insides began to twist. Another shudder rocked her. What Dana was telling them would never have crossed

her mind. She hadn't thought it could ever happen, or even be a possibility.

Could it be true?

That Rafe was to save her soul?

They would have a child, and if that child was a daughter, the Banshee would have a new soul to share.

When Rafe's gaze came back to her, Cara met it. Though he didn't immediately speak his thoughts out loud, Cara heard them as if he had.

"If we were to have a daughter..."

The thought of that sickened Cara the way it must have sickened her mother when the time came to pass along the dark spirit to its new younger, stronger host...

Because who could have wished such a thing for anyone they truly loved?

Chapter 31

Rafe rallied quickly and herded Cara toward the car. He was silent, though his mind whirled with questions, most of them having to do with sacrifice.

Cara's family had sacrificed their life in Miami in order to save others from harm. Sending Cara here had been about their wish for a hopeful future for their daughter, freeing her of at least one burden—ending her turn with the Banshee. Then there was the fact that Rafe's own family had been willing to tie their son to a Kirk-Killion and all that went with her by honoring promises they once had made.

Sacrifice.

As Rafe saw it, he was the big winner here. Cara was his. What was done was done, and the only direction open to them was forward.

He felt Cara's racing pulse through his grip on her hand and warned himself not to look at her face. If he did, he

would likely see her horror over what she had learned about their possible future progeny.

She'd be wondering how she could possibly pass the dark spirit to anyone else after having experienced what that kind of life was like, let alone asking such a thing of a child of her own. She might vow never to have children, which in turn might lead her to contemplate their relationship and possible ways to break the chains binding her to him.

Hell, he wasn't going to lose her. And anyway, that breakup couldn't happen.

Cara stopped when they reached their vehicles, and a new wave of tension ran through her. Rafe turned to search the driveway.

"Even I can smell that," his mother said. And she was right. Foul odors were drifting across the field, emanating from the area beneath the trees that they had just left.

Inner warnings came too fast for Rafe to acknowledge all of them, but one warning stood out and brought him a new round of fear. The only way for Cara to sever their bond was for one of them to die.

If Cara were to sacrifice herself in order to prevent a dismal childless future, perhaps she'd assume the Banshee might die with her. Where would the dark spirit go if that were the case?

"Don't you dare think that way," he said to her adamantly. "Please get in the car. We can outdistance this fight, at least for now, until we know more about it."

His mother didn't waste any time. She dived behind the wheel of the black SUV and started the engine. Rafe opened the door and ushered Cara inside.

"Go," he directed. "Take Cara home." He trusted his mother to take care of her, and she didn't argue.

Anyone who had been a cop, or in any way affiliated

with law enforcement, trusted others in the field to do the right thing and make the right choices. His mother took off in a whirlwind of kicked-up dirt and debris, jamming the car into Reverse, then wheeling it around to head down the driveway at breakneck speed. Cara's face in the window became a white blur.

Rafe got behind the wheel of his borrowed sedan but didn't follow the SUV. After starting the engine, he steered toward the trees, determined to see for himself what kind of abomination had come for his lover this time, and if there was anything he could do about it.

"He won't do anything stupid," Dana said as Fairview Hospital slid into the distance. "You don't have to worry about that."

Cara leaned back against the seat, feeling sick and thinking about jumping out of the car. She couldn't see Rafe or the vehicle he had been driving. It was entirely possible that Rafe's mother didn't know her son as well as she liked to think, and his next choice might surprise her.

"It worked," Cara said.

"Yes." Dana didn't pretend not to understand what Cara was talking about. Two families touched by tragedy had been joined at the hip. She and Rafe had become lovers, which had been one of the secret goals for bringing her to Miami that had been exposed at Fairview tonight.

"That must have been some promise your pack made to my family," Cara said. "I wonder what you think about it now."

"I think that had you come here under any circumstances, there would have been the same result. I see the way you look at each other. No one made you do that."

"Rafe knows what I am."

Dana nodded. "We all do."

"Yet you'd accept the consequences of such a pairing for your family? Welcome it?"

"Yes."

"Why?"

"Because everyone benefits, especially you, Cara. And because you've taken your turn with this spirit and deserve some freedom of your own."

"What about Rafe?"

"You'll have to believe me when I tell you that my son can take care of himself and has never once done anything he hasn't chosen to do."

"He chose me."

"Yes, he did."

"And that fell right into the original plan for bringing me here."

"Yes, though none of us could have been sure what might have happened," Dana said.

In Cara's mind, the two objectives for her visit to Miami had been tied together in a nice little knot. She had walked right into this, she realized as she replayed the events of the past few days in search of the details she might have otherwise missed.

En route to Miami, she had jumped from the car that had been sent to transport her and had ended up at the beach…when she now knew that beach was nowhere near the Landau estate. It was in the opposite direction.

This raised the question that nagged at her now. Had someone predicted that she'd try to escape and planned to have her taken in the direction where she had ended up that first night…which just happened to be in Rafe's front yard?

Could anyone actually have seen that far ahead?

Who would have had an idea about the kind of male she'd be attracted to, and vice versa? Her parents?

Had they…could they…have planted those dreams

about Rafe in her mind, so that she would recognize him the way she had when they met face-to-face?

Had their union been preordained by the parents who had raised her and who possessed the kind of power and talent to set such a plan in motion?

Cara's fingers closed over the door handle of Dana's car.

"Did you know?" she asked Dana. "Were you in on the details of his plan?"

Dana nodded. "It all came down to freedom."

"That's not the way I see it now. This plan was more like manipulation."

"You weren't forced to make the choices you made, Cara. Neither was Rafe. This could have turned out differently and been a big mistake, but I believe you'd be lying if you told me you'd have changed things."

Silence fell, as dark and weighty as the knot in Cara's stomach. Maybe Dana was right, and she would have fallen for Rafe in any circumstance without interference, but how was she to know that?

Dana broke the silence.

"Rosalind was eighteen and had never been to a city when she came here," Dana said. "You're also eighteen and have led the same kind of secluded life she did."

They were back to an area where streetlights kept the dark at bay. The sun would rise soon, and there would be a short period of relief from finding out what kinds of things the darkness had in store for her.

Closing her eyes was not an option. They had traveled away from Fairview, and yet Cara still strained for a glimpse of Rafe in the side mirror.

"You might have been conceived here," Dana continued. "Eighteen would therefore have been a magic number in all of this."

Cara's sickness doubled as that idea sank in. If what

Dana suggested was true, the timing had also been perfectly planned for this visit. She was mating age, and had been hungry enough for companionship to look forward to those dreams of Rafe, in spite of her anger over having them.

Her fingers put pressure on the door handle as thoughts seemed to coagulate...

By mating with Rafe in the bedroom her parents had used, was there a chance she also might have conceived a child—a werewolf child she could then pass the dark spirit along to? A child carrying Rosalind and Colton's superior genes?

She needed to pull over and throw up but couldn't speak.

"I'm sorry," Dana said. "If I had known about all of the logistics of the plan beforehand, I could have approached you about it. I could have spoken to Rafe and armed you both."

"If you didn't know the extent of this plan, who did?" Cara barely got that out. She was millimeters away from opening the door.

"Rafe's grandfather," Dana said. "Landau alpha at the time. And your parents."

She hadn't escaped by the time the gates to the Landau estate appeared, but it was never too late.

Cara pushed down on the handle.

There was dark and then there was *dark*—true darkness that sprang from bad origins. Rafe's car's headlights barely made a dent in it. Like a creeping fog, everything outside the windows was a deep, solid black. So it was a good thing that all Landau vehicles came fully loaded with weapons and a stash of silver bullets in a secret com-

partment under the floor that only Landau fingerprints
could access.

Things like that sometimes came in handy, and Rafe
was afraid this was going to be one of those times. The
foul odor he had detected had seeped into the car to choke
him. Death's detritus was all too familiar to him, except
that this time he wasn't in an enclosed room with a week-
old dead body. The space around him was wide-open.

"Where are you, you damn bloodsuckers?" he muttered,
yanking the wheel to the right to avoid a grove of ancient
trees in need of water. Once he had passed the trees, Rafe
stopped the car and left it to idle as he pulled up the floor
mat and pressed his thumb to the digital lock.

The compartment holding the small cache of weapons and specialized bullets opened with a soft click. He
reached inside for the gun, comfortable with it in his hand.

Then he got out of the car.

Cara stopped herself from making her escape, struck
by a premonition of her own.

"Turn around," she directed as the gate opened to let
them through. "Please. Quickly. Now."

"Cara..." Dana began.

"Rafe didn't follow us. He is out there, searching for
them, and shouldn't be alone. He told me he had never
seen a vampire before the incident at the beach. What are
the chances he's seen a demon?"

Dana didn't balk or argue. She rolled down the window
and barked orders to the guard. Wearing a worried expression, she turned to Cara. "Dylan is still in the park, but he
will hear me and come. Whoever is with him will follow."

They backed up and headed toward the road to Fairview. Cara didn't press home the point that Dana had been

wrong about Rafe and that they shouldn't have left him there on his own.

She shouldn't have left him.

Cara's pulse sped faster than the car. Rafe was going to protect his new mate and had sent her to safety. He was going to face demons for her, in her place, and all Cara could think about was that no matter what the plans had been, if Rafe were to die, her soul would die with him.

The SUV blew through several stop signs and a lot of traffic lights without incident or the police catching on. Dana had gone quiet, tucking her fears inside. Maybe she blamed herself for not seeing what Rafe was capable of. Again, this came down to choices, and whether anyone could accurately predict the behavior of another.

Cara couldn't sit still. How could she when she was sure that Rafe loved her? He had joined up with a monster hunter who was also a monster in most eyes. The thought of a budding love between them, so soon and so very unique, caused another kind of drumbeat deep inside, this time arising from fear.

Was Rafe doing this to give her the choices she hadn't had? Was he willing to sacrifice himself for her?

She felt the tingle of the warmth of the sun that now sat just beneath the horizon like an emerging ball of fire. Its presence was in the air she breathed. The closeness of sunrise was the saving grace in all of this. Vampires and demons couldn't function in daylight. They would burn to a crisp in the light of a new day.

And as far as she knew, another body had not turned up before the stars came out, as the dark spirit had predicted.

Which meant that body hadn't yet been found.

"Hold on," she messaged to Rafe on a channel she was sure he would hear. *"Hold them off until I get there. If you can... If you do...we can..."*

She didn't get to finish that message, and probably couldn't have anyway without the vocabulary necessary to tell Rafe how she felt. Love was new to her.

And it hurt.

Chapter 32

Rafe saw nothing past the beams of the headlights at first. There was no extra weight to the air here and no added foulness now that a breeze had arrived to cut the stink of whatever hid from him. He wasn't alone, though. Were senses told him so.

"She's gone," he called out. "You came here for nothing."

The almost total absence of sound was odd. There were no night birds singing and no crickets or other bugs doing their thing. Rafe's thundering pulse took up the slack.

"Either you crawl back to where you came from, or you come out to face me. What other choices are there?" he said with a firm grip on the gun he held behind his back.

Sudden rustling sounds behind him made Rafe turn. More came from his right, but he stood his ground.

"You know you can't have her. Think of me as the gate-keeper on that score."

Adrenaline turned his skin icy. Sensing these creeps without being able to see them made his stomach clench. Hell, were there vampires out here, or something even worse? What did demons look like, and how fast did they move? He had a nagging suspicion that he was about to find out.

Something slid past him, momentarily blurring the light from the headlights as it headed into the pool of blackness beyond the car. Rafe had no idea what it was. The thing had moved like a streak of misplaced air rather than anything hampered by a solid form.

He turned in a slow circle, watching, searching, waiting, for the next surprise. Each passing second put his practiced cop nerves to the test. "Everyone here has to behave," he muttered to break up the silence and calm his nerves.

Out of the corner of his eye, Rafe caught sight of another blur of movement and brought the gun forward with his finger on the trigger, ready to do some damage if it came to that.

"Show yourself," he said at a reasonable volume, figuring anything that could move so quickly might also have exceptional hearing.

More rustling came from his left. Then behind him. And again to his right. All signs pointed to his being surrounded, and he had how many silver rounds loaded in the damn gun?

Nerves buzzed like loose live wires. Rafe settled his shoulders and widened his stance. He took a deep breath. There was an annoying twitch beneath his left eye. But his hand was steady on the weapon that wasn't aimed at anything…because as of yet there was nothing to see.

He backed up to press himself against the warm metal of the car's side panel. If anything came from behind, it would have to leap over the car and he'd have time to address the threat. His cell phone was in his pocket. He should have made a call before heading in this direction, so his mother could summon backup and return. At least, since he hadn't gone far into the grove on the property, there was a chance that the small staff working underground at Fairview Hospital might have heard the engines and come out for a look.

As if that last thought had kicked up a disturbance in the atmosphere, a solitary form suddenly appeared in front of him. He hadn't even seen anything move, but this sucker was a familiar sight—gaunt, ghostly, white haired, white-faced and all fanged up. Though it might have been human once, it definitely didn't fit into that species anymore.

This was the vamp they had met in the park, the leader of a nest. The decrepit, odorous bloodsucker didn't seem to care about the gun Rafe aimed at its bony chest. After all, it had died once or twice before.

"Glad you decided to show up," Rafe remarked, alarmed by the sight in front of him but still steady enough to deal with this creature. "Too bad there's nothing here for you presently. Surely you've sensed that."

The bloodsucker returned in a mocking tone, "She will come. Surely *you* have sensed that."

The worst part was the ring of truth in the vamp's response. Cara might return when she discovered that he hadn't followed her. She could be on her way now if his mother also realized the potential of the danger he faced.

"She will never give you what you want," Rafe said. "You're wasting your time."

"I have plenty of time to spare. On the other hand, you do not share that luxury," the creature remarked.

"Luxury? Look at you. Time has not treated you well."

"Spoken by a werewolf with a limited life span," the vampire countered.

"At least I don't live off the life force of others. I don't troll the human race for my food supply."

"And yet I would not trade places with an animal that was never human to begin with."

"Yes, well, I don't think anyone would have offered you that choice," Rafe said. "And as a side note, Cara still isn't here."

The old vampire smiled, showing off a pair of chipped, yellowed fangs. Flat black eyes looked beyond Rafe in a way that made Rafe afraid to follow its gaze. He wasn't sure if the sucker had truly seen something or if this was part of an old ruse designed to shift Rafe's attention elsewhere, leaving him vulnerable to those fangs.

He had not heard a car arrive. He didn't sense Cara's return to the area when there was no way he could have missed her. Part of her soul now belonged to him, and he would fight every vampire on the earth if he had to in order to keep it.

Finally, the old creep moved, breaking the standoff with a sideways glide. Rafe adjusted his stance, determined to keep this monster in his sight, and realized shortly afterward that the vampire had detected something else. Not Cara or a car. The rustling noises he had heard earlier were back and seemed to come from everywhere. The strange thing about it was the fact that the vampire across from him appeared to be as wary of the sounds as he was.

This meant he and the vampires weren't alone, and it was possible the two of them weren't going to be the only species represented here.

The car wasn't going fast enough for Cara. But the old Fairview sign finally appeared in the headlight beams and the SUV skidded into a tight right turn.

"Wait," she again messaged to Rafe. *"Almost there."*

When no reply came, Cara sent her senses out to find him. What she located out there turned her skin cold. Chills engulfed her as Dana took another sharp right turn and the outline of the hospital loomed in the distance. Dana had no further questions now. She too was intent on finding Rafe.

Cara was out of the car before it came to a complete stop and sprinted for the trees. Behind her, Dana swore out loud and gave chase. This was a déjà vu moment for Rafe's mother, who had been here back then, when Rosalind was the central focus and monsters flocked to her like lemmings. Dana Delmonico Landau had seen what haunted these woods and was up for round two, bless her.

The distance from Fairview's chain-link fence to the trees was nominal. Cara covered it fast. She didn't stop to listen to the troubling sounds or to pay heed to the creatures that had gathered in such a doomed spot. Rafe was all she cared about. *Now* was the only thing that mattered. That, and the sound of Dana breathing hard behind her.

The vampires that had taken up residence here tonight didn't stop her. Passing the contorted faces of the demons that had come to party with her soul was a breeze. She slowed only after reaching the car Rafe had been driving. The engine was silent, but the headlights were on and the driver's side door had been left open.

The only thing missing from this scene was Rafe.

Cara urged Dana to be silent with a raised hand. *"Rafe?"* she messaged to him and then waited out an adrenaline rush more intense than the one that had gotten her this far.

Had that cagey old vampire found him? The scent of the creature tainted the air and brought bile to her throat. But that wasn't it, Cara suddenly understood.

"Demons," she hissed, as if uttering that word was an act of blasphemy. "We meet again."

Beside her, Dana said, "Shit."

And then the area became quiet again.

The next sound Cara heard was the voice of a vampire she had already met. She had been right in assuming the old bloodsucker would show up.

"I told him you would come," the pale-faced sucker said, appearing in the shadows the car's headlights didn't reach.

Ignoring the vamp, Cara closed her eyes to concentrate harder on Rafe. There were others here, her senses warned. The darkness was filled with a presence that even this ancient vampire would fear.

Vampires walked the earth hoping never to taste the tarnished fruits of the hell they would eventually descend to when their final death came. This was possibly the reason the old vampire desired to claim the dark spirit for himself...so that he could cheat death and continue endlessly on.

Demons were what everyone feared. So, how many of them had come to this place? It was curious how quickly they had located her. And it was a no-brainer that she would have returned to fight beside her lover.

Cara turned in a slow circle to place the positions of the hell spawn in their surroundings before opening her eyes. "Ten demons," she said to enlighten Dana, adding, "Not much of a party at all, really."

To the vampire, Cara said, "Where is he?"

"Right here," Rafe said, causing her heart to lurch as he sprinted from the shadows to draw up beside her.

Cara could have thrown herself into his arms now, the way she had always wanted to, yet she managed to restrain her careening emotions. Rafe was here. He was safe. Whatever happened next would be an anticlimax.

But…why was he safe with so many monsters around? How had he avoided them?

"Bait," he said, reading her thoughts and eyeing her steadily before nodding to his mother. "In order to catch a prize, everyone gets that you have to dangle the bait."

"They used him to get us back here," Dana said, frowning.

"The plan worked," Rafe agreed, brushing up against Cara's shoulder as if he also needed the comfort of a quick touch.

"You have a gun," Dana observed. "And bullets that will count. Why haven't you used it?"

"There's something else out here that I haven't been able to pinpoint. Another presence that has made our enemies as wary as we are."

"But now we have you, dark one," the vampire said without moving toward them. "One of us will be victorious when we shake that spirit from you and eat it alive."

Still, the vampires didn't advance to make good on that threat, and neither did the demons that looked on. So what was going on? Why were these monsters so anxious about doing what they had come here to do?

Cara spread her arms wide. "All you have to do is come closer, vampire…if you can coax the spirit from me, that is."

"Cara," Rafe warned.

She went on. "If you kill me in the process of taking what you want, you might kill the Banshee as well. Then where would you be? Demon fodder? Demons don't discriminate between the living and the dead. Can't you hear the sound of their jaws chomping?"

The vampire accepted the taunt by stepping forward.

Once the signal had been given, the rest of the bloodsucker's fanged friends rushed in from beneath the shelter of the trees.

Chapter 33

All hell broke loose.

Next to Cara, Rafe started shooting, picking off vampires by aiming at their pathetic chests, where their hearts used to beat. Four of them exploded before Dana raised the revolver she had stuffed in her belt and joined in. The sound of gunfire was deafening. The clearing filled with sticky gray ash, which prompted several more vamps to come running.

Given a party like this one, the demons weren't to be left out. Some of the ten Cara had counted flew forward, leaving their human disguises behind. Cara's claws sprang into existence like lethal switchblades as Rafe bumped against her. Wielding them like knives, Cara began her dance of death, swinging, slashing, ducking and lunging at each monster that came her way with a fury and a force they hadn't been expecting.

More vampires exploded. Clouds of ash rained down.

Only one demon burst into flames, having gotten too close to Cara, before the fighting shifted into high gear and the demons shrieked with displeasure over losing one of their own.

"Each kill weakens them," Cara shouted. Rafe and Dana were reloading their weapons in turns and fighting with their fists while they did. There was motion everywhere. Falling ash hampered sight.

So far, she, Rafe and Dana were holding their own. The Banshee hadn't wailed for them, so death wasn't imminent, though deep in her gut, Cara had a bad feeling about the outcome of this monstrous barrage. There was another presence out there, Rafe had warned, and she had known this from the start, but besides vampires and demons, what did that leave? Right then, she had no further sense of what sort of visitor could be out there, and there were too many monsters as it was.

Cara had never seen so many bloodsuckers in one place, except in her mother's show-and-tell of shared memory less than an hour ago. These vampires and demons hadn't attacked each other here, which would have been the norm. They seemed to have banded together, with the possible acquisition of a dark spirit as their common goal, though no love was lost between denizens of the darker species.

Cara's fangs appeared soon after the fourth vampire came at her. Black blood covered her cheeks when she used those fangs to tear at the hands reaching for her throat. She moved through the attackers in a whirlwind of fury. Attracted to this kind of power, the dark spirit she held back soared upward with an icy chill.

No. Not now. Not yet, Cara cautioned. She couldn't afford to lose her concentration. If she did, all would be lost.

The clearing crawled with supernatural attackers. Rafe now mainly used his fists, his fighting fueled by raw, wolf-backed strength. Next to her, Dana, showing no visible sign of fear, had become a fighting machine. And yet even the strongest werewolves didn't come equipped with an endless supply of energy, and their stamina would eventually wane. When it did, the remaining demons would approach, sensing that weakness.

For the first time in her life, Cara began to lose hope. She fought harder, growled with each strike, grunted as she dodged oncoming blows. Her goal was to protect her lover and the spirit that everyone wanted a piece of. She could not have Rafe harmed, especially now that she loved him. She couldn't let her family down.

Those thoughts had barely taken wing when a bolt of white lightning crashed through the crowd, tearing through vampires and demons like a guided missile bent on destruction. It wasn't actually lightning, though, but something made of flesh and bone that moved with the force of a terrible storm.

She had no time to find out what this new interruption was. Slowing down meant defeat. Yet the white streak seemed to be taking out monsters as if it was on her side.

When a high-pitched howl echoed through the clearing, Cara's ears rang with internal warnings. Her stomach turned over. But the howl had a strange effect on everyone in the battle.

Fighting slowed, as if the harrowing sound had contained a command. The vampire Cara held on to paused, shuddered and tried to backpedal. Rafe's demonic attacker lost focus and turned toward the trees. Dana lowered her gun.

Confused, anxious, wary and with their hearts in their throats, Cara and her companions also turned toward the echo, because every wolf on the earth recognized what such a sound meant. It was the song of triumph and of impending victory when the Weres here were still outnumbered and things didn't look good. And it had mesmerized everyone except Cara, who had heard that same sound once before in a dream sequence of her mother's memories about what had happened to Colton Killion in the park.

The aftermath of the sound was an uncomfortable silence that was dense and disquieting.

Rafe couldn't decide where to focus his attention. The echo of that howl went on and on, even though there were no walls out here for it to bounce off. The sound stirred his insides with hints of a forgotten past that no werewolf now knew. Images of mountains and valleys of trees flashed through his mind, there and gone so quickly he wondered if he had made them up.

All of a sudden, he felt connected to a larger picture that he could only manage to see the smallest part of, and the sensation lifted the fine hairs on the back of his neck. He wasn't the only one affected by the suddenness of new sensations. Every beast in the clearing had frozen in place as if they had been on the receiving end of a stun gun.

Cara looked to be as shocked as he was. His mother was holding her breath. As for whatever had moved through them like a lightning strike in the seconds preceding that howl…intuition warned that this also needed closer scrutiny. However, Rafe didn't turn to glance in that direction, already certain that whatever the flash was, it meant the three of them no harm. The curtain of ash that continued to fall told him so.

He was covered in the foul-smelling stuff. His arms burned with demon fire. The attention of the vastly reduced forces of their attackers had been lured away from Rafe's little threesome by whatever they had deemed to be a greater threat. Fear and excitement ruffled through their ranks. Fangs were again gnashing.

But none of them moved.

The echo of the howl they all had heard was finally broken by another more earthly sound. Cars on the driveway. Engines revved. Doors slammed. Voices called out. Rafe would have said that his pack had arrived in the nick of time if someone hadn't already hit the pause button that had extended to him, Cara and his mother a short respite in which to recoup their strength.

He looked to Cara to make sure she was all right. Her eyes were bright with excitement. Her face was tilted upward as she listened to what was going on. Did she anticipate another kind of arrival? Something he hadn't yet perceived? He had felt another presence out there in the dark, but hell, had that presence announced itself in a way that others here had recognized?

The thunder of running feet was uncommonly loud in the silence that had fallen. His father would come armed with weapons and packmates, ready to rumble. And yet even as the pack entered the clearing to shift the odds of victory in Were favor, the monsters made no attempt to face them. The arrival of reinforcements didn't seem to matter to these monsters at the moment. In spite of that strange fact, Rafe breathed a sigh of relief when his father stood beside him.

"What is it?" his father asked as several Weres warily gathered around.

"I have no idea...and yet at the same time, I kind of do," Rafe replied abstractly, moving closer to Cara as he reloaded the gun. This had something to do with her. He was sure of it.

"Fill me in," he said to Cara. It was clear that she knew

something no one else did. He saw this in the way her eyes pleaded with him to wait, and to stand down.

His nerves buzzed. His muscles twitched with the sudden inactivity. What was everybody waiting for, exactly? And was it a good thing, or bad?

When Cara stepped forward, he stopped her with a hand. She didn't look at him now. Her attention was riveted to the shadows across from them...and the slow approach of the creature that had caused such a ripple in the night.

Chapter 34

Cara's heart pounded frantically as the shadows parted. She took a shallow breath, then another in anticipation of an event she had thought she'd never see.

Her father was here.

A warm wash of familiarity hit her square in the chest as Colton Killion appeared. The ghost wolf had left his self-induced seclusion and had quite possibly saved the day.

It was he who had torn through the monsters like a lightning bolt of pure monster misery. No one could have equaled her father's exemplary fighting skills or brought such abject terror to his opponents. Without the ability to speak at the moment, her father allowed them all a good look at one of the fiercest werewolves on the planet, a Were who had died to his former Were self and returned as something else twice as formidable.

All white from head to toe and furred up like only the

rarest of pure-blooded Lycans, his height and the mounds of muscle clinging to his frame gave her father the appearance of an ancient wolf god. He stood in the blinking, fading headlights of Rafe's car like the legendary ghost everyone believed him to be.

And they all stared.

But he wasn't alone, and he hadn't been the lure for the creatures that had attacked Cara tonight. The ghost wolf, as stunning as his appearance here was, hadn't been good enough or strong enough to garner the kind of rapt attention the vampires and demons that had been left standing exhibited.

Her father, regal, terrible, in his colorless half-human, half-wolf form was merely the hors d'oeuvre before the main course. He was the guardian of a secret weapon that had once rendered monsters useless and had driven many of them so deep underground, it had taken almost twenty years for them to dare to emerge.

Her father had brought his mate. Cara should have known he would, because he never so much as left her side. Rosalind also had returned to Miami...and no one was ready for that.

The fear that drenched the clearing had its own smell and taste. One of the demons shrieked in anger. Two vampires hissed.

"Colton," the Landau alpha muttered with awe as Cara's father stepped aside to make way for his bride.

Cara felt the heat of Rafe's attention on her. "Christ," he said. "This is your dad?"

Rafe's remark faded as the headlights finally winked out, but no light was necessary for Rosalind's entrance onto the battlefield. She came as a large wolf on all fours with her black coat glistening and her ears pricked forward. Her delicate muzzle had drawn back in a snarl until her eyes, more human than wolf, found Cara. Then she reared up on her hind legs, shook her head hard and began her next shape-shift.

The black fur disappeared in the time it took for Cara to blink her eyes. Her mother's skin lightened to a smooth shade of ivory. Her limbs, slender and muscularly defined, took on a human shape. All that was left of the wolf Rosalind had been seconds before was her face until that melted into human cheeks, chin and long black lashes that rimmed a pair of light, serious eyes.

Rosalind Kirk stood before this gathering, tall and naked. Waist-length black hair infused with streaks of white partially curtained her torso as she raised a hand in greeting to Cara, then moved her arm to point at a pool of darkness beyond the trees nearest to the car. She spoke to those shadows in a deep, raspy voice. "You tried this one before, vampire. What made you imagine you would fare any better with my daughter?"

Rafe's hand slid to Cara's wrist, but she couldn't look at him yet. She didn't dare. The dark spirit inside her was twisting its way to the surface, drawn like everyone else to the sound of Rosalind's voice.

Rafe wanted to rub his eyes to make sure he was seeing correctly, but doing so would have meant letting go of his hold on Cara. *Legend* didn't begin to cover the pair of Lycans that had entered the clearing. He could not possibly have conceived of anything like this in his wildest imagination.

Still, Cara was his only concern. Cara's welfare. Her thoughts. What she might be feeling now when everyone here had gotten their first look at her parents.

At first, Cara seemed to be okay with the surprise appearance and the possibility of being reunited with her family. However, tiny quakes shook her arms as her gaze rested on the vampire that floated out of the darkness. Rosalind had called this old bloodsucker from its hiding place, and it was a bastard he and Cara had met before.

Still, Rafe kept his attention on Cara, whose shaking was getting worse with each passing second. He dropped her wrist and put his arm around her, able to feel how cold she was, thinking that odd when they had just exerted themselves and the night's temperature was soaring.

When her skin below the sleeves of her shirt began to darken, Rafe experienced a bobble in his stance. As the features of Cara's face began to rearrange, he fought the urge to shout for everyone to give them some space.

Rosalind was the most formidable presence he had ever experienced. The air in the clearing seemed to caress her, as if she had the power to call the smallest breeze. Colton, looking like a wolfish phantom, was a close second. And yet neither of Cara's parents could hold a candle to the daughter they had sent to Miami to find a mate. Because Cara had slipped away while he held on to her, and in her place was the dark thing that had glared at him from the tree in the park.

Exhaling a slow breath, Rafe looked this entity in the eyes, tightened his arm around her and said, "We meet again, Banshee."

Several things happened at once. The old vampire that had heeded Rosalind's call flew at Cara and the spirit that had taken hold of her. Rafe moved in front of her to ward off the first blow the vampire issued. He supposed a Banshee didn't require any assistance, and that as the right hand of death, she was the scariest, most dangerous creature here. But that assumption didn't take Rosalind and her many talents into account.

Cara's mother slid between Rafe and her daughter. Her

pale lips parted for a whisper of sounds, the meaning of which Rafe couldn't comprehend. With a free hand, Colton caught hold of the bloodsucker's coat and spun it around. The old vampire was slower than its younger companions and in need of a meal that its age prevented it from getting.

This vampire wanted the dark spirit for itself. Rafe understood quite clearly that if that were to happen, vampires would no longer need to hide. With a vamp leader in solidarity with a Banshee, all bets for human survival would be off.

He fought with all his strength to prevent that from happening, even though he wasn't sure if such a union was possible. Vampires were undead creatures, and the Banshee called the living to their deaths. Besides, Cara would die before letting the spirit go.

Colton was there with him, beside him, tall, huge, all wolfed up and mean as sin. Colton had the thing by its scrawny neck and, with a growling heave, simply tossed the bloodsucker away. When it came flying back, along with a few undead friends, Rafe felt Colton's hand on his shoulder. He was torn away from Cara before he realized the predicament that left her in.

He couldn't get back to Cara fast enough. He saw Colton step away from her, leaving way for three vampires to flood in. Rafe's heart stopped. Although he couldn't catch his breath, Rafe hurled himself toward his lover, determined to end this once and for all.

He should have realized that Colton had backed off because he knew Cara wasn't in danger, and that he needn't have worried. All four vampires stopped before reaching her. In confusion, they stared at two exact replicas of the dark spirit in corporeal form. There were two Banshees, each as darkly threatening as the other. It was like seeing double. So which one was the real death caller?

This might have confused the bloodsuckers, but Rafe suddenly got it. Rosalind, with her talent for shape-shifting and adopting the form of whatever creature she got close to, had become a Banshee. *The* Banshee? Maybe it was a glamour that Rosalind had used to fool them. Perhaps her abilities were advanced enough to actually become a copy of the dark spirit that she had once hosted. No one could tell which of the dark duo standing there was the real thing. The tables had turned. Instead of Cara having that thing inside her, she was now inside it.

That confusion was all it took for Rafe, Colton, Rafe's father and his packmates to spring into action. Working together in a coordinated series of lunges and growls, they sent all of the vampires and demons in the clearing to their final spiraling oblivion.

When the fighting was over and the air was thick with ash and smoke from the leftover flames of demon fire, Rafe looked to the Banshees with his senses wide-open and his heart drumming. Cara was in there somewhere, and his ravenous hunger for her hadn't weakened one bit. If this night had taught him one thing, it was that one sorrow didn't have to piggyback on another. He would work hard to make Cara happy if she'd stay. Hell, she had to stay, because of those chains that bound them to each other.

Didn't she?

He could feel the love Colton and Rosalind shared. That love beamed from them. Following the awareness of that was the key to Rosalind's disguise. Turning to face one of the dark spirits, sure he had to be right, Rafe said, "You must see now that our lives depend on trust, honor and the need for friends. Please come back to me, Cara."

Rafe's second request was to the dark-eyed thing that had taken hold of his lover. Searching for Cara in the intense and wavering gaze of that entity was like looking into the realm of death. Gathering his courage, he said, "You must allow this. If you do, it will ensure your protection and our fealty for the next several years. This, I swear to you."

Cool fingers feathered over hers. Cara shuddered again. Rafe's voice reached her in spite of the dark spirit's rise. Its familiar soothing quality made her heart skip. She wanted to return to Rafe. She had to. If she did, she would never leave him again. *"A vow. My promise to you, Rafe."*

Cara tried to send that message to him.

"Dark spirit. Help me."

The icy chill remained. It was possible she had gone too far and had been too lenient in allowing the dark spirit her freedom so many times in a row. She felt the spirit expanding. Freedom was what every species craved. *"I understand that. I do."*

Did she hear Rafe speaking to her? Her heart raced faster.

"Please come back to me, Cara."

"I will. I want to. Rafe, can you hear me?"

There was something more in the distance, a faint whisper that had to do with fealty and protection. That whisper wasn't directed to her.

She spoke internally to the Banshee. *"I have done my part. My family has done theirs. Now you must listen to me and return my freedom."*

Did the dark spirit listen? Had she understood? Like a running tap that was suddenly turned off, the burst of power she had felt began to recede. The flow became a trickle. Then a drip.

And when the final vestiges of the Banshee retreated, at least for the time being, and she could again breathe without pain, Cara opened her eyes.

Chapter 35

Rafe's breath hitched as Cara flung herself into his arms. Or maybe it was the other way around and he was the one who had rushed to gather her close. Either way, they were holding each other, their bodies pressed tight. His prayers had been answered by whoever had been watching this night play out, and for that he would be grateful for the rest of his days.

His lips hovered above hers. He was so very hungry for Cara and for the future he could perceive. He didn't give a damn about the others who were present—his pack-mates, his family and hers. This was what both families had hoped for. This pairing had been their plan all along, and rather than feeling used or manipulated, he was elated that it was going to work out. Cara had promised him that. He had heard every word.

As his mouth closed over hers, he heard his father say, "Thank you, Colton. It was you who placed the body near our wall, wasn't it, to alert us to demon presence? You've been here, watching over Cara from the start?"

Cara's lips parted. No sound came out.

In the hazy distance, his mother said, "A demon made the kill. If so, that poor human, good or bad, stood no chance."

Rosalind was there, too. Her presence was a powerful one unlike any other, living up to the legends surrounding her. She was so like Cara, only more so.

That thought also faded as Rafe deepened the kiss, needing to devour and reclaim what he had very nearly lost. His hands explored Cara's body, sliding over her back, her hips, her thighs. She growled softly to encourage him, and for a hungry wolf like Rafe, that was the ultimate seduction.

Could a death caller sense the pleasure moving through him, or classify it? Maybe he'd let her know.

Get used to it, Banshee...

He kissed Cara without letting her up for air, because every damn fiber of his being demanded it. And she kissed him back with a fervor that rivaled his. There was nothing tame about two werewolves mating. They would make love in human form tonight, and in a few days' time when the moon was full, they'd mate as wolves.

He was never going to take this for granted. It was enough, for now, to savor her taste...or so Rafe told himself.

Cara's body trembled as she leaned into him. An internal beat of pressure in his chest spurred him on. There was more about Cara to discover. There would always be more.

The sun was rising at last. Pink light edged the treetops, and there was new warmth in the air. In the back of Rafe's mind was a reminder that there would have been another death yesterday. The Banshee had predicted this, and Cara had let him know. Thank God his family was all here, and most of his friends were accounted for. So who was it going to turn out to be?

"A Were," Cara said when he gave her breathing room. "I don't recognize this one, and I'm sorry, Rafe. He fell near the edge of the trees before we arrived. Maybe he was watching the area? Someone from the hospital?"

He was sorry, too. Damn sorry that there had been a casualty here when the results of this fight had seemed so promising, and that it could have been someone he knew. He messaged that information to his father, who nodded with sadness.

There was nothing he could do about that death now. He would have to help his family tend to it later. He was finished with fighting for the time being, and with death and foreordained plans. Life lay ahead. He reached out to grasp it with both hands.

It was impolite to leave the others who had come to help in this fight, and to ignore both the latest victim of this battle and the keen observation of both sets of parents… but Rafe's emotional state demanded it.

Cara was hurting. She was alive and she was everything to him. Before he did anything else, he was going to prove that to her.

So he reluctantly took her hand. Then he turned, nodded an apology to everyone there, and ran.

Rafe had no idea how much time had passed as he rose from the comfort of Cara's naked body, panting from exertion and covered in sweat. Sometime during their wild, prolonged lovemaking session, daylight must have come and gone again. The night was quiet and almost eerily calm. Not even a breeze stirred the silence. Above them, the moon shone with a silver gleam, but it wasn't full, and nowhere near as powerful as what he held in his arms...

"No," Cara said, putting a finger to his lips to interrupt the sensations he was experiencing. "It's their memories you've tapped into. You're seeing the end of this through Colton and Rosalind's eyes. The spirit is showing you that picture, and it's nothing but a view of old memories, Rafe. We have to make our own."

Rafe blinked back his surprise. Hell, it had seemed so real. But he and Cara were backed into a corner of Fairview's chain-link fence, and not on the ground. The sky was still pink with a new dawn, and they were still hungry for each other and half-dressed. It turned out they hadn't even gotten to the best part yet.

Another thing to be grateful for.

"Keep your damn images to yourself," he muttered to a distant Colton Killion. "It's our turn."

A slow smile lifted the corners of his mouth. As Cara's eyes met his, her face lit up with a beautiful smile that showed no gleam of fangs. And it was one of the best things he had ever seen.

He laughed out of pure joy. As she laughed with him, Cara's green eyes danced with a mixture of longing and mischief. Yes, he loved her. Rafe loved everything about her. And with that acknowledgment, the next phase of their life began in earnest, punctuated by the sound of Cara's zipper on a slow, downward slide.

This mating was going to be no simple thing. Their love would have meaning for their pack's future, and also for the future of the werewolf species. If Cara bore a child, the dark spirit would again be passed on and a new breed of werewolf would continue to be loosed on the world. And the world would change.

Cara knew the ramifications and responsibilities of

housing the Banshee, and like Rosalind, would be able to help her daughter to prepare if he and Cara were to be blessed with female offspring.

Maybe this Banshee had a say in determining the sex of a child in order to preserve herself and her hiding place. If she had a say, did that make the Banshee a selfish entity, or merely a survivor?

Those were serious questions, but nothing he could come right out and ask. Not yet, anyway.

And hell…it was possible that dark spirits appreciated changing their hiding places now and then.

All that somehow seemed okay to Rafe as he left a trail of kisses across Cara's feverish neck, her chest, and in the valley of her breasts. She had thrown her head back, caught up in the throes of ecstasy. And her all-seeing eyes were closed.

For now, Cara was the only thing that mattered to him. *As for that future…*

Late at night when the moon called and death was imminent in the city, the Banshee would howl, the black wolf would prowl, and he and Cara would fight for the right to keep their secrets and be who they were, together, in a world that was only beginning to comprehend the extent of the populations of other creatures that lived among them.

The thing was…neither he nor Cara—the love of his life, and the lover in his arms—would have wanted it any other way. So Rafe lifted her up, listened to the soft patter of her pants hitting the ground, and despite any lingering activity in the distance, wrapped her long, bare legs around him.

"Future memory number one," he whispered to Cara, meaning every word of that vow.

* * * * *

If you liked
The Black Wolf,

Don't miss
Code Wolf,
*the final electrifying story
in the Wolf Moons series*

by Linda Thomas-Sundstrom

*Available November 2018
from Harlequin Nocturne.*